2/16

D0341771

YUBA COUNTY LIBRARY
MARYSVILLE, CA

No Sanctuary

Also available from MIRA Books and
HELEN R. MYERS

FINAL STAND
DEAD END
LOST
MORE THAN YOU KNOW
COME SUNDOWN

And watch for the newest novel of
romantic suspense from
HELEN R. MYERS

WHILE OTHERS SLEEP

Helen R. Myers

No Sanctuary

ISBN 0-7394-3484-5

NO SANCTUARY

Copyright © 2003 by Helen R. Myers.

All rights reserved. Except for use in any review, the reproduction or utilization of this work in whole or in part in any form by any electronic, mechanical or other means, now known or hereafter invented, including xerography, photocopying and recording, or in any information storage or retrieval system, is forbidden without the written permission of the publisher, MIRA Books, 225 Duncan Mill Road, Don Mills, Ontario, Canada M3B 3K9.

All characters in this book have no existence outside the imagination of the author and have no relation whatsoever to anyone bearing the same name or names. They are not even distantly inspired by any individual known or unknown to the author, and all incidents are pure invention.

MIRA and the Star Colophon are trademarks used under license and registered in Australia, New Zealand, Philippines, United States Patent and Trademark Office and in other countries.

Printed in U.S.A.

YUBA COUNTY LIBRARY
MARYSVILLE, CA

For Norma L. Wilkinson
Who has also known what it takes to stand alone.

AUTHOR'S NOTE

Like many, I grew up hearing the sage advice "Two things should never be discussed at the dinner table—politics and religion." An adage, I should add, that was rarely heeded by those who taught it to me. Then my family moved south of the Mason-Dixon Line and, a few years after we were married, my husband and I settled in east Texas, a place, I have wryly concluded, where there are more churches than pine trees. As hard as I try, avoiding the subject of religion here is more difficult yet—in fact it's virtually impossible. Salutations are typically followed by one of two questions: "What church do you belong to?" or "Who are your people?"

It is partly because of such troubling and inappropriate queries that this story evolved. My other inspiration came from actual crimes—two in particular. One to this day remains unproven, although I'm sure the U.S. Treasury Department continues to watch over it hoping for a break, and the other was brought to trial but failed to win a conviction. From there on, this is a work of fiction. To the best of my knowledge, Mission of Mercy Church does not exist in this area. But sadly, I have seen a few too many variations of it and of characters like Martin Davis and Madeleine Ridgeway. They present great fodder for a writer, but I despair for the innocent minds they abuse and corrupt.

ACKNOWLEDGMENTS

Several people need to be thanked for sharing their stories and expertise, or for going out of their way to try to arrange interviews—Darese Cotton, Karen Kelley and Linda Broday. To those of you who write in approval of my protagonists' "real" professional backgrounds, I hope you'll enjoy Bay and her work. All credit for its accuracy goes to my husband, Robert, a master craftsman and shaman with metal. Any error there and elsewhere is entirely my own.

The world is governed
by very different personages from what is
imagined by those who are not behind the scenes.
—Benjamin Disraeli

Prologue

Tyler, Texas
August, 1995

It was well past nine, hours after their usual quitting time—more if the battery-operated clock above the office door had stuck again—and yet Bay Butler reached for another welding rod. With two more ornamental lances to tack then weld into the division bars, she could call her half of the entry gate completed, and she wasn't shutting down until done. The gate had to be installed the day after tomorrow. It couldn't matter that every muscle and bone in her back and neck screamed from fatigue, or that her eyes had been on fire since the rest of the crew had gone home for the day. Never mind that sweat saturated her long-sleeved denim shirt and jeans, threatening to slow-cook her to death. It was August, this was Texas, and only a bankruptcy-intent fool air-conditioned a welding shop.

At least her clothes were providing some protection from the red-hot sparks shooting at her. Denim was not ideal for such work, but allowed flexibility of movement that the leather vest wisdom dictated a welder use didn't. Those contraptions felt as weighty as a warrior's breastplate, the arms as stiff and restrictive as the pauldrons, rerebraces and couters of any good knight's armor. The invention was also meant to guard against worse health problems down the road; however, thanks to her creditors, there would be no "down the road" for Bay if she couldn't work with reasonable speed and flexibility. Which was also why she replaced her wardrobe every few months; none of which, her CPA chastised repeatedly, was deductible because her shop wasn't union and denim didn't qualify as a uniform.

Two more lances…

It might as well be six and she had to visualize something pleasant to keep going. Once she dragged her butt home, she would fill the tub with whatever the faucet marked *C* offered considering this was Tyler and triple-digit heat had been the status quo for thirty-eight days straight. A tray or three of ice cubes from the freezer would help, as would the quart of cold milk from the fridge that was a few days past its expiration date. Whole milk, which was why she rarely drank it, the kind that clung to skin like a pearl's sheen. Then she would pop the tab on a tall Miller Lite to cool off her insides, and hopefully pass out from sheer exhaustion.

"Christ Almighty, will you knock it off, already?"

She paused in lowering the Darth Vader-like hood over her face and glanced behind her to see Glenn English glaring from beneath his own raised hood.

Behind him on the rolling parts table were five other ten-foot tall iron rods with the sharp arrowheads that would finish his side of the entry gate. It wasn't like him to be so far behind her, and he knew what was at stake. But as she accepted she might have to forgo the soak, maybe even the beer, she shouted back over the motors, "Go ahead and quit if you need to. I'll finish for you."

She made sure her tone was matter-of-fact; after all, he had someone waiting for him. Maybe Holly had committed them to an engagement and he'd neglected to share that tidbit of information. It wouldn't be the first time, and who could blame Holly for deciding that tonight she'd eaten one too many dinners alone, received one last-minute excuse beyond what a fiancée should endure?

"You'd like me to walk out on you, wouldn't you? A perfect ending to the martyr image."

Dumbfounded, Bay could only stare. She loved her work. What they were doing was hot and dirty for sure; but the opportunity it represented was a challenge, and a terrific business opportunity. Whatever his problem, she was willing to shrug it off to fatigue and the god-awful heat. Everyone in the shop had been snarling at each other on and off for weeks, thanks to the weather and the company's money crunch.

"We only have tomorrow to finish up," she said, drawing on the last of her own patience. "If this project doesn't go in on Friday morning, you won't have to worry about more overtime. We'll have to shut those doors for good."

It wasn't an exaggeration since they had yet to begin the painting-finishing process. The gate would be a navy gray, two careful coats of top-grade, weather-resistant flat—a third if, upon final inspection, Bay decided it was warranted. When that was completely dry, they would begin the painstaking hammering of the yellow brass wire wrapped in three strategic points along the length of each lance. She called the design *The Iron Maiden,* a little tongue-in-cheek acknowledgment after one of Glenn's remarks about her "ball-breaker" work habits and her dogged determination to keep the shop afloat. As luck would have it a few weeks ago, the grand duchess of all ball-breakers had driven by the small sidewalk-size version of the *Maiden* exhibited outside and stopped. On the spot, Madeleine Ridgeway had demanded a driveway-size model for her new estate. Nobody turned down Mrs. Herman Ridgeway, daughter and sole heiress to Duncan Holt's vast grocery warehousing empire.

"Friday," Bay said to Glenn with more emphasis. "And don't forget Mrs. R. needs access for the caterers and florists by early afternoon. That'll create a squeeze for us no matter how smoothly things go. What if Zamora shows up in the morning with the shakes, or the paint runs, or the wire snaps too often as we're hammering the trim?"

"Shit happens."

"Not when she signs the check."

"So she doesn't get her frigging gate in time for her party. You don't think the house is enough to keep everybody gaping?"

The answer to that was so obvious it didn't need

to be voiced. Nevertheless, Bay wanted people to see *The Iron Maiden* first.

As a hunch about Glenn settled deeper in her gut, she frowned. This wasn't about their intense schedule, at least not entirely. Something else was wrong. He'd been as thrilled as she was when they'd landed this job and they'd hugged and cheered, despite it coming only a few weeks after Bay turned down his marriage proposal. She'd thought, hoped, they'd cleared the air since. He'd certainly started up with Holly fast enough. Could there now be trouble in that paradise?

Heaven spare me from love.

They had to hang on. Once their financial pressures were behind them, they could think about expansion, a future that would allow for larger projects, independence. *Dreams.* The end of what she privately saw as a two-year leeching of everything creative inside her. She couldn't let him fall apart one check away from freedom and inspiration.

"I can't and won't do that to Mrs. Ridgeway," Bay told him.

"You think she wouldn't cut you loose in a heartbeat if it suited her?"

Glenn's cynicism worked like hot salsa on her empty stomach. If this abrasive attitude was his way to complete his emotional "disconnect" from her, to assure her that he'd learned his lesson, he needed to rethink his strategy.

"Look, I'm not a mind reader, and if you have something to say, I wish you'd can the sarcasm and get to the point...only not tonight. I'm begging you, Glenn. Let's get this job done."

He stood for several more seconds as though he wanted to press a point, but as abruptly as he'd flared, he reached for another lance from the rolling table behind him, slid it in place and dropped his hood. Striking an arc, he began welding again.

Exhaling in relief, Bay threw a load on her own welder. She began the bottom weld on her lance and was immediately lost in her work.

How long was it before she picked up on the change…the smell? Two minutes. Three?

It couldn't have been much longer. In any case, the strong odor, wholly unnatural to their environment and so clearly *wrong* prompted her to throw up her hood and sniff again.

She turned around. "Jesus."

Smoke was coming from Glenn's table, so much smoke that she couldn't see him. Nevertheless, the nauseating smell told her he was there. Swatting the hood off her head, she ran to his machine, flipped off the ignition switch and scrambled over lines to reach him. While her reaction was fact, her movements automatic, her mind froze on one thought. Heart attack. The stench gagged her as much as the smoke did, speaking too clearly of burning clothing and worse. As horror urged retreat, she grabbed the lead to get the stinger out from beneath him, at the same time pushing against his shoulder to roll him off it. In that instant something struck her forearm.

Through tearing eyes and suffocating smoke, she saw a metal rod—no, one of the *Maiden*'s lances.

The spear was impaled through Glenn's back.

1

Six years later
Gatesville Unit, Texas Department of Corrections
Gatesville, Texas
Wednesday, May 9, 2001

"Butler! Shut it down, you have a visitor."

About to drop her hood to weld the rest of a handrail, Bay Butler hesitated and glanced over at Sergeant Draper scowling at her from the doorway. At first she thought she must be hearing things, then the woman squeezed into a size-sixteen prison guard uniform aimed her baton. Bay shut down the machine.

What the hell...?

She couldn't imagine who wanted to see her. She had no family, so-called friends had abandoned her ages ago, and the most rabid reporter had long lost interest in her. Nevertheless, she knew better than to question when a prison guard gave a directive, particularly this one. Bay got along well enough with most of the staff—they left her alone, while she pretended they were part of the concrete and steel surrounding her—but Draper had made it clear from day one that she thought Bay belonged on Death Row.

Setting her hood on top of the welding machine, Bay approached the woman whose face would make a plastic surgeon think, "*Windfall.*" Keeping her own expression passive, she dealt with an unwelcome rush of adrenaline. Why hope? Hope, she'd learned the hard way, was for babies, brides and fools. Yet Draper knew something. Suspicion and trouble were unpleasant scents to season Bay's memory as she struggled to remember what she might have done wrong in the last six days, never mind six years. It had to be a trick of some kind; no one on the outside cared whether she lived or rotted here and she had no assets, therefore, no need for a beneficiary to encourage her early demise. Her life had been reduced to its lowest common denominator.

Six years…in another six weeks. Any more sixes, she mused, and she was going to start wondering if the Bible-thumpers—whom she avoided as diligently as she did prison troublemakers—were right about the antichrist already being present on earth. That, too, said bad things about her state of mind.

Wary, Bay followed the surly guard's directives down the hall. She knew better than to ask questions. As far as Draper was concerned, if you were at Gatesville, you were guilty and should serve your full term, and the guard did her best to make sure Bay understood that went doubly for her.

The cloudless Texas sky blinded Bay as she crossed the prison yard, and the packed clay tested her bones and joints as much as the concrete floors of the prison did. Gatesville was the state's main women's facility, located about an hour west of Waco, hard country that fooled you. Gently rolling terrain let you believe over the next slope was a lake, a stream, maybe an oasis of woods when the only break from the incessant sun was the scrub brush and rain-starved cedars. For as far as she could see the dusty, heat-scorched vegetation littered the land like storm debris. Bay never yearned for the soothing shade of the piney woods more than when she was ordered outside to fulfill state requirements for "fresh air and exercise."

The plant-bare yard was speckled with a number of women cloistered in a corner like chickens without feed and unionizing in protest. Several called to her, whistled and blew taunting kisses. Bay had a certain reputation among the inmates, not for any unpredictability or violent tendencies, but for her refusal to make group alliances. It wasn't a focused intent, she simply wasn't and never had been tribal, didn't join clubs and other variations of so-called support groups as a means of feeling secure. An only child raised in what any first-year psych student would recognize as an unorthodox manner, her social skills weren't only untapped, they remained buried rootstock, or worse, like invisible seeds on Mars.

Unfortunately for her, Bay resembled the very people who came from various ministries to attend to the needs of her soul. Slim to the point of gaunt, having saved her sanity by plunging herself in relentless work, she was as pale as a chronic anemic. What color she did have was welding burns. Add her artist's feverish, unblinking stare and she could pass for a seer, or someone in need of a white jacket with sleeves that tied, which explained why all but the most fearless inmates avoided her, as one would any unknown commodity. It was those predators, the ones who traveled in the strongest packs that refused to be permanently thwarted. Bay carried a few scars from them—the chronic ache of cracked ribs, a broken finger and damaged spleen.

It was her skill with metal that had kept her alive, that and the fact that the new warden, after a visit to the infirmary, had done her homework. Upon reading Bay's file, the woman assigned her to the prison mechanic shop. Ever since, Bay worked at repaying her by methodically cutting down on the list of repairs and improvements needed at the facility, those frequently put off due to budget constraints. The move hadn't stopped the diehards from their taunts, though. As she crossed the yard they stuttered, "B-b-b," or called, "Hey, Baby Butt Butler!" or "Yo! Bitch Bonnie Bay." But, as always, unless someone addressed her as "Bay" or "Butler," she tuned them out.

After the debilitating heat it was a relief to enter the visitors building, although the air-conditioning sounded as though it was ready to go at any second. Either that or souls from previous inmates were haunting the ventilation system. Still, it was a good twenty degrees cooler than outside, almost thirty better than at the shop. But what caused Bay to shiver was the reminder that she hadn't been in here since her first month at Gatesville and that she'd forgotten procedure. Hesitating once too often after a directive earned her Draper's scorn.

"Hell, Butler, has inhaling those gas fumes numbed your brain?" the guard snapped as they stood outside the last set of gates. "I said pass through."

Bay intended to...but she'd spotted whom she was being handed off to, a great hulk of flesh with a face that made Draper a beauty queen. Would he insist on a body search, too, before she was allowed to see if any of this was worth it?

Bay clenched her teeth and stepped into the cell-like corridor. Then she stood staring through the bars at the door of mystery while the WWF reject attempted to get his jollies, only to discover he was wasting his time, since she was flat going and coming.

Muttering in disappointment or disgust, he directed her to the visitation room. "Cubicle six," he recited in a voice that Disney Studios might contract to play a drowning grouper. "Stay seated, use the phones, no passing anything over the partition. No body contact whatsoever. Any infraction and the meeting's over. You give me any lip and the meeting's over. You try something stupid and you go into Solitary. Clear?"

"Yes, sir." Bay's automatic reply hid her consternation. *Sixth cubicle. Six-six-six.*

Her trepidation didn't ease once she arrived at the designated spot. Not only was the man waiting for her a total stranger, he had all of the markings of a lawyer, the successful kind. She took in the educated, pampered face, the manicured hands, the salon-styled, flaxen hair and the suit she figured cost more than her court-appointed attorney had made handling her entire case, and considered doing an about-face. What stopped her were his eyes. He resented being here as much as she did the prospect of having to speak to him.

As curiosity won out over pride, she sat down and matched him stare for stare. What helped was that he was as fine-boned as he was fair—her male counterpart. He picked up his phone, then waited for her to reach for hers. That's when she noticed the condition of her hands—black from grease and dirt. Certain that he'd noticed, she took her time to wipe them on her thighs, further staining the already soiled orange jumpsuit.

"I'm Lyle Gessler," he snapped as soon as she brought the receiver against her left ear. "Mrs. Ridgeway sent me."

All reluctance and embarrassment evaporated like summer drizzle on sun-baked Texas earth. If the name Ridgeway had clout in this state, it had double that with her. One thing she believed—the widow of oil tycoon Herman Ridgeway and daughter and sole heiress of the late grocery-distributor magnate Duncan Holt was the only reason she didn't call Death Row home. For Madeleine Ridgeway, she would listen.

"As you know, Mrs. Ridgeway has continued to protest your situation."

Continued? "She was supportive before and during the trial. But since...I couldn't say."

Mrs. Ridgeway had sent a note right after her arrest saying she would be following the trial and offer herself as a character witness for the defense, but Bay had refused for fear of public opinion turning on the good woman. Later she'd learned from her lawyer, court-appointed Mary Dish, that Mrs. Ridgeway had spoken to some influential political friends who had somehow convinced the D.A. that while a conviction was likely, a Murder One charge would be risky. For that, if nothing else, Bay would always be grateful.

"Then allow me to enlighten you. After saving you from a date with the Lethal Injection Boys, she expanded her own investigation—and at no small expense. It's a result of that, the evidence we've unearthed, that I'm here. Your conviction has been vacated."

Bay struggled to figure out what the hell that meant without looking like a fresh-hatched chick. She was sensitive about her lack of formal education. Schooling she had, having gone through the whole welding school apprenticeship and being mentored by some of the best journeymen in the business. But the rest of it, the college-range curriculum had been denied her. She'd used some of her time here trying to catch up, improving her reading skills and sense of history and politics, anything to fill the endless days; however, the sense of stigma remained.

"I don't understand," she admitted at last.

"We convinced the D.A. to agree with your defense attorney and request that your trial be set aside."

He might as well have announced her the winner of a jackpot lottery. "How?" she whispered, surprised she could speak at all. She'd had a full trial, the whole gamut of legalities and jury and media humiliation.

''What does it matter? The point is you're getting out.''

As much as she wanted to believe him, Bay stared at the stranger with the feminine nose and pinched lips reading him like a Times Square billboard. Not only didn't he believe what he was spouting at her, not only didn't he care if she did or not, he thought coming here undeserving of his time.

''Excuse me.'' She gripped the phone tighter, aware that manners counted in such moments and that she had to hang on to what was left of hers. ''I don't mean any insult, and I am...I'm in shock. What I'm trying to say is that no one listened during the trial. What's changed?''

''Facts.'' The attorney focused on the unopened file before him. ''It appears new evidence finally surfaced that was unknown at the time of the initial investigation. The deceased was recently discovered to have had a gambling problem. Apparently—''

''The deceased had a name. Glenn English.''

''—Mr. English's debts,'' Lyle Gessler continued frowning at the closed folder, ''had gotten so out of control that a collector was sent after him.''

''Bull.'' Bay would never have stood for that kind of behavior, and Glenn had known it because her father had been a compulsive gambler. Glenn had witnessed the worst of what that meant; in fact, he'd almost been as hurt by the effects of her father's addiction as Bay was. They'd come a cold sweat away from losing the business and Bay the pitiful roof over her head. No way would Glenn have allowed himself to become consumed by the same weakness. He'd cared, cared too much.

"Look, I don't specialize in appellate law, but Mrs. Ridgeway found someone who does. He, in turn, found the right investigators and we ended up with the testimony from a small-time crook by the name of George 'Catfish' Tarpley, who knew the hit man sent to settle things with Mr. English."

"Hit man?"

Gessler stiffened and leaning back glanced around to see how much attention she'd attracted from the other booths. Satisfied that it wasn't much, he whispered, "Do you mind? One Raymond Basque. Razor to those who use nicknames instead of Yellow Pages advertising."

Ignoring the snide retort, Bay shot back, "Someone with the kind of debt you're inferring would be warned several times, even at his place of business. I never saw or heard any—"

"Do you want to know why you're getting out or not?"

There was no arguing with that. Bay nodded.

"Like Basque, Tarpley's from Louisiana," Gessler continued. "But he has a record here that should have been long enough to make him a permanent resident. Several weeks ago he was stopped in Houston for a traffic violation. Police found an unregistered handgun in the car, and he was also in illegal possession of prescription drugs. Needless to say, once he understood that this time he was facing Texas's strikeout situation, he was anxious to plea bargain."

If it happened, no doubt; but to Bay it sounded too

pat. ‘‘The D.A. and a judge wouldn’t listen to me, why should they listen to a career criminal?’’

‘‘Because he helped close the book on Basque. Basque is dead...has been for over six years. He was found at DFW Airport with a single gunshot wound to the head the morning after fulfilling the contract on your friend. As luck would have it, at the time there was no reason to connect him to your friend’s murder because the Tyler police believed they had their killer.’’

The whole story was insane, and yet Bay saw the way Fate had played nemesis in her life. ‘‘How much did Glenn owe?’’

‘‘I have no idea.’’

‘‘It cost him his life, what do you mean you don’t know? Ten thousand? Fifty?’’

‘‘I’m pleased to be able to say such things aren’t in my general area of expertise.’’

Unfortunately, they were in hers. ‘‘Then let *me* enlighten you. To be worth the trouble of killing, Glenn would have to have been so deeply in debt he would be sweating blood by day and pissing it by night.’’ Bay had seen her father in that condition enough to know the signs. ‘‘He would have had a few scares, maybe a slashed tire or bashed headlight on a vehicle, and then if that didn’t get the message across, he would have had the crap beaten out of him. No way Glenn could have hidden all of that from me.’’

Although he turned a sickly yellow against his flashy suit, Gessler managed his own share of sarcasm. ‘‘I’m sharing confidences and insights I doubt anyone else on the case would. Your protests and censure beg the question of why I'm wasting my time talking to you. Perhaps Mrs. Ridgeway needs to be informed of that.''

Bay wanted to kick through the partition and grab the little snot by his platinum silk tie. In her dreams of justice, she'd found vindication and freedom, but not like this. Never at the cost of a dear memory, someone she'd respected and trusted. Glenn hadn't just shared everything he knew about working with metal, he stuck around through the bad times when others quit due to one too many late paychecks. That was why she'd made him a partner, and why she'd called him a friend. What could she do to disprove these filthy lies? Nothing here. She had to temper her outrage and find the real answers outside.

''This Catfish guy,'' she said, her throat aching, ''he's in custody on a commuted sentence? I can talk to him?''

''I told you, he was afraid that what he knew about Basque could be his death warrant if he went back to Huntsville, so he gave authorities various other tidbits that helped on several arrests and earned him a walk.''

She couldn't deny the validity of that. In prison, what you knew could get you in as much trouble as speculating about what wasn't any of your business and plenty of inmates lived in dread of returning to pay for their secrets.

''I don't know, it still sounds as though he got the best of you guys. How do you know he didn't?''

''We have the confirmation of a detective in Vice, one Nick Martel, who acknowledged he saw Tarpley and Basque in the exact booth at the all-night restaurant Tarpley mentioned when he described making Basque's payoff.''

The news sucked the air out of the room until Bay felt her lungs burning. A cop…it was one thing to reject the word of a career crook and liar looking for any angle to gain a deal on his sentence, quite another to refute a cop. Sure, guys who carried badges and took oaths lied—naive she wasn't. It would be a first for one to help someone in her kind of trouble, though.

''Would Martel talk to me?'' she asked.

''To what end? He didn't know English. He just saw what he saw.''

''Then what about Tarpley? Did they ask him who hired him to make the payoff?''

Gessler shook his head. ''All of his leads dead-end because no names were used and payment was made at arranged drop-off sites for exactly those reasons.''

Bay could see she would get little from the man and had to allow that maybe that's why he was sent. It could be that, like Tarpley, he was simply part of the conduit. For the moment it would be wise to let him believe he'd performed his role expertly. But Bay had known Glenn English. He may have cut a corner or two on projects in his time; however, his conscience always reminded him where and when, especially after becoming engaged to Holly Kirkland. And she was active in her church. The couple had been planning a modest wedding to save money for a house. It was inconceivable that he would have jeopardized her trust.

What to do...? So-called justice had already cost her six years of her life. If it took another big blunder to set things right, why not accept that as a gift? Sure as hell, she couldn't do Glenn's memory any good here. She also needed to get out for her sanity's sake.

"So what's next?" she asked, aware of a slight trembling in her legs. With her free hand she gripped her left thigh to control it.

"Sit tight for the formal paperwork to come through. You should be out by the end of the month, your record expunged."

Incredulous, she was slow to find her voice. "That fast?"

"I told you, Mrs. Ridgeway has been working on this for some time."

Free...and not just paroled, the sentence overturned. It was too much to take in. The only thing that saved her was the weight of her guilt. Glenn still wasn't coming back. Her friend died because she hadn't locked a door, wasn't more conscious of what had been going on with him...something.

"Just don't go doing something stupid like committing another murder before your release date," Gessler said, breaking into her thoughts. "Mrs. Ridgeway doesn't appreciate people who undermine her efforts."

Bay had to wait until the throbbing behind her eyeballs eased. "I didn't do the first one."

As Lyle Gessler hung up the phone, she could almost hear his mind cranking away. He was doing his job. She'd gotten the same message from what's his name, that detective who first questioned her that awful night. Despite his admitting to her that he'd believed something was fishy, he hadn't fought too hard, either, when the D.A. twisted his words into what proved the prosecution's strongest incriminating testimony. It was a miracle she hadn't gotten the death penalty.

As the attorney collected his things, Bay knocked on the window. "Thank you," she mouthed.

Gessler barely acknowledged her, but then Bay wasn't really talking to him. She knew who deserved her thanks and she would voice them in person as soon as possible.

2

Tyler, Texas
Thursday, May 31, 2001

Things had changed. Nestled in the luxurious dove-gray leather of Madeleine Ridgeway's white Lincoln Town Car sent to bring her home, Bay struggled to recognize landmarks as she was chauffeured around Tyler's Loop. If it hadn't been for the road signs, she would have sworn she wasn't even on 323. Gone were the woods interspersed with stretches of pasture that had first given the East Texas community its charming rural appeal years ago. In their place was row after row of shopping strips, large chain stores and enough fast-food joints to keep the stomach bulging and the wallet starved. As for traffic, Bay had seen less congestion this morning as they'd passed under I-35 by Waco—the current main expressway connecting Mexico to the heartland of the U.S.A. It explained the increase of apartments, though. With everyone shopping so much, who had the money for a mortgage?

As her hymn-humming driver Elvin Capps wove

his way between slower vehicles—most of them SUVs or pickups and all freshly washed—she dealt with a dizzying mixture of elation and alienation. ''Is there a plan for street expansion or another loop?'' she asked once the car stopped for yet another red light.

Darkly lashed hazel eyes met hers in the rearview mirror and crinkled at their corners. ''My, yes. There's always a plan. There's a plan to adjust the latest plan, and a plan to oust the people wanting to stick with the original plan. In the meantime the traffic gets worse, accidents more frequent, insurance rates skyrocket and—'' He punctuated his opinion with a shrug and sheepish smile. ''I'm no expert, ask Mrs. Ridgeway. Next to her church commitments, improving the roads is her biggest interest.''

Then no doubt something would get done. Bay believed if Madeleine Ridgeway could get her out from under a murder conviction, unraveling the political and economic bird's nest delaying a new multimillion dollar road system should be no problem.

The congestion didn't ease up once Elvin turned south on Broadway. Before they cleared the second traffic light, she witnessed several near collisions... and the city stretched onward.

''Good grief!'' Torn between a laugh and shout of warning as another impatient driver cut in front of them, she gripped the back of the front seat.

''Don't fret none,'' Elvin drawled, stopping before the intersection that featured one of the Ridgeways' gourmet grocery stores. ''You're in good hands. Jesus watches over this car.''

As he went back to humming the latest gospel tune playing on the radio, Bay reconsidered his earlier advice that she fasten her seat belt. Back in Waco, she'd rejected the idea as too close a reminder of driving shackled in the back of a patrol car. To avoid it now she averted her eyes from the traffic to the growing city's infrastructure.

Discount department store, super hardware store, super furniture store...American corporations were making a killing on cheap imports. Bay wondered...did she have a future in this kind of economical environment? Why would anyone pay premium prices for her one-of-a-kind creations when they could get slapped-together facsimiles for a fraction of the cost? Of course, the dream of having her own business again, let alone focusing on her sculpture was just that, a dream that would have to wait until she could manage to simply support herself. What she needed to think about was would anyone want to hire her? She'd been forewarned by the warden at Gatesville that the media knew of her release and was treating it as top-story material.

By the time Elvin steered the sedan past the electronic gates of the Ridgeway estate, some of Bay's euphoria over being released faded under the weight of her cloudy future. When they stopped beneath the two-car-wide portico of the sprawling three-story structure, Bay, feeling less worthy than ever, got out before the cherub-faced driver could make it to her door. Elvin Capps seemed a genuine dear, comfortable in that middle-aged, barrel-chested way that probably made him a top candidate by organizations seeking volunteer Santas at Christmas. What won *her* approval was his unmistakable devotion to Mrs. Ridgeway.

But as Bay eyed his crisp white shirt, khaki slacks and navy blazer, she experienced renewed doubt. For all of their simplicity, Elvin's clothes were designer quality compared to her cheap T-shirt and jeans. She might as well be back in her orange jumpsuit. How did she face Mrs. Ridgeway looking like someone even her chauffeur would find tacky?

"I don't know about this," she began. "Maybe I'll come back after I get properly settled somewhere."

"You get in there and let her enjoy the reunion." Brusque as he pressed the doorbell, Elvin was beaming as he stepped back to make room for her. "I'll be here when you're ready."

The door opened. A young Latino girl in a white uniform beckoned her inside, keeping Bay from questioning the latter half of his comment.

The maid led her across the foyer to a door on the left. Softly knocking, she opened it and gestured for Bay to enter.

On the far side of the high-ceilinged room sitting behind a huge rectangle of thick, smoky glass held up by a pair of marble elephants waited Madeleine Ridgeway. She sat framed in the mauve-ivory-and-silver decor, a sight to behold dressed in a silk tunic pantsuit that matched her platinum hair. Bay had never forgotten the elegance of the office; the woman had her gaping. Once Madeleine's trademark had been her long, steel-gray mane coifed in a sophisticated bun at the nape, à la dancing legend Martha

Graham. Today she wore it as short as a boy's, as short as her own, and almost the same color. Bay had the oddest sensation that she was seeing herself in thirty years.

"My dear."

Her mature alter ego rose from a gray leather chair similar to the car's interior and swept toward her with arms wide. The women were twins in build now, too, except that Madeleine stood inches taller even without high heels. Despite her initial shock, Bay saw that time had been kind to her benefactress. Her skin was as luminescent as the six rows of pearls gracing her throat, complimenting well-defined features that held just enough secret humor in those clear blue eyes, only a shade darker than her own, to keep from looking severe. Madeleine's smile broadened, diminishing the fine lines around lips painted a passionate burgundy. The life-size portrait on the wall behind her couldn't compete with her flesh-and-blood radiance.

"You made it. This morning I woke in a sweat dreaming they'd kept you."

As Madeleine drew her closer for an exuberant hug, Bay fought the impulse to reject. Displays of affection had been few and far between even before her incarceration, and that history compounded her awkwardness. But to her surprise, the harder Madeleine laughed and hugged, the deeper she felt a seeping warmth. It was a relief to finally break away before she turned into a blubbering fool.

"Mrs. Ridgeway. How do I begin to thank you?"

"Oh, don't start."

"I have to. I owe you everything."

"I only did what I had to do for my own peace of mind." Hands with rings on every manicured finger including the thumbs gripped Bay's upper arms, while intelligent eyes held her gaze with as much concern as warmth. "How *are* you, my friend? You've cost me many a night of sleep from worry."

Where to begin? Did she really want to know? Bay had narrowed her philosophy of life to match her social one—believe in no one and nothing save herself. This woman's kindness worked against that, as did the bite of seawater as it washed away the germs in a deep wound. Curiously, it left her weak in an unfamiliar and uneasy way. She needed time to regain her strength, not to mention her voice.

"I'm fine now." The recited words were from a dozen or so she'd prepared to aid her in getting through the initial days. "Great, thanks to you."

"Huh." After another hug, Madeleine Ridgeway pushed her to arm's length. "You're as substantial as a morning glory. Let me call Lulu and have her get Cook to make you a calorie-saturated omelet. Lulu is actually Lucia, but I only call her that in formal situations."

Bay thought fleetingly of the girl who'd worked here before. What had become of her? A job with the Ridgeways undoubtedly paid better than most service jobs and would be prized. "Really, I don't need anything."

"After such a ride? What about coffee, tea, a lemonade? I'm leaving shortly for a luncheon. Nevertheless, you're welcome to—"

Bay took a step back toward the door. "I won't

keep you. I only wanted to thank you...for everything. The ride, too.''

''Isn't Elvin a treasure? He'll take you to your new home. Any questions or needs you have just tell him.''

This was like stepping into a movie theater ten minutes into the film. ''I don't understand.'' At the prison they'd returned her belongings—a wallet containing sixty-three dollars, an expired license and equally useless credit cards, keys to a car, trailer and business that no longer existed. Her new residence would be wherever her exhausted body landed once she found a job that she could start immediately.

Madeleine threw back her head and laughed. ''I'm ahead of myself, aren't I? Blame it on sheer giddiness.'' Beckoning, she returned to the desk, picked up a manila envelope and offered it to Bay with both hands. ''This is for you. It's a little property west of town. The cottage isn't much larger than a dollhouse and it's as old as my poor bones, which should warn you that it needs substantial work beyond what Elvin's had time to put into it. On the plus side, it's on the airport highway and has a tin building out front close to the road that can serve as a shop.''

The envelope might as well have been a new warrant. Bay shoved her hands into the back pockets of her jeans. ''I can't afford anything like that, Mrs. Ridgeway. I'll be lucky to find someone to hire me to wash dishes on a trial basis, let alone give me a chance to work in my own field.''

''That's utter nonsense. Darling, surely Lyle explained it to you? Your record is cleared.''

''Then someone neglected to inform the reporters waiting outside the prison as I got out.''

''Well, the case did receive broad media attention from the first. It's understandable the discovery of that awful Basque man being responsible would stir things back up again. But it's died down considerably what with the other horrors going on in the state and around the world. That's the one thing you can rely on with the press—a short attention span for anything that doesn't provide juicy video and meaty sound bites. In any case, you have nothing to apologize for, let alone explain to anyone.

''I think you misunderstand me on another front, too,'' Madeleine continued with a knowing smile. ''The property described in that envelope has been deeded over to you. What's more, you begin work tomorrow on your first contract.''

''Doing what?''

''Get that hideous animal cage monstrosity called a gate off of my property and put up *The Iron Maiden.*''

There had been no missing the boring wall of metal bars as Elvin drove into the estate. Whoever contracted the job did competent work, but the design lacked the imagination and flair to do the estate justice, creating instead something better suited for the entranceway to a storage rental business.

''It takes more than a building and a dream to create what you're asking me to do,'' Bay said with unabashed regret. ''As much as I'd love getting the job done right for you, I can't. Probably not for some time yet. I don't have the credit record to obtain adequate equipment, let alone purchase the material. Then there's a matter of personnel.''

White gold and diamonds glittered and jingled as Madeleine waved away Bay's excuses. ''Some of what you need you'll find already there. I had Elvin look into the situation. The rest, I'll finance you. It's all in that envelope. You keep record of everything else and we'll work out a payment schedule later. As for staff, I have people who work the grounds, perhaps they can help until you find experienced staff. And don't discount Elvin. He may be all thumbs for what you need, as well, but in a clinch, he's the strongest thing on two feet.''

This was amazing, and impossible. Convinced the past could never be buried completely, Bay held tight to her angst. ''Mrs. Ridgeway, you'll never know—this means the world to me. But how can you, as brilliant a businesswoman as you are, take this kind of risk?''

''I'm not suggesting it will be easy. First and foremost I'll worry dreadfully about you being out there day and night by your lonesome. I'd be happier if you stayed here with me. The place is like a giant mausoleum with my dear son Duncan constantly traveling.'' The instant Bay started to protest again, Madeleine held up her hand. ''I know better than to ask. So I'll chew on carrot sticks to burn up frustration and chip my nails punching in your number on my phone.''

Dazed, Bay struggled to find new words of thanks. This marvelous woman was throwing her completely off balance with her generosity. ''Why are you being so good to me? Don't you realize this might hurt your reputation socially as well as—okay, I'll say it. What about your position in the church?''

''Ho-ho. No one there had better utter a peep, not one word. Not if they dare call themselves Christians in my presence. As for our pastor, Martin Davis has been wholly supportive of my mission since I first discussed the matter with him.'' Madeleine grasped Bay's hands. ''Stop fighting me. Yes, I can see you are. This is the least I can do for someone who's been so wronged. I'll never forgive myself for not doing more sooner.''

''The D.A. was intent on getting me convicted. It would have been double the nightmare if he'd injured you somehow in the process.''

''Then we must all put that terrible time behind us. Oh, I know you can't get back the years you lost, but you can rebuild your life. I know. I did it twice, remember, first when I lost my darling father and again when dear Herman passed so prematurely.''

Bay nodded remembering the story she'd shared about how each had devastated her.

''If it wasn't for my son,'' Madeleine continued, ''I wouldn't have found the strength to go on. I can be that rock for you, dear. I admire you enormously, your talent, as well as your endurance.''

''Maybe you should wait for proof there's enough of that endurance left to be worth your while.'' At the moment Bay was feeling a shadow of her former self, vulnerable and unsure.

''You need to find your footing, that's all. This is your opportunity.''

It sounded too good to be true and Bay had firsthand experience about that unwritten law. ''What about Holly? Once she learns what you've done—''

''She knows.''

One more shock and Bay was going to have to sit down. Holly Kirkland was aware that Madeleine Ridgeway was sponsoring her? Glenn's former fiancée would never accept her presence in Tyler, let alone being the recipient of such benevolence at the hands of this good soul. ''Mrs. Ridgeway, with all due respect, you're way off on your perceptions about her. This is going to—I'm afraid she'll see this as a betrayal.''

''You'll remember that aside from being a member of our church, Holly is an employee and, as a result, she has a firsthand comprehension of what our foundation is about. Of course, if you do experience any negative behavior—by her or anyone—I want you to report it to me immediately.''

Bay couldn't do that any more than she would have run to Sergeant Draper for help. ''I've always handled my own problems.''

''Admirable, but no one disrespects my wishes. There, there.'' Embracing her again, Madeleine ran her hand over Bay's back in slow circles as though calming a high-strung thoroughbred. ''It'll all work out, you'll see.

''Now in this envelope are keys, phone numbers I felt you might need, a bit of cash and a checkbook with a modest deposit to get started. It's not charity. I know you too well. We'll take it off what you'll bill me for the *Maiden.* You'll also find the hours for church services in there.''

Bay handed back the padded envelope. ''I don't do church.''

''You have to attend, dear. I've talked you up to the entire congregation, and I should tell you that our membership contains some of the most influential people in the city and beyond. Why do you think there aren't vans from either of the local networks parked outside my property right now? Don't you realize that as soon as you got into my car back at Gatesville, they knew where you were going? In any case, seeing your sweet face and how some things turn out for the good will provide sustenance to our congregation's faith.''

Bay thought that was the longest stretch in any rationale Madeleine could have tried on her. ''I'm sorry if this disappoints you, Mrs. Ridgeway, but I've never been religious.'' She couldn't remember the last time she'd been to a service and guessed it was her mother's funeral. Her father had been lucky she'd arranged for a graveside prayer for him.

''Madeleine,'' her benefactress intoned. ''How often am I going to have to tell you? Having witnessed your art and your courage, I consider you an equal. As for religion—''

A knock at the door stopped her. Releasing Bay, she stepped around her to greet the newcomer. ''Martin. Your timing is divinely inspired. Help me assure your newest lamb that she's as wanted as she is needed.''

Into the room stepped a short man with the merry

eyes and chipmunk cheeks of a fairy-tale elf. Although his fifties-style pompadour barely reached Madeleine's choker, he grasped her hand between both of his and bestowed a kiss to rival any gallant performance in a royal court. Before Bay could worry she was about to suffer the same greeting, he patted her hand. "Praise God for this day. Madeleine has worked tirelessly to bring you out of Satan's den. Welcome, child. Welcome home to where you will be loved and nurtured."

Somewhere on the south side of his fifth decade, the auburn lights in his lush hair suggested he used a stylist for more than a good cut and blow-dry. His summer-gray suit also spoke of attention to detail and complemented Madeleine's silk suit. Accident or had they color-coordinated over the phone?

"Don't be shy, dear," Madeleine said. "Martin is as genuine as his smile. At our Christmas gala more children want to climb onto his lap than Santa's."

"Merely due to besting his girth, Maddie."

Charming as the self-deprecation was, Pastor Davis could hardly hope to squeeze Saint Nick or the Pillsbury Doughboy out of a TV screen. He was simply, pleasantly plump.

"And you know better than to push," he continued. To Bay he said, "We've always succeeded because we don't pressure. Our message speaks for itself."

Madeleine's skepticism came out in a ladylike sniff. "If only I had half that success with some of the politicians in this city. The cold hard truth, Bay, dear, is that aside from the gift Martin's sermons present, you need to understand that you'll meet business contacts through your affiliation that wouldn't necessarily be accessible to you elsewhere.''

Pressing a hand over his heart, Martin Davis groaned. ''Maddie! How many times do I have to tell you that you're my earthbound angel, not a networking guru?''

Bay held her breath wondering how her benefactress would take this, even gentle, scolding. Astonished, she listened to the older woman's girlish laugh.

''You know me, Martin. I can't just juggle two or four projects—lucky for you, too. In any case, it's no fun if I don't have to dodge a few bullets now and again.'' To Bay she added, ''You have to let me show you off. I expect you to sit beside me in the family pew, and ignore what Martin says. Modesty is his vice. He'll be wounded if you're not even slightly curious to hear how he's become the rudder of the fastest-growing congregation in the Southwest.''

As Bay stood between the two, she knew she was trapped. Worse, she had no energy—correction *confidence*—yet to fight.

3

After a small, but awkward pause, Martin Davis cleared his throat and leaned toward Madeleine. ''Do you think she needs to see us looking wounded and fearful?''

''Oh, no.'' Embarrassed that they must see her as an ungrateful bitch, Bay caved in. ''I'll come. I mean, thank you...for the invitation. For everything. Really.''

With a satisfied nod, her champion directed her toward the door. Bay thanked Madeleine Ridgeway again and let the shy Lulu show her the rest of the way out.

As promised, Elvin was waiting. The process of being handed off from person to person and passing through doorways triggered another unpleasant sensation, one she quickly reasoned away. There was no comparing this to prison, especially when she eyed the sprig of mint dangling from Elvin's mouth.

A scan of the landscape had her gaze settling on the thigh-high brick flower box on the far side of the portico. Amid the sea of red and white geraniums, she spotted lavender, parsley, dill and basil. So Madeleine didn't waste space any more than she did time or contacts. For a second, Bay wished the sprig was a cigarette so she could bum one. From someone who'd never taken up the habit to begin with, that spoke fathoms.

His hands thrust deep into his trouser pockets, Elvin rocked back on his heels and grinned. "You're looking like you did a few test rounds with a champ."

Not willing to admit how right he was, Bay asked, "I guess you know where to go?"

"Spent virtually every waking hour there for the last two months."

As he tossed away the wilting herb and headed for the driver's side, his cheerful reply triggered a nagging something in Bay's overtaxed, underfed brain. Then it clicked. "I only heard of the possibility of my release a few weeks ago," she said from the back seat. She slammed shut the passenger door. "Even then I wasn't certain it was a sure thing."

Elvin shrugged as he keyed the engine. "So it felt shorter to you. I got through it by practicing my music. Speaking of—" he turned on the radio to another gospel station "—if you don't mind, I need to listen. I'm trying to get these folks to consider my stuff."

A frustrated artist, Bay mused, studying the back of his head. She noted that while his hair was similar in color to Pastor Davis's, it lacked the neat cut and styling. At best Elvin's shaggy mane seemed to be combed by his stubby fingers. Not great hands for a musician, Bay surmised. Nervous, too. They were always active, like his hazel eyes. "Go figure," she murmured.

"What's that?"

"I suppose you can't study too much."

With a nod, Elvin sped back to the Loop and turned left, this time passing the street that led into town and Bay's old shop. Ignoring the pang of yearning, she watched as they continued on, until they reached the turnoff for Pounds Field. For a regional airport, the area retained its rural atmosphere, the traffic lighter than in town.

About a mile farther, past a nursery, a produce stand and a ballpark, Elvin made another left turn into a wooded property.

Bay had been browsing through the contents of the envelope and had already read that the land consisted of one-point-three acres, narrow but long, meaning limited highway frontage. As far as she was concerned, any frontage made the gift a gold mine.

Her first glimpse of the tin building that was to be her shop had her agreeing with Madeleine's appraisal—the decrepit shack needed work, new doors to start and sturdy locks, particularly once she started buying equipment and material stock. In contrast, the house was a haven, adorable as a dollhouse, freshly painted a cheery yellow with white trim and adorned with lacy iron supports that held up the white awning. Parked under the connecting carport weighed by an opulent trumpet vine was a black Chevy truck.

"That was mine," Elvin said. "Mrs. R. gave me one of the newer estate trucks in trade for getting the place in shape on time. But there's plenty more miles in that sweet thing."

Elvin's tone warned that he still saw his slightly worn baby as a Cadillac among trucks. "I see. Well,

I'll take good care of her, thank you." Forewarned, Bay would be prepared for impromptu under-the-hood checks and see that the ashtray and floorboard stayed as tidy as her profession allowed.

"All righty...so the phone and lights are working in there and you've got water. You'll have to transfer things over in your name, of course."

"I'll get to it right away."

"Mrs. R. had me stock the kitchen and whatnot. Do you need me to come in with you and show you around?"

Preoccupied with shoving papers back into the envelope, Bay belatedly met his gaze in the rearview mirror. Maybe it was the play of light or her overtaxed nerves, but in that instant she saw something in Elvin Capps's face that had the hairs on her arms lifting.

"Earth to blondie...? Hey, you having an out-of-body experience or something? I asked—"

"No."

"Criminy. Sue me for doing my job."

As she felt her face heat, Bay ducked her head, wishing for once that she had long hair to hide behind. "What I mean is, you've done so much already. I think I can manage from here." She scrambled out of the car convinced he must think her certifiable. It would serve her right if he rushed back to his employer to report what a bad decision she'd made.

Elvin lowered the front passenger window and leaned over to peer up at her. "You've got my number in that stuff. Use it. It's my job."

He cut a sharp three-point turn, and Bay finally

relaxed as he broke into yet another song. *Butler, Butler,* she thought. If the harmless, starstruck Elvin Capps could spook her, how did she hope to function around everyone else?

The Town Car eased out into the road and rolled out of sight. Exhaling, Bay rubbed at the house key she'd all but imprinted into her palm and headed inside. She took her time unlocking the front door, savoring the solid feel of the dead bolt. She was less pleased with all the glass. What was the point of locks if all you had to do was chuck a rock to get in?

Her paranoia passed as she checked out the inside. True to his word, Elvin had been working hard. Though small and probably a good forty years old, the place was spotless and as appealing as it looked from the outside. The cloud nine, listen-for-angel-harps white color scheme might be too perky for her, but she could overlook that for the time being. It was a hundred times better than where she'd been.

So much room...

Wandering from the kitchen-dinette area through the rest of the house, she opened cabinets and closets, finding that while the majority of the house remained unfurnished, Elvin had made sure she had the essentials—a broom here, an extra set of sheets and a few towels there. The closet in the bedroom with the queen-size bed that took up most of the room had her staring outright. Clothes, too?

On impulse Bay reached for the top drawer on the chest beside the closet and found everything from underwear to cotton socks, unnerving even though none of it was what anyone would call provocative. Seeing it was the correct size—she checked the A-cup bras and panty hose—she told herself this had to be Madeleine's handiwork.

She returned to the closet and noted more details—size six jeans, small T-shirts, the jogging shoes were a size seven…the powder-blue silk shift with matching three-inch pumps had her staring. Could she make it out of the house without breaking her neck, let alone navigate a church parking lot?

Although disconcerted that someone knew her body so well, the urge to rid herself of any physical link to Gatesville prompted Bay into stripping. Leaving her things where they fell, she went straight into the bathroom and took her first private shower since her arrest. The water smelled of chlorine, but the luscious peach-scented shower gel offset that. She used a quarter bottle of the fragrant goop repeatedly scrubbing her entire body until her blood hummed and her pale skin glistened.

The fluffy, white towel she wrapped herself in afterward was another first. Best not to get too fond of such luxury, she told herself. As soon as she was back to wrestling with stubborn engines and equally greasy metal, these towels would be relegated to the back of the closet and she'd be drying off in cheapo navy blue or black towels that would become shop rags soon enough.

Dry, she slipped into new panties, skipped the bra, and dragged on a bright-red T-shirt and jeans, then stood barefoot before the dresser mirror to stare at the skinny, spike-haired stranger before her. Was this what thirty-two looked like out there in the free world? Her gaze dropped to the mascara and lipstick set out on the dresser and she made a face. So she'd never been what her father and the good ol' boy-types called "a show pony"; she couldn't let that worry her now. Of all the things on her agenda, men and romance ranked last and off the list.

Scooping up her release clothes, Bay returned to the kitchen and dropped everything, including the loafers, into the plastic trash container by the door. Wasteful as that was, she needed to be physically separated from things that reminded her of prison. Then, to get her mind off what she had done, she started a serious inspection of cabinets and drawers, the pantry. The small four-pack of wine in the refrigerator startled her. Chardonnay.

"Your idea, Elvin?"

It would seem the church's position on drinking was more lenient than the Baptists' but in this instance bad judgment regardless. It would be too easy for her to fall into bad habits while in this early, vulnerable stage. About to close the door, she changed her mind, took out the carton and deposited it on top of the rejected clothing. Retracing her steps, she took a bottle of chilled vegetable juice out of the fridge and poured herself a glass.

Settling at the butcher-block dinette table, she tucked her legs into a lotus position and looked around the room and finally beyond the slats of the miniblinds, out to where the lush woods bordered the narrow yard.

Mine.

She still couldn't believe it. As her eyes began to

burn and her throat ached, she raised her glass. "Glenn...I don't understand any of this, but if you can hear me, I haven't forgotten, not you or the promise I made."

The heavens didn't smile with a rainbow of light, no chair fell over from some invisible hand. About to take a sip of her juice, the phone rang. Wincing as she clicked the glass against her teeth, Bay set it down and stared at the white wall unit by the counter as though it were a prison alarm bell. What now? Only Madeleine knew her number, and she should be in her meeting. Elvin, she decided, pushing herself off the chair. He probably forgot to explain something he thinks is critical. She didn't want to talk to him or anyone else today; however, she figured that if the call went unanswered, Madeleine's watchdog might be hammering at the door within minutes.

Bay snatched up the receiver on the fifth ring. "Hello?"

No one replied.

"One more chance, and then you get to talk to dead air. Hello!"

Bay heard enough background sound to tell her that someone was there; nevertheless, the caller remained silent. Frowning, she waited several more seconds, then, just as she was about to hang up, the caller did.

Somebody figured out they dialed the wrong number, she told herself. Her first call as a free woman and it's a mistake. Grateful that at least they hadn't tried to sell her something, she settled back in her chair.

The sun remained bright, the breeze playful as it

turned the trees bordering the property into a shimmering sea of emeralds, and yet her isolation suddenly mattered. Those patches of dense shadows for instance...was something or *someone* moving around out there?

As her cozy oasis changed before her eyes, Bay's imagination cranked into overdrive. What if the call hadn't been a wrong number? People knew she was out of prison. Madeleine had said so, and had also admitted it was possible that not everyone agreed with the court's decision just as Bay believed for her own reasons that the Tarpley story was a lie. And now that she thought about it, Bay believed it had been traffic sounds she'd heard. The caller could be on a cell phone standing in her very woods watching her.

She should have asked Madeleine more questions, found out exactly what the press knew and were saying about her, asked Elvin to stop for a paper. Considering the increased craziness going on in the world, she could be shot as she sat here, and it would be a day or more before Elvin or Madeleine found her.

With her heart beginning to pound like a full-fledged panic attack, Bay grabbed the blind's wand to shut out the view, then she flew to the door to close that one, and to test the dead bolt. It wasn't enough and, as she had on her first few nights at Gatesville, she withdrew to the most hidden corner of the room and curled into a tight ball in an attempt to make herself invisible.

"You're okay. You're okay," she recited pressing her forehead against her raised knees. She just needed to give herself some time.

But minutes stretched into hours and darkness fell and, still, Bay couldn't bring herself to move.

4

Opening her eyes to red numbers inches from her face was a shock. Once 4:00 registered, Bay went on to wonder how anything electronic, let alone something with a cord, had gotten into her cell. Belatedly, music drew her attention—and it wasn't coming from the clock. In prison you learned to numb yourself to the nonstop noise, the shouting and screams, but music didn't fit, either.

Rising up on her elbow, she saw subtle shifts of light on the door. As the thick fog dulling her senses receded, she made the connections—a door, not steel bars, sounds from a TV, not inmates and guards. This wasn't prison.

The plush, queen-size bed must have seduced her, once she'd given up her corner in the kitchen and decided she could risk going to bed. She remembered turning on the TV for background noise and supposed an experienced burglar could have cleaned out the place while she'd slept. It was her deepest sleep in over six years, but now thirst and hunger drove her out of bed.

Moving through the house like a guest, she turned on the stove hood light in the kitchen and went next for a bottle of water from the refrigerator. She drank half before putting on water for coffee. Once she located the jar of instant and a spoon, she chose a thick mug from the two in the open cupboard and measured out a heaping serving of granules. Significant caffeine was a must regardless of where she slept or how little. She could survive not smoking and had the discipline to monitor her drinking, but Java was her weakness. She liked the flavor in ice cream and in candy. If she could find that someone had invented a coffee-scented bath gel, she could be content.

From the TV came the sound of sirens. Bay hit her knee on the side table as she grappled for the remote and flipped the channel. She had to flip often, soon discovering how much noise, bloodletting and sex was on at night. When she came upon an old, familiar Western, she left it there and returned to the kitchen to pour the boiling water. A movie buff from childhood—once she understood she was responsible for her own entertainment, as she was her education—she remembered being enthralled by the on-screen chemistry between Gregory Peck and Anne Baxter. Unfortunately, time and experience had worked like thirty-six-grit sandpaper on her romantic ideals. As she watched the passion grow between the two lead characters, she could only see the potential for problems down the road…reality making any commitment between them one long conflict.

"Nobody is going to call me to reinvent the wheel," she said stirring her coffee.

Although she left on the set, she carried her mug to the dinette window where she peered through the blinds as she had earlier. Encouraged by how the security lights lit the property, Bay unlocked the door and settled into a plastic chair under the covered patio. Out on the highway traffic was virtually nonexistent; a freight truck rumbled by as she took her first sip of her brew, and after about a minute a car passed going in the opposite direction. Otherwise, sound effects were provided by night critters mostly from the creek that Bay guessed had to be to her right somewhere in the thickest section of woods. The thought of what went along with streams and dense vegetation had her tucking her feet beneath her. It was a nice night, though, even if city lights did obliterate star viewing.

Therein was a good message, she decided. There was nothing out here to dream over unless you invent it. Encouraged, she returned inside to find a pad and pencil and proceeded to list everything required to run a decent welding shop, and to stock it with ample supplies for the average walk-in business.

Before she knew it, the eastern sky went from indigo to fuchsia. Eager to see what Elvin had accomplished out in the shop, she washed up, slipped on sneakers and, with a third mug of coffee in hand, set off.

A foul smell greeted her as she slid open the shop's door, the mix of humidity, old oil, dead rodents and who knew what else. But once she turned on the fluorescent lights, all Bay saw was the welding machine. It stood precisely in the position that Glenn's machine had stood the night he was killed.

She turned away from the troubling coincidence

and studied the rest of the shop. Nothing else triggered the same revulsion in her, not the bottles of argon, oxygen and acetylene that stood just inside the door, probably where the delivery truck had left them, and it was simple practicality for the leads to be on the worktable. That table stood six-by-ten feet, larger than the ones they'd used in the old shop, and the red gang box, every bit her height, was a far more modern model than she could afford before.

As she grew more relaxed, she inspected the rest of the building. On the far side in a portable rack lay a modest inventory of stainless sheet metal; beside that was another rack with pipe, a fair quantity. Bay knew it was for Madeleine's gate.

She glanced back at the welder and decided it was an accident, that's all. Where else would Elvin put the thing?

Energized, she opened the shop doors the rest of the way, snatching up the notepad and pencil from the scarred desk that would serve as her office and began a more serious test of her memory of the design.

It was nearing noon before she stopped working. By then she was soaked with sweat and starving, and yet she felt better than she had in years. Not only did she have the initial cuts for the gate completed, she'd had her first walk-in customer, a man desperate to repair a broken headache rack on his truck. The small job earned her a fast seventy bucks—to be immediately spent on renewing her driver's license and buying paint for a sign, she decided. Pleased, she locked up and returned to the house.

After devouring a turkey sandwich and a glass of milk, she showered and tugged on clean jeans and a white T-shirt, this time over a bra. Then she drove into town to get her license renewed.

By the time she reached the DMV some of her anxiety returned. She fully expected them to know her on sight, but having her prison record lingering on their computers would be as bad. To her surprise and relief, though, the clerk reacted like someone who didn't watch TV, let alone subscribe to a newspaper, and when she brought up Bay's file on the monitor, the woman's expression remained passive.

''Okay. Uh...it's been over four years since you were a Texas resident, you'll have to take the written test again. Do you want to try it now or take a book home to study?''

Bay thought that was like asking how many shots you'd like at your execution. ''I'll give it a try,'' she told the young woman.

She made only one error and after the eye test, the clerk instructed her to step behind the strip of yellow tape on the floor for a photo. Done, Bay signed the computerized form, paid the fee and pocketed her temporary license.

Thanking the clerk, she turned to leave...and looked straight into the eyes of Jack Burke. Jack Burke, the detective who'd arrested her for Glenn's murder. Jack Burke who had grilled her for hours upon hours with relentless and redundant precision.

Jack Burke who, when she was sentenced, had the nerve to say, "I'm sorry."

Ducking her head and wishing for a pair of sunglasses to hide behind, Bay cut a sharper right. Time hadn't affected his reflexes, though, and he countered her move, knocking her off balance.

"Whoa."

At least he had no problem keeping her from cracking her jaw on the tile floor. Six years might have taken their toll other ways, but physically he remained as she remembered him, big enough to make her feel like a dry twig on a sapling and outweighing her by a good eighty-plus pounds.

"Sorry about that."

"No problem." Keeping her head low, she tried to move on.

His hold tightened. "It *is* you."

She could feel his recognition by the tension in his hands. Hadn't he heard she was getting out? Not caring one way or the other, she tugged harder and scrambled for the exit.

Ignoring the "Wait a minute!" he called after her, she pushed through the double glass doors and once outside broke into a dead run. Weak-kneed and sick to her stomach, she shoved the key into the truck's door lock.

She didn't bother turning on the air conditioner or taking time to roll down the window. The seat belt had to wait, too. Jamming the key into the ignition, she turned over the engine and drove. The need for escape had never been stronger—and grew worse when she spotted him in the rearview mirror running after her. Afraid he was about to grab on to the tail-gate, she burned rubber merging into traffic, almost hitting a Brinks armored truck.

She was free, but that was temporary. Weighed with a new gloom, she drove in a mindless, circuitous route and after a good half hour of haphazard turns she located a familiar street. In order to delay her return home a little longer, she stopped at a discount store for the paint. Another encounter was inevitable, though. Detective Jack Burke had been in the right place to obtain her new address.

It happened sooner than she expected. She hadn't yet reached the front door when the white pickup truck pulled into her driveway.

5

Doubt and worry buzzed like deer flies in her head as Bay waited for the worst. If only Madeleine would call now. She'd phoned early on to see how Bay made it through the night and once hearing Bay's plans to go for her license, promised to check in later. Sparing the busy woman a recap of her neurotic first hours here was easy—Bay would like to forget her foolish reaction herself—but she would feel better if Madeleine knew *he* had arrived, her worst analogy of a bad penny.

He stopped at the far end of the house and killed the engine, all the while watching her with the same intensity she used on him. When he climbed out, she saw he'd taken off his tan suit jacket and loosened his tie, but that just made the gun on his belt obvious. She was no less resentful of his size and how capable and trustworthy he looked. Sure, she thought, trust him to ruin your life. One thing, she had to admit time hadn't been all that kind to Jack Burke. Thanks in part to him, though, she didn't have enough generosity of spirit to feel sorry for him.

He still possessed the kind of face movie directors chose for a big brother, strong, the features defined without being craggy. But his probing brown eyes looked sunken and the shadows beneath them suggested whatever was ailing him had become chronic. Then there was that faint scar running down from his lower lip to his chin, which had her wondering who else he'd ticked off since he'd helped put her away.

He moved with a smooth grace like someone used to physical work that involved the whole body. Rolled-up sleeves exposed tanned and well-toned arms indicating that whatever he did to keep fit, it wasn't at an indoor gym. That healthy quality was offset by a slight slump to his broad shoulders, and the line bisecting those dark eyebrows cut deep enough to tell her that he frowned more often than he smiled.

He stopped a spare two yards away from her, his hands loose at his sides. She couldn't keep from folding her arms across her chest and resented him for that, too.

"You didn't have to run."

"Then why are you here?"

"For the moment, I guess only to make sure you're okay."

Right, Bay thought, and on top of her already huge generosity, Madeleine had convinced the mayor to throw a parade in her honor and give her the key to the city. At least he hadn't driven up in one of those unmarked cars. Regardless, the guy had *cop* written all over him and she wished they were standing farther back from the road than they were.

"I guess it's a bit much to hope you believe me?" he continued.

She didn't see a reason to respond to the obvious.

"Guess not. So much for my declining skill at small talk."

"You think that'll make it easier to haul me in?"

His troubled frown became one of confusion and made the ridge along his straight eyebrows resemble a mountain ledge. "Why would I do that?"

"To put me back where you think I belong."

"Then you don't know what I think."

"Please." Disgusted, Bay looked away. "Stop wasting my time. If your plan is to bug me day in and day out until I leave your precious town, forget it. If it's to make me feel guilty because a good woman believed in me and helped me, is continuing to help me," she added extending her arms to encompass her surroundings, "you can give it your best shot. But understand this, Madeleine Ridgeway will hear about it and she has connections."

"I'm acutely aware of your *friend*'s connections."

"What's that supposed to mean? Never mind. I don't care. Your bitterness about having a case getting turned around is your problem. You should have done a better job with the investigation to begin with."

"You're right there. Look, I realize you've had plenty of time to add to your hatred of me, but if it would give you any—"

"It won't."

"Bay..."

"No!" Rising anger emboldened her. "You have nothing to say that I want to hear. In fact, I was hoping never to have to see you again. Since my lucky streak seems to be short-lived, I think I should at least have a right to ask you to stay away from me."

"I'm not going to be able to do that."

The quiet words shook her more than an angry outburst would have. "That sounds like a threat."

"I could try to explain if you eased up on the defensiveness a bit."

"There's nothing to explain. I'm out. It's over."

"I don't think so...and if you're half the woman I think you are, you don't believe it, either."

The truth struck so close she barely refrained from stepping backward. "I don't know what you're talking about."

"Uh-huh. And the moment you heard your partner described as a weak gambling addict who risked your friendship and trust, not to mention his relationship with the woman he was about to marry, you didn't want to spit in the eye of the person reciting that crap to you?"

So he did know. And he was telling her that he didn't believe the story Catfish Tarpley had to tell any more than she did. It grated that they should agree about anything, but she wasn't going to let him know what she thought until she did some digging herself.

Instead, she played it cool and drawled, "Haven't visited many lifers, have you? If you did, you'd know we'd do just about anything to taste freedom again."

"Sorry, kiddo, you're not going to convince me that you've grown that hard."

"Don't call me that."

"It's the way I saw you that first night—a scared, little kid—and how I still see you."

Bay stared at the ground between them and tried not to wonder at the sadness in his voice. He couldn't care, not then or now. This was a ploy of some kind. She simply wasn't smart enough to figure out what and why.

"Why can't you just go away?" she whispered in a voice that sounded too much like the child he'd described.

"Because I owe you."

He had that much right.

"Do you know I didn't hear about the confession until it made front page in the papers? A little odd, don't you think? The case detective being left out of the loop?"

She shrugged. It wasn't her problem if his fellow cops didn't want to talk to him and that, as a result, he'd been professionally embarrassed.

"Tyler's not a three-cop town anymore," Jack Burke continued. "We don't know everything the others are doing, but for a convicted murderer who once garnered national press to have her conviction reversed without the detective on record being informed, let alone assist in the new investigation, is unusual, let me tell you."

"Maybe your superiors were trying to avoid any more PR damage than was already done."

"A valid point. So is the unwritten rule that people don't do favors for strangers."

"You think my release was a *favor?*" She dropped her hands to her sides, but her fingers curled into fists.

"Do you know your hero, Catfish Tarpley?"

"No, so you see he wasn't out to help me, he was

resolving another murder in order to help himself. What validated his testimony was that it was confirmed by one of your own. Someone in Vice.'' Seeing a look of distaste flash across his weary features, she drove her own verbal knife deeper adding, ''Do you know him?''

''I know of him. Generally, I stay away from those guys and they choose their own friends, too.''

''Sounds like a chicken way of saying you don't think much of Detective Martel.''

''It's the diplomatic way of not drawing conclusions before I have all of the facts. Who came to the prison to give you your good news?''

''My...an attorney hired by a friend.''

''Madeleine Ridgeway. She has been quite the friend to you,'' he added surveying the property.

Bay pointed her keys at him. ''Don't. Don't you dare condescend to me again. You and your *facts.* You never took the time to learn them before, why should I believe anything's changed?''

''Have you forgotten I challenged the DA's line of questioning during your trial? You don't remember how I said something didn't feel right about your case?''

''I remember he made chopped meat out of you,'' she sneered.

Jack Burke dropped his chin to his chest. ''I didn't have the experience to help you. And just prior to that they'd dumped a helluva caseload on me to where—'' he swore under his breath ''—excuses. Christ, listen to me.'' He met her gaze, his own full of misery. ''All I can say is that I'm sorry.''

Bay drew herself to her full five foot four. "Feel better now? Good. Now get lost."

His left hand moved in an almost unconscious gesture of supplication. "I'm serious about what I said. What I'd like—"

"What I'd like is to move on to the rest of my life."

"Doing what? Driving the streets Glenn English drove, reliving over and over the first instant you saw he'd been turned into a human shish kebab?"

"You son of a bitch."

"Someone has to snap you out of this daydream where you've turned into Cinderella and all's well with the world."

"If you believe that's what I'm doing, I'd be surprised to hear you've resolved any cases in your career, Detective."

Jack's eyes narrowed. "If what you're suggesting is true, all the more reason for us to talk. Don't stick your nose where it doesn't belong, Bay. You're not up to it. You're a ghost of your old self and that wasn't much to begin with. Hell, they put teens in the hospital for weighing what you do."

"You're one to criticize."

"Damned straight I look like crap. Know why? Because I've been living with what happened to you and my part in it 24/7."

Bay stared. She didn't want to believe him, but his voice almost shook when he spoke.

Nodding, Jack began heading back toward his truck. "I'll give you some space. Think about what I said."

"You think about this—I'll never accept your apology. Never!"

He paused and said over his shoulder, "That I can live with. You ending up like your friend is a different story."

6

Sunday, June 2, 2001

If it hadn't been for her lingering indignation over Jack Burke's visit and subsequent allegations, Bay might have wimped out of meeting the Ridgeways for church services. But she awakened on time that morning and despite feeling as substantial as an undercooked soufflé, made herself shower and slip into the clothes Madeleine had purchased for her. Then with only a hefty dose of caffeine to bolster her, she headed toward the southernmost city limits of Tyler.

While summer remained weeks away, heat had established itself in the piney woods. Bay saw it compounding the waves rising from the traffic creating a blinding glare that had her wishing again for sunglasses despite the early hour. So much traffic, she thought with disbelief. The steady stream surpassed anything she'd noticed so far around the airport, almost matching rush hour on the Loop, and many of the vehicles were pulling into the turning lane where she needed to go. Of course, she already knew the church was large, but seeing it for the first time left her openmouthed.

Mission of Mercy rose above the dogwood and pines, an unbelievable mix of the gardens of Babylon and Hollywood's rendition of Camelot. The snow-white mountain of granite glistened brighter with tall, lead windows and taller belfries interspersed with balconies adorned with planters full of red and white geraniums and assorted lush flowers. Bay estimated the whole structure took up a full city block and stood a good eight stories at its highest point.

Torn between awe and dismay, she waited for her turn to pull into the multiacre grounds, and unlike most of the traffic, chose a parking space as far away from the front doors as possible and nearest to the first street exit. "Mercy," she said, peering through the tinted windshield for a better look at what she'd only glimpsed on TV. "No need to fly out to Disney World when it's in your own backyard." No one would convince her that God listened better in something like this; however, the playoff game-size crowd streaming toward the building obviously thought otherwise. Forget worrying about sitting with the Ridgeways, she would be lucky to find them in that swarm.

Wondering about how many people the building could hold, she joined the parade; that's when she spotted the less gaudy two-story complex behind and to the left of the church. Satellite dishes and microwave towers identified its purpose as the nerve center or communication studios from which KWRD transmitted their message for Mission of Mercy. Bay had done a little homework over the last few days watching TV so as not to disappoint or embarrass Madeleine in front of others, and had gotten an earful about services as well the church's ministry. KWRD transmitted to much of the South and Southwest, also Mexico, several Central American countries and Colombia. Services or alternative spiritual programming were available virtually around the clock. Aside from live services, there was a talk show where Pastor Davis was joined by either his wife, the perpetually smiling Odessa, or Madeleine herself. Then there was home-shopping programming where a "faith representative" reviewed audio tapes, books, musical cassettes and CDs available for purchase. Years ago, Bay would flip by those channels thinking, "You see one of those, you've seen them all." But she'd felt a strange mix of emotions as she'd watched this time because she'd met Martin Davis and knew Madeleine, who was such an important member of the church. Bitten by the celebrity bug, she thought with a cynical twist of her lips.

Her conflicted emotions blossomed into outright panic as Bay entered the sprawling vestibule and remembered from commercials how the congregation was often shown during the taped services. Bay hadn't seen Madeleine or her son in them and hoped they sat out of camera range. The idea of finding herself in front of cameras again had her clenching her fingers tight to keep from scratching at the sudden itching along her neck.

"Praise God and welcome, sister. Do you need the assistance of a senior?"

Bay paused before the beaming man clutching a

Bible. The glorious sunshine streaming in through the huge glass panes of the vestibule intensified his flushed, shining face and made it impossible to miss that his gray eyes were feverish with anticipation. "Senior what?" she asked.

"That's our term for deacon or elder."

A hand, as warm as the voice near her ear, cupped her elbow. Startled, Bay glanced around and experienced the double impact of Duncan Ridgeway's dimples and amused blue eyes. It wasn't the first time she'd seen him. He was the darling of East Texas media and she'd glimpsed numerous photos of him at the Ridgeway estate. But one-dimensional images didn't do justice to the face best suited for color and animation, a leonine mane attractive from any angle, and intimate eyes that sparkled like a Caribbean sea as they observed the world with untiring focus. His was a face every fund-raiser yearned for, the kind of face that women would describe as romantic and men would see as competition but too friendly to resent. No wonder the ministry was doing so well, she thought with a mixture of artistic respect and cynical amusement.

"This is Mother's very special guest, Ed," Duncan Ridgeway said to the other man. "Thank you for looking out for her." To Bay he said, "I'm—"

"Duncan. I recognize you from your photos."

Even grimacing he charmed. "Of course, you've been to her office. She's worse than a small-town talent agent who's only success has been one client with a walk-on part in *Cats*."

"Oh, I think she has more reason than that to be proud of you. You favor your father, though."

Duncan touched his ringless left hand against the tie matching his pearl-gray suit. "That does my heart good. He was a lovely soul...but had just enough wickedness to make him the life of any party. I'll tell you a few of my favorite stories sometime. Right now we'd better get inside. Mother was about to dispatch Elvin to your house."

"I'm sorry. I didn't realize I was late."

"You're not. She's chronically networking-orientated and thinks everyone else should arrive for services thirty minutes early."

Duncan moved his hand to the small of her back as he directed her through the doorway and into the nave or what she'd heard referred to on TV as the Grand Hall. "She has her work cut out to convince me."

Duncan chuckled as he acknowledged the wave of someone in an aisle seat. "So I heard. Don't let her change you. Your strength is part of what she admires most."

"She'll probably end up labeling me stubborn."

"Challenge keeps her young. To know Mother is to understand her middle name is Strategy."

Bay was as conscious of Duncan's touch as she was of the stares aimed their way. She wanted to believe that it had little to do with her, that like his mother Duncan Ridgeway possessed a charisma that drew the eye, as did their stature in the church. But there was no missing the whispering, and when her gaze locked with Holly Kirkland's dark stare, her step faltered.

"Are you all right?" Duncan asked.

"Yes." She wasn't but she wouldn't let him know.

Glenn's fiancée had matured, advancing from girlishly pretty to striking, her lush dark hair cut stylishly short and her makeup subtle, since her dramatic coloring didn't require more. But it was her white suit that struck Bay strongest. It would be perfect for a quiet wedding, which left her wondering if Holly had chosen it to remind her that she wasn't the only one who had something stolen from her.

Reaching their front row seats turned out to be something of a relief after all.

"Darling." Madeleine reached out her hand and drew Bay down onto the plush theater seat on her left. "I'm so glad you could come. Doesn't she look enchanting, Duncan? She could be your baby sister."

"As radiant as you look today, more like yours."

Madeleine laughed throatily as her son lowered his lanky length into the chair on her right and she patted his long thigh affectionately. She could have been the mother of a bride in her silvery-blue silk suit, positively glowing with happiness. At the same time, the cynic in Bay couldn't help but note that framed by the royal-blue-and-white color scheme, the three of them created almost too perfect a photo opportunity. Almost on cue, the KWRD TV cameraman swept their way and lingered.

"Oh, no."

Although she'd whispered the protest between stiff lips, Madeleine heard and leaned toward her. "Chin up and smile, darling. Think of something else, lunch for instance. Cook is preparing the most divine lobster salad.''

Cook must not be in need of spiritual support or networking, Bay thought enviously. To Madeleine she replied, ''Thank you, but I'm not sure I'll have an appetite after this.''

Duncan leaned forward and pointed behind him with his program. ''If you need to leave in a hurry, that door to our right leads to the vestibule. Don't try the fire exits, or you'll trigger the alarms and then you *will* have more attention than you want.''

''Oh, sweetheart, don't encourage her.''

Grinning at his mother's protest, Duncan winked at Bay before sitting back. The choir stood and began singing. Thankfully, the cameras turned to them and Bay worked at getting her heart out of her throat and back where it belonged.

''How're y'all this blessed of all mornings?'' Martin Davis said approaching the dais, once the choir finished. ''I told my darling Odessa as we got in the car, no one could have gotten out of the wrong side of the bed on a day this fine. Moments later at the first traffic light, I stopped rather than drive through yellow, and the guy behind me gave me the finger.'' After a pause for laughter, he continued, ''It just goes to show you that everything can be perfect, you can obey every law, follow the rules...and somebody's still gonna have that finger ready. Reminds me of what happened to the apostle Peter while...''

For the next twenty minutes, Bay rode a strange sea of emotions as Pastor Davis navigated his way through the service with the energy of a decathlon athlete and intelligent wit of Johnny Carson. Blatant, however, was how for all of his country boy charm, ambition ran like a heady wine in this minister's veins. Bay caught glimpses of his shrewd speculation as he studied his congregation gauging how firmly he had them in his control; nevertheless, she found him more tolerable than most evangelists on TV. If she was a neophyte attending with an open mind and heart and in need of familial attention, needy in general, she could see herself succumbing to Davis's brand of, "Trust *me* and the Lord will bless *you*" manipulation. At least he didn't reduce her to yawns. Where did he envision himself to be in five years? As grand as this place was, somehow she didn't think thriving, but modest little Tyler, Texas, was the end of his visionary rainbow.

"Well, now, I dare you to tell me that you weren't inspired?" Madeleine said as they rose along with everyone else.

Bay gazed around the huge auditorium. "These are such soothing cool colors to counterbalance the pastor's passion, did you pick them out?"

Duncan laughed and linked his mother's arm through his. "Good for you, Bay. It's so refreshing to meet someone who refuses to say anything she doesn't mean. Mother, when I get you to the car, I'll drive to the house with Bay, show her a back way so she's not trapped in that infernal midday traffic."

After a brief unreadable stare for her son, Madeleine gave Bay a shrug. "So you're right, it wasn't his best sermon. Now we'll have to listen to Odessa worrying all through lunch that he offended the little white-haired ladies in the congregation with that finger reference.''

''See,'' Duncan whispered conspiratorially to Bay, ''it's catching.''

''Keep on,'' Madeleine drawled. ''I'm sitting Odessa next to you. Now let's stop to say hello to Holly, I gather that's why she's lingering behind, since lately she's one of the first out of here. She'll be at lunch,'' she explained to Bay. ''I want to know how she's liking being part of the TV production team. I hated encouraging Martin to move her out of the church office, but the other ladies confided that there were simply too many mistakes being made. Lyle and Granger will complete the table.''

''Granger?''

''Patterson. Publisher of the town's new magazine. Tyler's answer to *D Magazine* and *Texas Monthly.*''

Duncan was no longer smiling. ''Mother, is that smart? Bay is still getting acclimated and you dangle her in front of a shark.''

Madeleine looked wounded. ''How can you suggest that? Besides, I'll be there to intercede if he does push her for an interview. Honestly, Duncan, it was his only open date for the next month and I have to get him to join our church before the Baptists grab hold of him. Holly,'' she sang, ''aren't you looking absolutely divine. You remember Bay, of course.''

''Who could forget?''

''Hello, Holly. You are looking well.''

The unsmiling woman didn't return the compliment; in fact, except for a brief, hard stare, she ignored her. Her manner warmed several degrees as she focused on Duncan. ''If you can spare the time, I'd like to talk to you after lunch.''

''Sure.''

Nodding, Holly retreated via a side exit. Watching her, Madeleine sighed.

''I do hope I won't have to have another talk with the girl. It troubles me that despite claiming to understand she was wrong about Bay, she behaved so coldly just now. I'll have Lulu adjust the seating arrangements as soon as I get home and rely on you, Duncan, to make sure Holly doesn't indulge in too much wine. Monica, Steve, how are you? Did the kids get settled in D.C. all right?''

Amazing, Bay thought, as Madeleine moved on to another couple and another subject. How did she keep everything straight and remember everyone's names? And there was a constant stream of Monicas and Steves, all of whom fell into either an awkward silence or artificial friendliness as Madeleine introduced them to her, until Bay simply held back to stay out of her line of vision.

Once they finally reached the car, Duncan turned his mother over to Elvin, parked curbside, the engine idling in order for the air conditioner to cool the interior. In the last second, Madeleine grasped Bay's wrist.

''Don't think I didn't notice what you did back there. You must be bolder, darling. Look people straight in the eye and defy them to judge you. Naturally, I abhor gossip, but the Scrantons? His brother is still doing time for annuity embezzlement.''

"Oh, Madeleine. I'm just not the psychological pugilist you are. All I want to do is to work with my metal and to take some time figuring out where I fit in."

"Mm. I can see you need coaching."

With a fond pat on the cheek she slid into the car. Only when Duncan touched her elbow did Bay realize she was standing there caught in the hopeless avalanche of his mother's overpowering personality.

"She is one of a kind," he said staying close as they stepped off the curb.

"Is it absolutely necessary that I attend this lunch? This hasn't been my idea of a fun morning and the last thing I want to do is add to the friction between Holly and your mother."

"The only reason Holly remains with us is due to her. We've all tried to help Holly get on with her life. At first I thought she was, but in the last year or two...well, you saw for yourself how she behaved."

"Your mother hinted at an addiction problem."

"No need to hint. If you're around her long enough, you'll find out for yourself. Bay, something you should know...Holly and I went out a few times."

The news came as no surprise. Holly oozed sex appeal and while slim, had all of the curves in the right places. Bay thought her as exotic as an imported delicacy. "It's none of my business," she said without jealousy.

"It could be." At her startled glance, he smiled. "So much for my ego."

"No, I—I'm not looking for a relationship, Duncan."

"And as my mother's point man, I have the family business as well as the public relations for the church to oversee, which takes me out of town more than I'd like. But you intrigue me, Bay. Everything Mother's said about you and your challenges growing up, I feel like an old friend of the family has returned home. In any case, I didn't want you to hear rumors elsewhere and not know the truth, that I couldn't take things to the next level with Holly due to her unpredictability. Our family and the church's international status makes us too high profile to allow such conduct. Cold-blooded, huh?"

"Not at all. I'm hardly in your league, but I worry myself, how my record will taint my ability to attract enough lucrative accounts to establish a viable business here."

"What record?"

His innocent tone earned him another sidelong look and Bay could only shake her head in wonder. Maybe after a while she would believe her past no longer existed, at least on paper; it would take much longer to convince herself that someone as suave and successful as Duncan Ridgeway would find her a worthy replacement to Holly when he could have any beauty he wanted. She had to be crazy to warn him off. The Ridgeways were already making things easier for her, and Duncan could make that doubly so.

"What's that frown for?" he asked.

No way would she tell him her mercenary thought even though she was disgusted with herself for having it. ''Holly. I appreciate the confidence. I always liked her and I'll do what I can not to complicate things for your family.''

''A sweet thought,'' he said with a heavy sigh. ''I fear that's no more in your control than it is in mine.''

The words haunted Bay for the rest of the trip to the Ridgeway estate.

7

It was the last chance Bay and Duncan had to talk one-on-one. Once they arrived at the house, Madeleine took over again leading Bay from one guest to the next. Contrary to Madeleine's earlier criticism, she liked Odessa Davis best. Diminutive, eternally sunny and as plump as her husband, she exhibited a genuine affection for him even when gently chastising him about his sermon as Madeleine warned she would.

Despite having left the church first, Holly arrived shortly after the Davises and didn't participate in any conversation unless asked a direct question, something no one seemed eager to do. Lyle Gessler appeared from somewhere else in the house and planted himself behind Madeleine like a substitute guardian angel. Bay caught him watching her several times and, while his expression remained lawyer passive, his aura of disdain for her brought a chill that made the air-conditioned room almost too cold to bear.

Granger Patterson was the last to arrive and offered no apology or explanation for delaying lunch. Tall enough to tower over Duncan, his sun-streaked blond hair also bore interesting silver highlights, a close match to his eyes. Bay guessed him to be in his mid-sixties, except that his hands and neck suggested a decade beyond that. Cosmetic surgery? From what she'd read in the news, an increasing number of men were opting to go under the knife for business reasons. Bay disliked him on sight, but not for that reason. Once they were introduced, the man simply gave her no other choice.

"Ms. Butler." He shook her hand in a firm, but brief exchange. "Tyler's lady of the hour."

"Closer to a reluctant fifty-nine seconds if I'm lucky."

"Clever soundbite, though it wouldn't work as well in print as on TV."

"I didn't realize I was being interviewed."

"Would you like to be?"

"Absolutely not."

"All right, we can talk price."

"That wasn't an attempt at negotiation."

The slight duck of his head signaled his cynicism. "I don't put much stock in modesty. I care about the story, not politics or agenda."

"Okay, then you know I haven't voted in several years and my only agenda is to stay away from carnivores. If you can manage to insult me accurately, we might end up having a conversation."

His laugh sounded like someone strangling. "I'll have my secretary set up an appointment."

"Not about a story."

"It could be lucrative for you. Madeleine tells me you're an artist as well as craftsman."

"One who's booked to September."

"You'll be old news by then."

"Lucky me."

Being rejected didn't phase Patterson. At lunch he sat on Madeleine's left and Bay on her right, and while their hostess did her best to keep his attention, he remained doggedly intent on including Bay in their dialogue. Not only was Madeleine visibly annoyed, but it kept Bay from speaking to Lyle Gessler. Intercepting sharp looks from Holly at the far end of the table beside Duncan made it all worse.

Rich food and stress took its toll and Bay excused herself before dessert could be served hoping to find aspirin in the guest bathroom to ease her throbbing head. The perfect hostess, Madeleine had several pain relievers displayed on a crystal tray for guests. Two tablets and a few moments with a cool washcloth against her forehead gave her the ability to head back to the others.

On her way past the sunroom, she spotted Holly at the wheel-cart bar. "Could we talk for a moment?" Bay asked, as the young woman poured herself what looked like vodka from a crystal decanter.

Ignoring her, Holly downed the double shot of liquor. "No need to practice your 'Free at last, free at last' speech on me. Unlike the very interesting Mr. Patterson, I'm not buying theatrics. I get enough at my day job."

So much for Madeleine's claims. How could she misread Holly this badly? "It's true. I really want—"

"To be friends? Nice trick, considering we were never going to be that when Glenn was alive."

"I wanted to, so why not? We both cared about him."

Sheer hatred flared in the other woman's eyes. "*I* loved him. You threw him away."

"We were friends, Holly. It was never meant to be anything else. He understood in the end and I was so happy for him when he met you and recognized that he was really in love."

"Ms. Butler, Holly," Lyle Gessler said in the doorway. "You're about to miss dessert. Mrs. Ridgeway would like you to return to the table."

Rejecting the arm Lyle offered her, Holly did that immediately. Bay saw her opportunity and tried to delay him.

"Mr. Gessler, a moment, please. My case file," she told the attorney as he paused. "I'd like to see it."

"That's impossible."

"Why?"

"Because I don't have it."

"Who does?"

He nodded toward the dining room.

"You haven't kept a copy?"

"There was no reason to. I was the liaison. My area is corporate law, not trial law."

"Thank you," Bay replied despite his condescending tone. "I'll speak with Mrs. Ridgeway then."

She wanted to leave there and then, but somehow got through the white chocolate mousse with raspberry sauce, and the tedious wait for the other guests to depart. Finally, as Martin Davis and Odessa took their leave, she let Madeleine walk her to the door—only to be handed another rejection.

"It's over, darling. What good is reminding yourself of the unpleasant? It's certainly not going to help your future."

"I'm still searching for clarity and perspective. I know Mr. Gessler gave me the abbreviated facts, but this is my life we're talking about. I went from no future, to unlimited possibilities in a matter of minutes. I'm still coming to terms with how that happened."

"I agree. Let her have it," Duncan said coming up beside her.

Madeleine looked as though he'd encouraged her to burn down the house; however, she recovered admirably. "I happen to know Bay's sensitive and artistic side and I think exposing her to any additional unpleasantness would only be detrimental to her creativity."

"That's complete rot, Mother. Look at her—Bay is as levelheaded as you are. She'll be fine."

"Well." Madeleine clasped her hands in an inverted V. "I see I'm outnumbered. Then you get the file for me, won't you, dear? It's on my credenza, I believe."

As he left with a quick arm squeeze for Bay, Madeleine's smile grew rueful. "Promise me that you won't spend the rest of the day on that thing?"

"I won't." Bay didn't feel so much as a twinge of guilt at voicing the lie. "I'm sorry about Holly."

Madeleine sighed. "Holly reminds me of a bird determined to fly straight into a window convinced that what it sees is continuing sky. We've paid for her therapy, made all sorts of compromises and adjustments so she could continue with us, but—'' she shrugged ''—I'm close to being out of ideas and, I fear, at the end of my patience.''

''Maybe if she could meet someone else, she could move on.''

''What's the likelihood of that under the circumstances?''

To Bay's relief Duncan returned, saving her from having to respond. ''Thank you,'' she said hoping they didn't see the slight trembling of her hands as she accepted the folder, which somehow looked thinner than the one she'd seen Lyle Gessler page through at Gatesville.

''What's your schedule like later in the week?'' he replied.

She didn't know what her expression looked like, and Madeleine's wasn't much better in that she'd now mastered her emotions. ''I...well, I'll be working, I suppose. I owe your mother the gate she's been waiting for.''

''You can't work around the clock and you have to eat. I'm out of town until Wednesday. How about if I call you Thursday and we'll see about dinner? You haven't committed me to something, have you, Mother?''

''Of course, not.'' Madeleine embraced Bay. ''You two work it out. I have some calls to return. Thank you for making my morning so enjoyable, my dear.''

As she retreated into her office, Bay frowned at Duncan. ''She doesn't approve.''

''She's annoyed with me for forcing her hand and giving you the file.''

"Speaking of being upset...you don't have to take up where she's leaving off. I'm not in need of constant entertaining, never mind caretaking."

"Good Lord, is that how you see this?" With a new gleam in his eye, he took hold of her upper arms. "I see I have my work cut out for me."

A part of her, the ghost of the awkward schoolgirl, didn't want to be having this conversation. The injured woman warmed with secret triumph and feminine curiosity.

"You're staring at me as though I were under your microscope," Duncan said, touching the tip of her nose. "This is where you make my day by giving me something refreshing to look forward to instead of another ghastly dinner meeting."

"You'll be disappointed."

"Try me."

8

The phone was ringing as Bay returned home and opened her front door. Not bothering to take the key out of the lock, she grabbed the receiver.

"Hello?" She placed her slim shoulder bag and the folder from the Ridgeways onto the kitchen counter. "Hello?"

Once again she heard subtle but indistinguishable background noises to assure her that someone was there.

"Not today, thanks," she muttered hanging up.

She'd had enough, enough of people pushing her buttons, of those trying to play mind games and all of the manipulation. All she wanted to do now was slip out of what she would heretofore call her "torture slippers" and change into the loosest, skimpiest outfit she could find.

"Mercy, that air conditioner is cranking away," she said carrying her things down the hall. At the register she found out why.

The temperature was set all the way to the coldest setting. How had she managed that? What an idiot, she thought quickly adjusting it back up to seventy-nine. She must have knocked it somehow as she was hurrying to leave and wobbling in those shoes. Dreading what this would do to her electricity bill, she continued to the bedroom...and froze in the doorway.

The window nearest the bathroom was open.

Sultry air was seeping into the room, offsetting the chill in the hall and yet goose bumps rose on her bare arms. Now *that* she knew she hadn't done.

Her heart slamming against her breastbone, she retreated to the kitchen for some kind of weapon—the heavy-duty flashlight kept by the door for her left hand to deflect a blow, and a knife with the longest, sturdiest blade for her right. Once leaving Gatesville, she'd hoped she was putting this part of her life behind her. She should have known that was too good to be true.

This time Bay checked room by room, starting with the kitchen's broom closet and the linen closet in the hallway. At the same time she looked for other signs that someone had left taunting clues of his visit. Once she got as far as the bathroom and determined she was the only one in the house, she closed the window, tested the lock and began checking drawers, her imagination in overdrive.

Everything else appeared untouched. In a way that upset her more than if she'd seen her things ripped or soiled. And now what did she do, call the police? That was a joke.

"Hi, this is Bay Butler, former convicted murderer. Could you send someone out here to fingerprint the place? I just got home and my bedroom window is open and my air conditioner is heading for cardiac arrest."

No, aside from there being no provable crime, the word would go out on the police radio and with her luck some ambitious reporter would join in the rush out here. That would cinch her being the joke of the day on the morning TV and radio talk shows. As for calling anyone else for help, to what end? There was nothing anyone could do unless she'd had a video camera operating here in her absence to catch the person in the act. Madeleine would insist she move into the big house after all or send Elvin out here to play bodyguard and both of those ideas were unacceptable. The camera idea was a good one, but a luxury she simply couldn't afford.

"Damn it!" she seethed. She'd earned the right to live alone, to maintain her privacy. *So think. What was the point of this?*

Intimidation.

Jack Burke? That speech the other day could have been a crock and if he couldn't get her back behind bars, he wanted her out of Tyler worse than Holly did. As for her, she'd been at church with the rest of them. No, whoever called minutes ago had been her intruder wanting to see if she'd gotten home and how she was taking this. Likely that wasn't Burke, because he hadn't known where to find her that first day. Several others did, but everyone she could think of had the alibi of being at the church. Could she be guilty of not checking that window after all?

Brooding over that, Bay changed into a loose nightshirt and panties and in the end concluded that the biggest favor she could do for herself was to study that file and see if there were any clues.

Minutes later she leaned back on the couch and stared at the papers spread across the coffee table. Something was very wrong. There were things missing. Unfortunately, she couldn't put her finger on exactly what. Besides not having a college degree, she was no student of the law. All she knew was that the file wasn't as thick as the one Gessler brought the day he'd come to speak to her. From her perspective, there should be a report on Tarpley's testimony, another from Razor Basque's case file, and Nick Martel's statement… Shouldn't there be a notarized, thumbprint-in-blood something or other?

As the day took its toll, Bay rubbed her face with both hands. How could it be that Gessler's memo to Madeleine summarizing everything—almost as abbreviated as his verbal report to her—was the closest thing to information in there aside from her own trial record? The court edict vacating her verdict was nice to see in black and white, but of no other help. Where was any of the background paperwork from that trial lawyer Gessler referred to? Had Gessler removed it before turning the file over to Madeleine? Why? A woman like Madeleine would want all of the data, since she'd financed this endeavor.

The implications made Bay's stomach roil. If Madeleine removed or had someone remove documents, she would have to know Bay would ask for the file. She'd looked so surprised and unhappy about it… Surely that hadn't been "strategy" as Duncan put it? As for him, he'd been quick to retrieve the file, had supported her right to have it. Her suspicious mind had them pulling a good-cop-bad-cop routine. Ridiculous.

The most direct way to get answers would be to ask. Bay headed for the kitchen phone, but stopped before picking up the receiver. Calling was out of the question. Madeleine would see this as an outright accusation, and Duncan probably would, too. Bay would have to be ready to walk away from this property, maybe lose *The Iron Maiden* contract once and for all.

Oh, God, she thought. Pulling away from her would subsequently cost her business from any other church member too, forcing Bay to Dallas or Houston where there were larger metal shops. Getting answers about Tarpley, Basque and Martel long-distance would be more difficult yet.

Returning to the living room, she paced in front of the coffee table, eyeing the unsatisfying spread. She needed a break. She *needed* a real ally, someone to point her in the right direction even if he didn't have the answers himself. Maybe Nick Martel had only been a fringe principle in all of this, but he was a detective and could give her some advice.

Jack Burke's less-than-glowing remarks about the Vice cop replayed in her mind, but she pushed them away. "I don't want to date him," she said, with a growing sense of commitment to the idea. "I just want to pick his brain."

And if he seemed at all sympathetic, maybe she'd ask for his advice about her intruder.

9

Monday, June 3, 2001

While she'd had a profitable day, thanks to another walk-in customer, Bay was anxious to lock up and head across town.

Shortly after four, she tucked the money into her hind pocket and crossed the driveway to the house. Another few customers like the one who'd just left, she thought, and she could consider that camera after all. Walk-in traffic rarely challenged her as an artist, but as a craftsman, she enjoyed testing her skills against practical applications, as well as doing the best job for the customer. Usually, she knew more about what metal could and couldn't do than the person asking for her help, and that had been the case with the guy whose truck, full of franchise auto parts, had been broken into overnight. She showed him how simply repairing the damage would leave him vulnerable to additional vandalism and various options to discourage that. The guy didn't blink at the cost—a smart move considering what he stood to lose in inventory.

After a quick shower, Bay changed into a white T-shirt and jeans, stuck a pencil under the miniblinds on the door and carefully locked up again. The concept behind the poor man's burglar alarm was that if she got home and was equally careful unlocking the door, she'd find the pencil exactly how she'd left it—or know she needed to use caution before proceeding any farther.

Driving to the Loop, she passed three gas station/convenience stores before stopping to use a pay phone, following the theory, "better neurotic than traced." After putting in the proper change and dialing the number on the scrap of paper she'd brought with her, she waited for the connection.

"Yes," she said to the central switchboard operator, "I'd like to talk to Detective Nick Martel, please."

There was a pause on the other line. "I'm sorry," the woman replied slowly. "I don't seem to…do you know which department he's in?"

"Vice."

"Let me connect you with them. This is a new list and I don't see him on here. But I'm pretty new, so hold please."

The phone rang and rang. Finally a man's curt voice snapped, "Vice."

"Nick Martel, please."

Once again she was subjected to one of those telling pauses that suggested this wasn't going to be easy.

"Who's calling, please?"

"Oh, no. Don't tell me he's gone for the day?" She hoped whining in the little girl's voice worked.

"Who is this?"

Bay hung up. Maybe she could have pulled this off giving the guy a fake name, but something in his tone warned her not to. What to do next? she thought, watching the traffic speed by. There had been no listing in the phone book for any Nick or N. Martel, and while she appreciated the ironical link between names and occupations, she couldn't assume Martel's Welding was any relation to Nick.

Disappointed, Bay decided to drive around downtown to see if inspiration would strike again. Taking the next left meant passing where her old shop had stood. Madeleine had warned her that it had been torn down and replaced with a used car lot. Just as well, Bay thought. Likely Glenn would have approved, considering that he'd been a vintage car junkie and hated the new models that got progressively more expensive to buy and costlier to repair.

She drove around the square and then inspected some of the side streets, using the opportunity to refresh her memory and note the changes as she had in other parts of the city. As she passed a grill, she saw a couple of cops exit their private vehicles and enter for what she assumed was an early dinner. Or a few beers, she amended, remembering that though the churches had succeeded in keeping liquor stores out of the city, restaurants could sell drinks on a membership basis. Thinking it might be a cop hangout, Bay slid into the first parking slot available. She could go in and order takeout. If things didn't get uncomfortable, she would ask the uniforms if they knew Martel.

Once her eyes adjusted to the dim lighting in the brick-walled restaurant, she counted at least five officers. Relieved that she didn't recognize any of them, she placed her order and went to the first table.

It took a few tries to be heard above the fifties rock-and-roll music, but finally two of the men shook their heads. The third eyed her with curiosity. "Why don't you go to the station and ask there?" he suggested.

"Well, I wouldn't want to intrude."

The three exchanged knowing glances, and losing nerve fast, Bay thanked them and moved on to the other table where a man and woman in uniform sat. Neither of them were of help; however, as Bay began to leave, the woman called her back.

"You look familiar. Have we met?"

"I get that all the time," Bay replied and quickly withdrew. She spent the next several minutes sweating blood waiting for her order to be ready. About ready to lose her courage and sacrifice her purchase, the waitress pushed the white box across the counter at her.

Snatching it up, Bay took the longest strides she could to get out of there...and came face-to-face with Jack Burke.

He looked from her into the eatery and then at her again. "What are you doing here?"

She held up the box.

Jack lifted his left eyebrow. "You passed any number of burger joints coming here. I know better than to hope you were looking for me, so that leaves who?"

"That's my business."

"Did you specifically ask for Martel in there?"

"What if I did?"

"What kind of luck did you have?"

She looked away. "None."

"Because he's gone."

"What?"

"I just found out myself. He's left Tyler, left Texas and moved his family to Portland."

Bay gripped her foam box until it began to crack. "I don't understand."

"That makes two of us. Did anyone recognize you in there?"

"They're working on it."

"All right, hit the road. I'll pick up something myself and meet you back at your place."

"No. I told you, stay away from me."

Before she could step around him, Jack gripped her arm. "With Martel gone, you need me more than ever."

It was a mistake to look up into his face. Their close proximity allowed too much—intimacy, a full awareness of his strength, what a clear rich brown his eyes were...how hard his heart pounded against her hand. Nothing spectacular that she didn't see or experience before, and yet her body responded as though she'd been in incubation for thirty-two years and had tasted fresh air for the first time.

When his gaze shifted to her mouth, she jerked free and escaped to her truck. Out of the corner of her eye, she saw Jack Burke continue inside as though nothing had happened.

"There's a lesson for you," she muttered shifting into reverse.

If he showed up at the house, she wouldn't let him in. She would shut the miniblinds tight and pretend she didn't hear him. The only thing she liked worse than being embarrassed was realizing she'd been wrong. She wasn't a lost cause. She could feel temptation.

Her alternate fuming and self-chastising came to an abrupt halt as she pulled into her driveway and saw Madeleine's car in the driveway and Elvin about to put a key in the door lock. It set her heart pounding for an entirely different reason.

She beat her palm against the horn. It stopped him and he waited for her to drive around the sedan and into the carport.

"Where've you been?" he demanded as she came around the corner.

Bay stopped, disliking his tone as much as she did knowing he had access to her house. Hadn't Madeleine signed the deed over to her?

"Mrs. R. called. Repeatedly," he continued.

Grateful that she hadn't stopped on the way home to toss her dinner box into the trash, she held it up for Elvin to see. "I ran an errand and picked up dinner."

"The refrigerator's empty already?"

What was this, Prison Lite? Holding his gaze, she countered with her own subtle accusation. "What are you doing with a key to the house?"

"Mrs. R. felt we should keep one in case of an emergency."

Then she should have told her. Bay didn't like this at all and, inevitably, thought of the window and thermostat. Here was someone who was exposing his access, but why would he do something so taunting and costly? Did he think her undeserving of his employer's generosity? No, Bay reminded herself, Elvin had been at the church, and he wasn't stupid. All she had to do is mention what happened to Madeleine and he would be exposed. There was one thing she did have to make clear.

Bay held out her hand. "Could I have it, please?"

"Not without Mrs. R.'s say-so."

"She deeded the property over to me. Are you aware of that?"

The stocky man shrugged, his lower lip beginning to protrude. "Not any of my business. All I know is she wanted to keep a key and she sent me over to check on you."

"Then let's call her, shall we?"

"Go ahead."

That wasn't the reaction Bay wanted. Chances were he would follow her, and aside from not wanting to be alone in the house with a virtual stranger who might have a side to him that his employer didn't know about, there was that pencil. She wasn't about to give away her secret tricks or expose her concern.

Hoping her confident pose could outlast his, she nodded to the phone in his shirt pocket. "I'm sure you have that thing programmed, go ahead and use yours."

With a flash of impatience, he spun away from her. "I don't need this crap. I'm off to take care of the rest of what I gotta do. You're still breathing and Mrs. R. needs me back at the house to drive her to a function this evening. The rest is your problem to settle with her.''

''Elvin, do not leave here with that key.''

''If that's what she wants, you'll get it,'' he replied over his shoulder as he headed for the car. ''Next time.''

After he'd had a chance to make a copy? ''No. Now.''

He stopped just as abruptly and, staring at his back, Bay felt a flicker of doubt. She'd provoked him, she could sense it in the tension in his back muscles against the white cotton of his shirt. Idiot, she seethed. She knew better than to challenge an unknown commodity.

As she fingered her keys, adjusting them in case she needed the self-defense, a white pickup pulled into her driveway. The problem was she didn't know whether he was an answer to a prayer or more trouble. How had he made it here so fast?

Jack took his time emerging from the truck. ''Everything okay?'' he asked, casually approaching them.

''Just peachy, Detective.''

As soon as Elvin resumed his retreat, Bay understood: like a cunning coyote, he was cutting his losses, meaning to use Jack's arrival to avoid further dialogue over the key. No way could she spend another night here knowing he or anyone else had that kind of access.

''Elvin.'' When he paused again, she continued, ''The key, please.''

"Oh, right, right." Pursing his thick lips, he pretended to dig into his right pants pocket and came up with the single key, then brought it back to her. "You be sure and call her, hear?" he said winking as he handed it over.

"Oh, I will."

"No hard feelings. I was just doing my job."

That's what she wanted to believe; however, watching him drive away, Bay wasn't convinced. Unable to resist scratching the itch where the key touched her skin, she met Jack Burke's serious scrutiny and forced herself to stop.

"Where's your takeout?"

"I changed my mind."

"You never meant to eat there in the first place. You spotted me."

"What was the deal with the key?"

"Like he said, a misunderstanding."

"Try again. He covered it well, but I know he didn't want to hand it over. I also know he's Madeleine Ridgeway's driver, Bay."

"What a coincidence. By his reaction I'd say you were no mystery to him, either. Translation—if I don't phone Madeleine fast, how long do you think it'll be before she calls me demanding to know why you're here?"

"And what will you tell her?"

"That I can't decide who's the bigger pain in the backside, you or my good friend Elvin."

Once again Jack held her gaze. "Confess, Bonnie B. You were relieved to see me."

"I'll be equally relieved to see you go." Casting

him an ominous look, she returned to her truck to get her dinner. If there was one thing that ticked her off, it was being taunted with her idiotic first name, the result of her mother buying a paperback version of *Gone with the Wind* at a garage sale during her pregnancy.

When she rounded the corner again, Bay found him at her front door. "What do you think you're doing?"

"I can wait until you've made your call."

"You can leave."

"We haven't discussed Nick Martel yet."

"You said he's gone. There's nothing else to say."

"Do you suppose your friends the Ridgeways are aware of that?"

"I have no idea."

"Then they didn't suggest you approach Martel?"

"Hardly. Madeleine didn't even want me to have—"

When she didn't continue, Jack said, "Go ahead."

Bay shook her head, unwilling to mention the missing file documents. She didn't want to make something out of what could be a simple misunderstanding, until she knew the truth.

"Nick Martel had nine years invested with the Tyler PD," Jack said. "You don't walk away from that so easily, uproot kids from school—"

"School is over for the summer."

"But they had friends, activities...his wife worked. They owned a house."

"Where?"

He lowered his head like a bull lining up his next victim to charge. "Forget it."

"I have a right to know. He's not listed in the phone book."

"If he had been, would you have walked to his front door and introduced yourself?"

"What would be so wrong with that? The man helped me. At the least I'd have liked to thank him."

"Maybe he doesn't want your thanks. Maybe he wouldn't want you on his front steps saying things he didn't want his family to know about. You're street smart, honey, but you're still a puppy."

That was one dig too many. "Overincubated," she snapped back, "that's me."

Jack closed his eyes. If she'd thought him haggard before, she found new gradations for the term. A spasm of sympathy mixed with her shame. "Oh, hell, go home, Burke. That was a low blow and as much as I distrust you, cheap shots aren't my way. Here, take this, too." She shoved her dinner at him.

"What makes you think I have any more of an appetite than you do?"

"Eat it anyway. Look, I'm realizing you're the only one listening to me and taking me seriously, though we may not agree on the bottom line. So at least feed that brain if not your diminishing brawn, and maybe if I can get over wanting to break your face, we'll talk in a couple of days."

Jack dug into his left shirt pocket and drew out a card. "My home number is on the back. I was going to stop by and drop that off regardless," he said at her narrow-eyed look.

"My timetable," she muttered, and not waiting for an answer, Bay hurried inside.

Unlocking the dead bolt and not giving a fig that the pencil flew across the linoleum floor, she slammed the door behind her and reset the lock. Her stomach was queasy and when she held the card up to look at the clean, bold numbers scrawled on the back of his business card, she couldn't read them because her hand was shaking too much.

"God," she whispered.

What had she just done? Complimented the man, and almost made him a promise. What was next, sleeping with the enemy?

10

Tuesday, June 4, 2001

Once again work brought Bay back to some sense of stability, but not before she'd experienced another rough night, one comparable to her first. It didn't help that she had the distinct feeling that Madeleine was avoiding her.

Yesterday, after she'd settled down and made sure Jack had gone, she'd dialed Madeleine's number and got the machine. Guessing she could be in the shower, Bay waited and tried again several minutes later without luck. Despite leaving a message both times, she had yet to receive a call back. She suspected Elvin had reached her first and reported a version of what happened that didn't sit well with Madeleine. Fair enough, but what irked was not being asked for her side of the story.

For the rest of the morning, Bay worked like someone with a fever, determined to finish cutting the final shafts for the *Maiden.* Once that was accomplished, she sprayed them to slow rusting.

It was minutes before noon when she finished, as

good a time as any to break. Locking up, she returned to the house and on impulse dialed the estate again. This time Madeleine picked up.

"Darling. I was just thinking about you," the woman said.

Somewhat thrown off by her warmth and cheer, Bay stumbled over her reply. "That's...thanks. I did call yesterday."

"Twice, I heard your messages this morning. Sorry, dear, I had unexpected guests that stayed too late and then I had to rush to get ready for a benefit. It's been variations of the same thing this morning. Never mind, it's all for a good cause. How are you? I'm so relieved that Elvin found you safe and sound."

It was the opening Bay was hoping for. "I wasn't lost, Madeleine. Like Elvin, I had errands to run. Don't forget, I am running a one-person shop at the moment."

"I need to get you a wireless phone."

"Don't you dare. You've done enough."

"And have enjoyed every minute. But I hear something in your voice...you were peeved by Elvin's attentiveness yesterday."

"Maybe he could have been slightly less dictatorial."

"Ah. He does take his position seriously. It's his way of showing gratitude, I suspect. He didn't have the smoothest run of luck, either, before he came to us. I'm sorry if he seemed overzealous. That's not the only thing that upset you, though, is it?"

"I do wish you had told me there was an extra key to this place floating around."

"Yes, I should have...and then you'd react as you are now."

"Wouldn't you if our positions were reversed?"

"I'd be insufferable," Madeleine replied with a self-deprecating laugh. "Forgive me for thinking like a—well, at least a caring friend."

She was proving to be that over and over. Bay, in turn, suddenly felt like bug excrement. "I'm no good at this Madeleine. I'm sorry. Of course, your generosity and kindness constantly dumbfound me."

"You just haven't learned how to let someone care about you."

"True enough."

"I do enjoy our chats. They're so honest compared to the bulk of my days, all of those meetings and socials where you spend too much time stroking someone's ego and not enough on the important issues."

"I'll bet your track record of accomplishments is double that of anyone else's. You inspire everyone around you to work harder and do more."

"Oh, you *are* good for my ego. Speaking of...what on earth is wrong with that detective person? Elvin told me he came by. Believe me, I gave Elvin a good talking to about leaving you with him."

"No, that was fine. Detective Burke left shortly after Elvin did."

"Good. But what did he want? I can't imagine him paying an innocent social call."

"Pretty much." Bay didn't want to be so evasive, but she didn't want to lie, either. "He doesn't seem well. Have you seen him at all during the last several years?''

''Once or twice. Briefly. As you can imagine, he isn't one of my favorite people, either.''

''I used to spend a good part of my day willing him to know the same misery I did. It was a shock to get back and realize maybe he has.''

''Don't you dare waste your time pitying him. There's a price to be paid for people in his line of work and in his case, a debt, too. Oh, let's not talk about him anymore. I have some exciting news for you. One of our congregation members has called to ask about you. I think I did a good job at convincing him that you were the right person for what he needed. His wife is a serious gardener, the kind who enters shows and such and she has specific needs for her greenhouse, carts and things. Doesn't sound all that artistic—''

''Work is work at this stage.''

''I thought you'd think so. Now don't sell yourself cheap. Trust me, Bruce can afford your price. Besides, keeping Celia out of the kitchen is worth a good deal to him. Don't you dare tell Martin I was uncharitable toward one of our members,'' Madeleine added on a laugh. ''She's a delight, really. Provides many of the flowers at the church.

''Now, when do I get to see you again? You must come to dinner Sunday after services, but that's such a far way off. Besides I want to talk about what we can do once the *Maiden* is finished.''

When Madeleine finally cut herself short because her luncheon guest had arrived, Bay's head was spinning as it usually did after spending time with her. She felt better about their relationship, but thought the woman was being generous regarding Elvin and would continue to watch him.

Her single disappointment—aside from having to endure another Sunday morning of feeling as if she were under a microscope—was that they hadn't returned to any subject or individual that would allow Bay to comfortably ask about her file. Just as well, she decided, washing up before she inspected the refrigerator. This wasn't Madeleine's problem anymore, and there should be a way to find out what she needed to know without involving her.

Bay found that all-important first step after lunch. Madeleine's friend Bruce didn't show, but a local drag racer did. He brought his damaged car in need of new panels.

"You did work for my old man, Doug Crow, back when you had the shop off of Erwin," the young man said. "I remember him saying you were good and you didn't screw him price-wise."

When he grimaced at his own words, Bay waved away his apology. "Crow…sure. Conveyor control boxes, I remember. Thanks for stopping by. There's just one problem that I can see…."

She explained that she didn't own a break yet to bend the sheet metal and would have to locate a shop willing to lend their equipment. That meant a slightly higher fee than if she did the work here. Since the material would gobble up everything she had in her account, she also explained she would require that part of the cost up front.

The younger Crow reached for his wallet. ''Sounds fair.''

About two hours later, after Bay went over his car with him, discussed his racing times, his concerns with aerodynamics, any gripes about drag, and took all the measurements she needed, then double-checked them, he left and she locked up. There were several shops she could approach; however, only one drew her personal interest as much as her professional concern and she wanted to get there early enough not to annoy the owner if he was trying to close on schedule.

Martel's Welding was located on the north side of the Loop where the industrial companies were situated. While hardly small, the shop was dwarfed by the trucking company on its east side. Bay's pickup was one of only six in the dirt lot when she parked to the left of the first overhead door. Either they were starting earlier to help avoid summer heating problems or this was another business to suffer a financial punch from some world trade treaty. If it was the latter, Martel might be willing to sell her some of his overstock at a discount and charge only a small fee for the use of the equipment.

Mike Martel was a slight, middle-aged man whose salt-and-pepper mustache contained more hair than was on his head. Bloodshot, black eyes studied her with some skepticism, but no outright rejection when she introduced herself.

''Sure, I remember your family's shop. Who in this

trade doesn't listen to gossip about the competition? I'd heard good things about your work, and I'm not judging you about the other—'' his shrug had to be something handed down through DNA ''—you're out, then, God bless. But listen, you've been away from the business a good while. I've got problems enough without risking expensive equipment to someone who's rusty.''

''I worked in the prison shop.''

Martel's chin dimpled as he compressed his lips. ''Come over here.''

He took her to an unoccupied workstation, near a heliarc welder. Nodding to the partially formed copper that was, according to the sketch, eventually going to be a fancy vent-a-hood, he said, ''Set up the machine as though you were going to do this job. There's a few scrap pieces on the side that you can use.''

Bay understood. A smart shop owner didn't take anyone's word when it came to expensive material, either. She would be no less cautious if their situations were reversed. Selecting two small strips of copper, she slipped on the welding hood. Next she adjusted the welder machine's lever to the DC straight polarity, reached over to turn on the argon bottle and flipped on the welder's power switch. Striking an arc, she fine-tuned the machine's temperature, jerked her head to flip down the hood, and went to work.

About two minutes later, she pushed up the hood with her left hand, shut off everything, and stepped aside to await Martel's inspection.

''You can weld,'' he said as though reporting on

the blue sky. Then he added, "I should hire you to finish this hood. I'm having nightmares that the guy who's doing it doesn't screw it up the way he did his last project. Okay, let's talk business."

Everyone else had left by the time Mark Martel extended his hand to seal their agreement. "I gotta admit some curiosity," he said with a sidelong glance as he walked her out. "Of all the shops you could have gone to, why not skip this one?"

So he knew her story better than he'd first admitted. Bay liked that he was willing to expose that. "I considered it. I told myself the name was a fluke, that you weren't likely to be related to Nick Martel. But I wanted you to be, just as I decided if you weren't, your location and quality of equipment was the best for me."

"You—" Martel pointed at her "—you could be trouble, I think. Those eyes," he explained. "They get to the conscience."

"It's only my desperation. I can't forget my partner. He was a decent man. His life was stolen, his reputation stained."

"And Nick has run away after doing the right thing for a change. Doesn't sound good, does it?" Martel rubbed the back of his neck. "What can I tell you about Nick...he's my older brother's youngest son. My brother and his wife have both passed, so I can't recommend you talk to them. I'd heard Nick was somehow instrumental in getting your case put aside, and I'm guessing you know he left Texas right after that. Why, I don't know. Nobody in the family knows. That's Nick's way."

Bay thought that interesting phrasing. "I owe him a thank-you. Have you heard from him since he left for Oregon?"

The older man shook his head. "Nothing. But Nicky was always the lone stranger in the family, and since his folks died and he married, himself, he's had less and less to do with us."

That information somehow fit with Jack Burke's enigmatic statements about the man. On her way home, Bay found herself juggling her relief at having found an alternate workspace where she was welcome and a greater concern that Jack could be turning into her biggest ally. It was a scary thought.

Once Bay arrived at the house, she decided she owed Burke a call to let him know she agreed with his opinion of the former Vice cop. But when she picked up the phone and began to dial, she heard a voice.

"Hello? Bay?"

"Duncan."

"You sound surprised. I told you I'd call."

"Yes...how are you? Where are you?"

"In transit from Tampa to Atlanta. In fact things are going so well, I'll be back in Tyler a day early, that's why I'm calling—to confirm dinner on Thursday."

"Oh, no."

His laugh-choke had her realizing she'd answered too honestly.

"I'm sorry, I didn't mean that. Duncan, I appreciate the gesture—"

"You think I'm calling out of pity?"

"Maybe as a favor to your mother."

He uttered another guttural sound. "I'm nuts about my mother, but I'd tell her to take a flying leap if she intruded in my personal life."

"This from the man who warned me that Strategy was her middle name."

"But I know all of her moves."

Bay almost smiled. His gift for the quick comeback made him easy to talk to and interesting to banter with. Still… "You know this is a waste of your time. We really have nothing in common."

"We both had second helpings of dessert last Sunday."

He would remind her of that. She'd never had white chocolate before and after the first taste thought she'd finally understood what the word *orgasmic* meant.

"That was meant as a joke."

"I know," she said with a pang of sadness. "But it proves my point. We don't travel in the same circles, our lives aren't compatible…."

"You can't know that yet. We've barely had a chance to talk without someone else around. You know what your problem is? You're scared. I respect that. It's just dinner and friendship I'm aiming for right now, Bay. You don't know how rare it is for me to sit across the table from someone who doesn't want something from me."

Bay winced, wishing he hadn't said that. She didn't want to feel sorry for him or anyone. She didn't have enough energy for herself let alone to spend it on concern for another, and she had so much to do. Besides, she did want something from him.

"Friendship is all I could ever offer you," she said, almost apologetic.

"Maybe...and maybe you'll surprise yourself. What kind of food do you like to eat?"

"Whatever's put in front of me."

"This is going to be so great."

11

Wednesday, June 5, 2001

What was great was feeling things were finally going her way for a change.

The following day Bay worked half the morning in her shop on the *Maiden,* then moved to Martel's where she cut Doug Crow's panels and formed them.

Carrying them home and stacking them in the shop, she locked up and went to the house. As she gulped down a big glass of ice water, she checked the time. It was almost four o'clock. She could call Crow and have him bring over the dragster as soon as he got off from work, but then it would be dark by the time she finished attaching the panels. The lighting in the shop wasn't sufficient yet for that kind of work, and she decided to leave a message on his machine for him to drop off the vehicle on his way to work in the morning.

With that done, she showered and headed for the mall. She needed something to wear for tomorrow night. Spending money on clothes when she needed tools and equipment for the shop seemed the most ridiculous of extravagances, but she'd committed herself to Duncan and—

The phone rang, interrupting her debate with herself.

"Hello?"

She balanced the receiver between her ear and shoulder so she could refresh her drink. She had the glass halfway to her mouth when she realized no one was responding.

"Hello?"

Not again, she thought putting down the glass.

She circled the counter to hang up the phone. "You are not going to ruin my day," she said to the unit.

Waiting several seconds to make sure she'd disconnected, she picked up the receiver and set it on the counter. Now if her caller tried to harass her, they could listen to a busy signal, she thought heading for the shower.

Thirty-some minutes later, her hair still wet, Bay passed the phone that was now emitting a loud buzz, stuck the pencil in its special spot and locked up. She'd left several lights on inside, as well as the TV hoping that would discourage trouble even if a possible intruder saw the truck wasn't there.

The mall didn't appear crowded; however, parking anywhere near the main entrance was a challenge. She lucked out and found a slot two aisles away, then did a complete walk-through since she didn't have a clue as to what was where anymore, let alone know what she wanted.

The outside security lights were on by the time she reemerged, a plastic bag slung over her right shoulder and two shopping bags in her left hand. As spongy as the evening air felt against her skin, Bay breathed a sigh of relief to have the shopping ordeal behind her. She now owned three dresses—the sum total of her entire wardrobe her senior year in high school. It seemed a good idea to buy something she could also wear on Sunday, and not wanting to embarrass herself by showing up in the same outfit twice in one week, she'd found a second dress.

Ridiculous, she thought mentally shaking her head at herself. She'd just spent nearly all of her available cash doing something she didn't want to do because she had to go somewhere she wasn't wild about going.

Out on Broadway, traffic was as heavy as usual and, despite everyone needing their lights, no one's driving etiquette had improved. Bay heard three horn blasts before she was halfway to her car. She was glad she was done shopping and could head back to the house and not anywhere else. Her feet hurt, and her eyes burned from the stores' fluorescent lighting and dry air. She wanted to deal with impatient drivers about as much as she wanted to try on another dress or pair of shoes.

A long horn blast followed by the squeal of brakes disrupted the calm night. For a few seconds, the near collision at the traffic light by the entryway of the mall drew Bay's attention, but they were a few seconds too many. Pausing before she draped her bag over the side of the truck to get out her keys, she was slow to sense something—a presence, a shifting of air and shadows. In the next instant, she was being knocked off her feet.

Disbelief and fear momentarily paralyzed her, but there was little time to gasp for breath let alone scream. She hit the ground fast and with such force the shock and pain brought back images of her last attack, the dread and horror of the violence that followed. Fortunately, adrenaline surged and she began the fight for her life. Unfortunately, this attacker was experienced, and stronger than the two women who'd been intent on teaching her a lesson in Gatesville.

Already feeling as though her skull had cracked open, she cried out again as a hand pressed her stinging cheek harder against the hot asphalt, and a hefty knee crushed into her back denying her air and threatening to rupture the very organs that had yet to heal completely. Blinded by helpless tears of agony, she didn't see the shadow loom closer, only smelled foul breath and spittle against her ear.

"Leave well enough alone," he growled.

Then, with ruthless force, her attacker grabbed her short hair, snapped back her head and again banged her face against the pavement. This time, gratefully, everything went blank.

It was pain that told Bay she'd survived...and pain that made her wish she hadn't. She tried to retreat back into blissful oblivion, but when that proved impossible, she attempted to beg whoever was screaming and shouting to stop, to silence the sirens, as well. What came out, though was an odd keening...and what was that metal taste? She'd lost her ability to discern, and managing enough short pants to survive seemed to take more effort than it was worth.

Tears and something else distorted her vision, but she grew aware of flashing lights and then the shadow loomed again. She tried to scream, to cry, "No more," but what came out was gibberish.

"Ma'am, lie still. An ambulance is coming. You'll be all right."

No ambulance. No hospital.

"Ma'am, you're hurt. You have to lie still."

Easy for him to say, she thought with increasing lucidity. She was the one who was having the metal rod driven through her brain.

The next thought Bay had was that she'd been sleeping and had experienced the worst dream. Then her vision focused and she realized she wasn't at the house. The light hurt her eyes and the blue wall of curtains around the bed... What was that all about?

Slowly, as it registered, her heart started pounding. She heard beeping and metallic clinking, voices, and smelled odors that triggered an even greater anxiety. This was a hospital.

"She's coming out of it," a soft voice said off to her left.

That brought someone over on her right, a face she knew. "Wh-where'd you come from?" she croaked. Her throat was as dry as her lips stiff.

"You had my card in your pocket," Jack Burke replied. "How are you feeling?"

"How do I look?"

"Pretty scary."

"Feel…worse."

Bay started to lift a hand to her head, but Jack took hold of it and closed it within both of his.

"Your right temple needed stitches. The cheek is scraped, but they left that open and you don't want to wipe the ointment off."

"How many?"

"Stitches? Seven. Your new lucky number."

Groaning, she tried to pull free her hand. Jack refused to let go.

"Water," she entreated.

He looked over his shoulder.

Bay heard that same feminine voice say, "I'll get her some. The doctor should be here in a minute."

"Hear that?" Jack asked. "Hang on. It's coming."

"Mm." What else did she have to do?

Jack became her focal point, a shopworn one. He looked like he'd been up so long his five o'clock shadow had graduated into the legitimate beginnings of a beard, and his dark-brown hair was a ruffled mess and falling over his forehead. He also was suffering from one of the worst cases of bloodshot eyes she'd seen since she turned down Glenn's marriage proposal.

"Time?"

"Not quite one. Bay, I have to ask you some questions in case the doctor decides to run me out of here. Did you get a glimpse of them?"

"Them?"

"Whoever it was that you rubbed the wrong way this time."

He was failing as a comedian, but she didn't mind

the concern in his voice. Only it sounded as though he'd followed her over the same rock quarry she'd been dragged through. There was also no missing the way he kept stroking the back of her hand with his thumb.

"Could have been a salesclerk," she managed weakly. "Didn't want to take cash. Tried to bully me into signing up for a credit card."

"Sometimes it's best not to buck the system."

"Tired of the safe and narrow. Burke, what's wrong with my mouth?"

"Your lip is split. Two more stitches."

Raggedy Ann. She couldn't turn her head without experiencing a white-hot pain, so Bay averted her burning eyes as memories blended with her present misery. Raggedy Ann was what the kids used to call her in grade school when her father sent her to school in jeans mended with duct tape. On top of her assorted bruises earned from chores in the shop, the state of her clothes was one blemish too many. Humiliated for the last time, she learned to change out of her things as soon as she got home and hand wash them in the sink to ensure she would never have to experience ridicule again.

"Stay with me." Jack's grip tightened.

"Yeah."

"The doctor is concerned about your spleen. Any additional abuse to it and you'll need it removed."

"Huh."

"Bay...look at me. He said your ribs show recent injury, as well. You were attacked in prison, weren't you?"

"Ancient history. I never saw him, Burke. Tonight. Heard him, though."

Jack's expression was already stony. Now he worked his jaw. "One person. I'm following you. What did he say?"

"'Leave...leave well enough alone.'"

Bay didn't get to see more than the shock in his eyes because the doctor arrived. Thorough, but busy, he seemed pleased with how she was rebounding; however, he recommended she stay overnight due to her concussion, and her fragile state overall. It sounded like the standard hospital speech and Bay would have none of it.

"Out," she demanded to Jack.

"You're crazy. You're in no condition—"

"Get me out."

Jack looked at the doctor, who threw up his hands in an it's-your-funeral manner and went off to his next patient.

"My terms this time," Jack told her.

Motivated by images of the three-ring circus she knew would be posted outside by morning, she murmured, "'Kay."

Having spent more energy than she had in reserve, Bay drifted in and out of consciousness and wasn't sure how long it was before she was released. She did rouse long enough to note it wasn't by way of wheelchair or gurney. As soon as Jack returned from settling her bill, he carefully lifted her into his arms and, with a male nurse's help, sneaked out via a rear exit where he'd parked his truck.

"I spotted a reporter lurking out front," he explained, using a blanket from the back seat to ease the pressure of the belt seat crossing her body. "I'm going to set your seat all the way back to keep you out of view.

"Okay?" he asked once he settled in on the driver's side.

"'Preciate this, Burke. Pay you back."

"You want to pay me back, call me Jack. The rest...I'd be pleased if you let me do this for you."

Both requests made her self-conscious. She didn't need that when some of the local anesthetic and medication were beginning to wear off. Added to the attack on her abused nerve endings and she didn't know where to look let alone what to say. At the moment being alone in a cell sounded almost appealing.

"It might help to talk."

"I'm closer to a cussin' mood."

"Well, before you retreat too far from me, tell me this, do I call the Ridgeways?"

He would do that for her? "No," she murmured. "Thanks."

"Because?"

"Press. Politics."

"You're protecting them from supposedly being tainted by you? In case that blow to your head gave you amnesia, you're the victim in this situation."

"Pride."

She could feel his gaze shift to her and recognized comprehension in his eyes. Pride was something they had in common, not that she wanted to discuss it. She'd figured that part of him out years ago, even respected it, with a healthy dose of bitterness, of course. He'd done his job to the best of his ability, done it so well that when he said he'd changed his mind, people thought he'd lost it, had been taken in by the murderess with the deceptively innocent looks.

"Talk to me. Haven't I earned the right to know?"

"I don't, how am I supposed to tell you?"

"You're wanting to write this off as a simple mugging."

It wasn't his fault that the words grated on every wound, opened the dam to too much emotion. "You kiss asphalt as hard as I did tonight and tell me it's simple."

"Good, and while you're remembering that, understand muggers rip off women in designer clothes, women who have more diamonds than buttons and drive cars that cost what I make in two years. Women double your age who aren't able to give them a crotch cramp with their knees."

"Me, either. Attacked from behind."

"But what money you had is still in your jeans, next to your temporary driver's license and my business card."

Oops.

"And the stuff you bought? It's in the back seat."

She would have gladly passed out but as luck would have it now, Bay stayed conscious.

"He was specific, Bay. Do you get it?"

"Loud and clear. What do you want, a highway billboard?"

"Then what have you been up to since we last talked and you promised to call me?"

They would have gotten to this point eventually,

regardless, but Bay didn't know when she'd ever be ready. "I'm not going to apologize for looking for answers or making space for myself."

"You gave me your word you'd call."

"The phone rang."

It was the most ludicrous thing she could say and yet true. "I was going to call you...today. No, yesterday. No, last night...but the phone rang."

"And that changed things?"

"Don't know. But it was the same nobody as before and before that."

Once again he shot her a sidelong glance. "You're getting calls?"

"Big surprise."

"How many?"

"Not bad. Not hate mail. Technology, I thought at first."

"At first? You're barely out a week. What else has happened?"

"Little things I can't prove. An open window, a tampered switch."

As Jack sped through town studying the rearview mirror as much as he did the road ahead, his grip on the steering wheel tightened. He didn't only pass the mall, when he reached her driveway, he never let off the accelerator.

The maneuver jarred Bay more than another blow. "What are you doing? Hey, I need my truck!"

12

"You won't be in shape to drive it for two or three days," Jack said continuing down the highway.

"Burke, I do not like this. Take me to my house. Now."

"Forget it. I'm too tired to do a proper check of your property, and I know no one will look for you at my place. Am I right?"

Apparently, since she didn't know where he lived herself.

"Damn it, Bay, why don't you have Caller ID?"

She forced her attention back to him. "Can't afford it yet."

"Why didn't you report the other problems?" At her droll look, he grimaced. "You could at least have told me. I would have taken it seriously. I can't believe you've stayed there knowing someone has free access to you. Did you tell Madeleine Ridgeway any of this?"

"No. She mother hens me enough as it is."

"Well, she needs to be told you suspect her driver. Don't deny it."

Him, her attorney...virtually anyone in Tyler who knew of her case and might think she didn't deserve to be back. That used to include him, but somehow she couldn't wrap her mind around that notion anymore. She'd been struck in the head once too often, that's what her problem was. The man who'd helped ruin her life was kidnapping her and she was actually feeling safe...physically if not emotionally.

"Tomorrow you tell her," Jack ordered. "I can't believe she stuck you out here as it is. Shit."

He made it sound like the property was at the farthest corner of civilization. "It's a great place. Better than anything I could afford on my own." Better than anywhere she had ever lived. "Hell, a week ago I couldn't afford a park bench."

"Can you afford a headstone yet? Because it sure sounds as though someone is tempted for you to relocate somewhere else—permanently. You might as well put a sign out front next to the one you did—Single, Unarmed Woman. Damn it, Bay, this whole thing reeks."

While she could have done without him hitting the steering wheel with his palm to punctuate his opinion, Bay couldn't argue about her situation being disturbing. She also appreciated his concern—it continued to bewilder her, but less with each passing day. That didn't mean she was relinquishing her freedom again, not to him or anyone, especially her right to make her own decisions.

When the silence between them grew uncomfortably long, Jack purged a long breath. "I shouldn't have yelled. I know you have the mother of all headaches."

"Mm. Doesn't mix well with whatever stuff they

gave me, either. If we don't get someplace soon, you're going to have to pull over."

"We're here."

Less than a quarter mile down the road, he made a left turn into a fenced property, crossed over a cattle guard and drove up a long dirt driveway to a brick one-story house set back several acres from the highway. A few hundred feet behind it was a barn and to the left of that was a full-size house trailer. Both house and trailer were dark except for the floodlights.

Jack hit the garage door opener on his sun visor and eased the truck into the immaculate and almost empty garage on the left side of the house. "Stay put," he said, once he shut off the engine. "I'll unlock the door and come around to help you."

He was out of the truck before she could say otherwise, leaving Bay to make a few new conclusions about the man: he wasn't married because no way would he be bringing another woman home to a wife, and he sure wasn't a pack rat. There wasn't so much as a lawn mower on the other side of the two-car garage. Except for the closed trash bin and broom leaning against the wall by the left entrance, the place would have looked like no one lived here.

Releasing her seat belt, she tossed the blanket over her shoulder and brought her seat to its upright position. Those few movements had her swallowing hard against her lurching stomach. Afraid she might get sick in his car, she opened the door...and heard an immediate bark and long, throaty growl. She had the briefest glimpse of a black beast, gleaming and muscular, and slammed the door shut. Seconds later, the big dog was leaping up against Jack, who came to her side of the truck and reopened the door.

"Down, Bud. Try to be a gentleman. This is Buddy," he told her.

Bringing up her hands to protect her face, Bay otherwise went rigid with terror as the dog with the pit bull head and the glossy coat of a mink sniffed every inch of her that he could reach. That proved to be anything he wanted, since he easily reached Jack's shoulders when he jumped.

"Oh, my God. Oh, my God," she moaned.

"Don't be frightened. He's a big baby."

No baby she'd ever seen had teeth that resembled a lumberjack's chain saw. "Could you—I don't have any experience with animals."

"Stretch out your hand and let him learn your scent, then I'll get you out of there. He's just impatient for you to love on him."

"He's in for a big disappointment." However, willing to do anything to keep the animal from getting completely in the cab with her, she followed Jack's directive and eased forward her hand. Not surprisingly, it was shaking. But seeming to smile, the dog sniffed, and literally wrapped his tongue around her for a wet handshake before leaping up into her lap.

Bay opened her mouth to scream.

"Bud, you're a pig," Jack said, hauling him off her. "Get down and wait until you're invited."

With equal ease, Jack scooped her out of the truck and this time Bay didn't protest. She even wrapped her arms around his neck ready to climb up on his shoulders—no matter how much it hurt—to escape the animal who was bouncing around them, a maneuver that brought him frighteningly close to eye level with her.

"You mean it? You never had a dog when you were a kid?"

Jack nudged the door shut with his hip and pushed the garage door button with his elbow before carrying her inside. Bud zipped past them, hopping a few more times before darting off.

"No." Her father hadn't believed in wasting good gambling money on food for them; Bay couldn't imagine what he would have said if she'd asked for any kind of pet. Anyway, considering their cramped and grim quarters, she wouldn't have subjected another living creature to those conditions.

"I guess I've never been without one. Bud's a stray that showed up here about a year ago, so starved he crawled on his belly better than he could walk. I won't put you down until I get you to the bedroom. You're about the size of his favorite chew toy and I'm afraid he'd knock you clear off your feet. Let him check the house and then he'll be ready to go back outside and hunt gophers and moles. That's his favorite nighttime activity. He likes to sleep during the day, at least until the worst of the summer is over."

"The couch'll do." They had passed through a utility room/pantry and the kitchen and she'd spotted the leather couch in the den. There was no way she was going to let him put her in his room.

"The guest room has it's own bath and it'll be closer if you need to get up. There aren't any sheets on the bed—I don't have company—but I'll take care of that in a few minutes.''

''No family to visit?''

''Nope. Like you, I was an only child. This place belonged to my parents, but they're gone now.''

''I'm sorry.'' They couldn't have been very old. He wasn't more than thirty-four or -six.

''My father flipped over the tractor and it crushed him. Drove that thing too fast near the ravines. My mother always told him he would break his neck one day. After a while she remarried and turned this place over to me. She had another six happy years and then she came down with cancer. It could have been treatable, but she waited too long.''

''How sad.''

''Yup.'' Entering the second door on the right, he went straight to the bathroom where he set her on her feet and turned on the light. ''I'll go give Bud a treat and let him out, then—''

Bay gasped at what she saw in the mirror. Dear God, she was hideous. Horrified, she stumbled to the toilet, but on her empty stomach, all she did was choke.

''Come on, Bud, out.''

Jack vanished with the dog, and a grateful Bay struggled to regain control. It was a good minute before she had the strength to get to her feet and over to the sink where she rinsed her mouth as best as she could. Finally, miserable and weak, she slumped onto the edge of the tub.

Jack returned, his eyes reflecting concern and sympathy. Bay averted her face.

"Don't do that," he said.

"I'm so ugly."

"You're hurt. It'll be much better in a few days. In a few weeks, you'll barely be able to notice anything."

Bay didn't reply. She was so close to losing it, she didn't dare.

Jack disappeared again, apparently sensing she needed some space. She heard him moving around in the bedroom, making the bed. When he returned, he switched on the night-light vanity mirror.

Bay was relieved, until he kneeled before her. "What are you—?"

Closing the toilet, he placed something on the seat lid. In his right hand was a pair of scissors. Bay gaped as he took hold of the bottom of her T-shirt and began cutting.

"Burke!"

"It's a bloody mess...and I don't have a clue as to what that other crap is. You must have fallen into spilled soda or overflow from an air conditioner. Anyway, there's no way you can slip it over your head. You can have my T-shirt, which will cover you from neck to knee and appease any spasms of modesty."

"Convicts lose the right to know what that is," she muttered looking away again. "Guess it doesn't matter, anyway. There's not much to cover."

Jack sighed and once he had her ruined top peeled off her, he eased his T-shirt over her head and helped her get her arms through the short sleeves.

Then he shocked her again by reaching behind her

and through the soft cotton to release the catch of her bra.

"Damn you."

"Sometime when you're feeling better," he said, holding her gaze as he reached into her left sleeve to peel her out of one strap, "I'll show you that what you have is just fine with me." With that, he eased her out of the other strap and pulled the bra out of her right sleeve opening. "Shocked?"

"Pissed."

"That's better than embarrassment. Up." Lifting her by her elbows, he got her to stand, then released the snap on her jeans.

"For crying out loud!" Bay wrestled with him for control. "Burke!"

"Jack. Call me Jack and I'll let you do it yourself."

"Jack," she seethed.

He let go and although she got the zipper open, her instability almost sent her backward into the tub when she tried to slip out of her athletic shoes. Shaking his head, Jack crouched to do it for her. He peeled off her socks and, ordering her to hold on to his shoulders, got her out of the jeans.

"Now," he said rising, "do you want to throw up air again, or lie down?"

"Lie down. Please."

He delivered her to the bed where the top sheet was turned back invitingly. After tucking her in, he returned to the bathroom and collected her things.

"Do you think you could get down a little broth and crackers?"

"No. I just want to be left alone."

Without another word, he walked out, leaving Bay wishing he hadn't, wishing he'd stood his ground and argued with her. She was an ungrateful bitch and a fool. It was too soon to be alone or to close her eyes. All she saw was flashes of her world turning upside down, and she relived the first pain as she'd hit the ground. When added to the throbbing she felt now, it was almost too much to bear.

She could choke back the sob that rose to her throat, but there was no stopping the tears that slipped from the corners of her eyes.

13

Although bone tired, Jack knew there was no way he would be sleeping anytime soon and let himself out through the French doors in the den. He crossed the covered deck he never took the time to enjoy, descended the two cedar plank stairs and strolled across the barren yard, seeing it with new eyes. Thirty-five in another month, he thought, and the place looked like someone twice that age lived here. He had yet to replace any of the trees and shrubs he'd let die during the years of family illness, drought and life's general kicks in the teeth that had taken everything and everyone who meant something to him. He owned eighty-eight acres of rich bottomland and beyond the corral, he knew things remained generally okay despite the rough weather patterns lingering on; good enough for a speculator to have recently offered him over a quarter-million dollars for the place. As Jack walked beside the pasture fence, he accepted that it might have been smarter to take the money and relocate like Nick Martel. And maybe his instincts were wrong about Martel; could be Martel's career was on an upswing and he'd been invited up to the Pacific Northwest.

While yours, you dumb shit, is in the crash-and-burn mode.

Getting called into his lieutenant's office today had thrust him that much closer. If he'd ever been at a career crossroads, it was now.

Over by the trailer he heard a door open and close. Nearby, Bud let out a brief, welcoming yelp and loped over to greet Simon Jimenez. Man and dog soon joined Jack. A decade older, the thrice-divorced Mexican-American lived alone in the trailer that he'd called home for five years after deciding that connubial bliss wasn't for him. Preferring "quiet cattle to barking women" it was Simon who kept things going on the old homestead.

The trim, average-built man met him at the empty corral's gate. "How'd it go?" Simon asked.

"A woman was hurt tonight. I brought her back with me." He'd buzzed Simon on the intercom to let him know he'd had an emergency and needed to go to the hospital.

"Bud's all excited." The ranch hand grinned at the dog butting his head against his thigh. "He wanna talk about her."

"Like you speak Dog."

Simon's grin widened. "I speak Bud. He take to her like he do the calves?"

"Yeah, she's almost their size, too." Jack knew he owed him some explanation. Simon was about the only friend he had left now that he'd alienated almost everyone at the station. Leaning on the gate, he rested his right foot on the first rung and began, "You know a couple of years ago when you said I was eating myself up from the inside? Well, she's the reason. Because of me, she did six years of hard time before some important people got her case overturned."

Simon whistled softly. "Get all the knives in the kitchen and put 'em in the trailer, man."

"That's not what worries me."

"Something sure is."

"She's started her own investigation."

"And that's how she ended up in the hospital?"

Jack nodded.

The shorter man dug his hands into the back pockets of his jeans and studied his dusty boots. "So now you gonna try and help her?"

"I have been all along." He'd just had a lot of roadblocks thrown in his way.

"Sounds like you got it bad for this little kid."

"She's not a kid anymore, she's thirty-two." Jack doubted Bay ever had been a child and wondered how long it would be before she trusted him with her story, not the bullshit one the D.A. had told to help get her convicted. The embittered-abused-child-turned-sociopath stereotype he was never buying. She'd endured neglect and a few rough backhands or two from life, that he could figure out, but she wasn't a classic case study. He could see in her eyes that she ached for stability...and love. She simply wasn't going to waste her own resources again on losers.

"How bad is she hurt?" Simon asked.

"Just don't wince if you cross her path or I'll skin you worse than she's been."

Simon crossed himself. "You want I keep the dog away?"

"No, I need his instincts. Yours, too. Wish I could tell you more, but the damned thing is I don't know how big this is."

Simon studied him for a long moment. "Understood. Until you tell me different, the shotgun comes out of the pickup and stays at my side. Coyote, pig, two-legged varmint...I be watching."

Jack had once needed Simon for the two-legged variety when they'd had problems with poachers. They'd resolved the situation, but it had cost him the old friend he'd had before Bud.

Gripping Simon's shoulder to signal a gratitude he couldn't begin to voice, Jack continued his walk. He was too restless to stay put for long; his thoughts were being pulled in too many directions.

When he'd first gotten the call tonight and heard Bay's name and the word *hospital,* his heart had dropped like a wrecking ball. After all of these years, he understood what Simon had grasped in minutes—it wasn't only moral principle, an obsession to try to fix a wrong that had been eating at him. He had a terminal case of Bay Butler, one so bad that he wouldn't be going easy on the asshole who'd terrorized her tonight the way he had those redneck creeps who'd tried to steal his cattle a few years back. No, there wouldn't be anything left for medics to shuttle to any hospital this time.

Sucking in another deep breath of the humid night air, Jack made a slow tour around the house, letting Bud do his own inspection with his keener nose. As he walked, questions raced through his mind, like who knew Bay would be at the mall tonight? The attacker's motive was clear, but what a risk he'd taken of being spotted. How much simpler to have waited until she was back at her place and alone. Jack wanted to know what that meant. He also wanted a list of every single person she'd talked to since he last saw her. He *needed* to know where she was planning to wear those outfits she'd bought tonight, particularly that little black number.

His dour mood notwithstanding, he gave Bud an affectionate rub, sending him back to his hunting, and went inside. The house was as quiet as if he were alone, but Bay might as well have been standing beside him, he was that aware of her presence. Then he heard something....

Hurrying down the hall, he heard the sound again. As he feared, things weren't going well; Bay's writhing was getting her all tangled in the top sheet, and she was alternately whimpering and moaning. From a dream or pain? Pain, he concluded as he came to the edge of the bed and their eyes met in the dim light.

"I woke you, I'm so sorry," she rasped.

Her voice was almost an octave lower, it bore so much guilt. That was something they had in common, Jack thought shaking his head. They both carried a ton of guilt. "You didn't. I've been outside talking to Simon. He does most of the ranching work," he explained at her confused look. "Lives in the trailer. Where does it hurt?"

"Throw a dart. Wherever it lands is bound to be an improvement. Better yet, just let me be dog meat to that pit bull of yours."

Jack watched her struggle to sit up. The sheet had been dragged almost to her knees and his T-shirt up around her waist exposing the slimmest band of pink. Quickly tugging it down, she struggled with the pillows and the cotton tightened across her firm breasts, emphasizing nipples as hard and perfectly round as small pearls. "He's not a pit bull, he's a mix of Lab and mastiff," he said turning away to the closet as heat collected in his groin. "And the only thing he's liable to do with you is lick the rest of you raw."

Bay shuddered. "Then lend me your gun."

Jack pulled two more pillows from the top shelf. They didn't have any covers, but he stacked them behind the others to make her more comfortable.

"What you need is something to soothe from the inside." Since it wasn't going to be him, Jack beat a fast retreat to the kitchen.

Ten minutes later he returned with a tray.

"Do you do windows, too?"

She looked at him as though he'd just stepped off a flying saucer. He liked that he was a mystery to her. Confusion was a cousin to curiosity, and curiosity was addictive. The idea of being her addiction brought a crooked smile to his lips as he sat down on the edge of the bed and transferred the tray onto her lap.

"Bachelors learn to be self-sufficient...not that I can remember the last time I did the windows, except where Bud presses his big nose."

There were two mugs with steaming chicken broth on the tray and a package of crackers already torn open. He'd put a straw in Bay's mug and she was eyeing it with bemusement.

"Broth tends to be a bit spicy and I figured it wouldn't sting your lip if you used the straw," he told her.

"Thank you, but what I was wondering is where you're finding the patience to be so good to me at this hour, after a full day on the job and everything. Don't career bachelors rank high-maintenance women lower than bad oysters?"

"I didn't say career."

"Oh." Bay reached for the mug, ending up using both hands to keep from spilling it. After taking the smallest of sips, she sat there with her hands clasped like a kid in Sunday school.

"Have a cracker."

"No, thanks. You go ahead."

"Then ask your question."

Bay opened her mouth, shut it, and after a few seconds asked, "Are you involved with someone?"

"No. She would definitely say no."

"What happened?"

"I blew it."

"She couldn't handle you being a cop?"

"Something like that." Jack sipped his own broth while watching her digest that. "What about you? I mean about what you said on the stand?"

"I don't remember everything I said, but I remember the oath I took."

"So you've never been in love, not even with English? He must have been crushed." Jack watched

Bay's beautiful eyes grow shadowed with a different kind of pain.

"Never tell a guy who wants to go to bed with you that you only love him like a brother. He tends to wind up with a three-day hangover."

"If I said that to a guy, it'd probably be a week-long one."

The ghost of a smile lit Bay's eyes. But as quickly as it came, the light vanished. "I wish I could convince Holly that I was never any threat to her. I tried to talk to her on Sunday at the Ridgeways. She still hates my guts, though."

Seeing a new thought flick across Bay's face, Jack asked, "What?"

"Nothing really."

"Tell me."

"Duncan said they went out a few times."

Duncan, the golden boy of fund-raising and deal making, Jack thought sourly. "Why did he share that with you?" The instant Bay lowered her gaze and reached for her mug, it hit Jack, as brutally as a jackhammer to the skull. He didn't have to ask about the sexy bit of a dress.

The green-eyed monster of jealousy stung at him like an extra-potent jellyfish. "I see. You are on the fast track, aren't you?"

"What's that supposed to mean?"

"The trip to the mall earlier in the evening. You caught his interest and now you have to keep up with show-pony protocol."

"That's not fair."

"Bet that's what Holly's thinking having learned lightning can strike twice."

"There is nothing between me and Duncan."

"Yet. But the Ridgeways have exposed you to a different world. It's only natural for you to be tempted. The house, the shop, those are already hefty gestures of affection for a girl who grew up in a trailer. Who'd blame you for thinking you'd roughed it long enough and might like to live in the big house where you could focus on your pricier sculp—"

"You son of a bitch."

Bay slammed her mug onto the tray hard enough for the contents to strike and sting Jack. Shoving the tray at him, she left the bed with the same passionate energy, but her left leg stayed tangled in the sheet and she went sprawling across the carpet.

"Bay—" Ignoring the sting of the hot broth, Jack rushed to help. "Are you okay?" As soon as he spoke, he knew it was an inane question; even if she hadn't reopened any wound, he'd inflicted a worse injury. At least the beige carpeting was plush and reduced the odds of the former.

"Get away."

"Let me make sure you're not bleeding again."

"I'm not, but you will be if you don't get your hands off of me."

"I was only trying to—"

"I am *not* a whore."

He began to protest, to insist he'd never said that…and realized his guilt by inference. It hit him like a close-range .9 mm chest shot. Wanting her himself, he'd struck out at her the instant he feared she might be attracted to someone else. ''Jesus,'' he whispered.

Bay used his bewilderment to make her escape, rushing down the hallway and out the back door. She was on the deck when he caught up with her.

She didn't scream when he grabbed her, but she swung. After one impressive punch to his left side, he was able to trap her in a fairly stable body lock. That's when Bud reached them raising hell and bouncing from one side of the deck to the other as though unable to decide which of them he was rooting for.

''Bud—shut up!'' Jack snapped.

Simon brought up the rear, shotgun in hand. He took in the situation with typical aplomb and asked, ''Am I supposed to shoot her, you, or go back to bed?''

''You're supposed to figure out when to mind your own business,'' Jack snarled.

''No, don't go,'' Bay entreated as he began to retreat. ''Please help me get out of here. I want to go home.''

Returning to the base of the steps, Simon gazed up at her with dark, sympathetic eyes. ''I don't think that's safe for you, miss. You should try to rest. Boss,'' he added to Jack in a harder tone, ''easy does it, okay?''

Ordering Bud to come with him, he retreated to his trailer. Jack could feel Bay's despair as she watched him, but at least she'd stopped fighting.

''I'm going to get you back inside.'' His lips

grazed her nape, but he'd be damned if he would apologize for that.

While she trembled at the caress, she said coldly, "I'll walk. You have my word I'll go quietly, *Detective.*"

The formal address cut as it was meant to; nevertheless, knowing her word was good, Jack released her and she returned inside. Any relief was short-lived as he saw her head straight for the navy leather couch set against the picture window to the right of the French doors. Keeping her back to him, she curled into a tight ball in the left corner.

Sighing, Jack locked up and began pacing the length of the den, from the home entertainment system he never used to the entryway to the dimly lit kitchen. He combed back his hair with both hands as he searched for something to say that wouldn't make her despise him more—or terrify her. Rejecting everything that came to mind, he settled on the coffee table that had held pretzels and popcorn for hundreds of movies, baseball and football games watched with his father. Simpler times.

Resting his forearms on his knees, he said quietly, "I would give anything to take back the last ten minutes."

Bay remained silent.

"I apologize. That's inadequate, but if you believe nothing else, I wish you'd believe that I would rather turn in my gun and badge first thing tomorrow than hurt you again."

"Do you know how hard it is to try to do the right

thing and find your footing at the same time?'' she asked, her tone weary.

''Somewhat.''

''Yeah, right. Detective By-the-Book Burke. For your information, I tried to turn down that property. I felt undeserving and worried there would be strings attached. There are, but they don't offset what I owe Madeleine Ridgeway, which is my life. Literally. And all she wants are the gates for her estate to finally complete the look of the property. To ask her to wait months, maybe a year or two until I had my own business built up again on my terms would be nothing but an exercise in foolish pride. She could have taken my design and had it reproduced almost anywhere. If she's that honest and steadfast with me, who am I to turn up my nose because I won't be able to say I got where I'm going without anyone's help?''

''What strings?'' Jack asked.

''Attending Mission of Mercy, for one.'' For the first time she glanced over her shoulder at him. ''Sounds trivial, doesn't it? I know joining the church officially is next and I already know I can't do that.''

''I don't think anyone should step into a place of worship except for one reason.'' At Bay's surprised look he smiled. ''There was bound to be something we agreed on.''

''Yeah, well, I'm worse. I'm not comfortable where members are courted for their position and their financial statement, not their spiritual needs. I know everyone tries to clean up to look their best for church, but most of the congregation could go straight from services to one of Donald Trump's hotels for brunch.'' No sooner did she say that than she dismissed the observation with a flick of her hand. ''Forget it. Even I can hear the reverse prejudice in that. From what I've seen on TV, they do amazing good work with orphans and educating poor kids in third-world countries.''

''Do you believe everything you see on TV?''

Bay frowned as much as her injuries allowed. ''You're insinuating...?''

''Have you noticed the number of infomercials on TV these days?''

''They're hard to miss when you keep the hours I do.''

''Then you've recognized the parallel in marketing styles?''

''That's more cynical than my attitude.''

Concerned that he would upset her again, Jack backed off. ''Ignore me. It's been a long day.'' His gut told him he had to have the same faith as the one that had kept her so sane and decent despite everything. ''Here are my keys.'' Rising, Jack dug them out of his pocket and set them on the coffee table. ''If I frighten you more than whoever attacked you, you know where the truck is. I'm going to clean up the guest room, and then I'm going to bed.''

''No, I'll do it.'' As soon as he made room for her, Bay eased herself to her feet. ''It's my mess and you have to be at work in a few hours.''

''Not necessarily.'' At her uncertain glance, he shrugged. ''I've been demoted. For all I know, they may not give a damn if I ever show up again.''

14

Thursday, June 6, 2001
8:30 a.m.

Good intentions had little effect on exhaustion, and Bay and Jack were late getting out of the house the next morning. Subdued as they met in the kitchen where he had two steaming mugs of coffee ready, Jack remained preoccupied and Bay was simply hoping the second and final sample packet of Darvocet the doctor had given her would kick in soon and ease the killer headache that had returned.

Half an hour later Jack drove her into the Broadway Square Mall's parking lot where the black pickup stood in a lonely reminder of the night's events. Bay already had the keys in her fist and her purchases from yesterday on her lap. Last night she'd hesitated asking him about his sudden announcement.

''I'm sorry,'' was all she said. After their argument, she didn't feel she had a right to intrude in his business. This morning she knew she had to say something.

''I want you to know that I appreciate all you've

done,'' she began. ''The news about your job...if I'd known—''

''We'll talk at your house.''

''You don't have to shadow me.''

He reached into his glove compartment and drew out a pair of sunglasses. ''Here. You should have said the glare is killing you. They're plenty big and won't touch anything tender. If you get woozier than you are, pull over. I'll be right behind you.''

Bay would have sworn he had barely glanced at her since she emerged from the guest room. ''The pills should be kicking in soon. I'm sure I'll be fine.''

''Don't make me nuts by telling me what you think I want to hear. If I need one thing right now, Bay, it's the truth from you.''

''Okay. If it's not too much trouble.'' She wasn't thrilled with the idea of returning to the house by herself, but she wished he didn't make her feel like bloodying his nose one minute and curling up in his lap the next.

''And just leave that stuff on the seat. I'll take care of it for you.''

She made it back around the Loop without running anyone off the road. Jack's sunglasses made the difference, and also hid her wide-eyed shock when she pulled into the driveway and saw a sleek black Jaguar parked in her driveway. Duncan Ridgeway appeared from the far side of the house, a piece of paper in one hand, a cellular phone in the other.

''Help,'' Bay muttered under her breath.

She drove around his expensive car and pulled under the carport. By the time she shut off the engine, he was at the door.

"Dear God, what happened?"

"It's a long story."

"Who's that behind you?"

"Detective Jack Burke."

Bay didn't think anyone could make Duncan look bewildered and at a loss for words, but she'd done it. His confusion grew into annoyance as Jack pulled around the Jaguar, too, as though Jack was signaling Duncan was expected to leave first. Duncan's consternation didn't ease any as he took in her attire, specifically the huge man's T-shirt over her jeans. Smart move to put on the bra after all, Bay decided. She'd been tempted to stuff the thing in her pocket for the sake of comfort, thinking Jack had seen just about everything there was to see anyway.

"Duncan, what were you doing in back of the house?"

"I heard noises. When I didn't see your truck, but heard voices and music, I didn't know what to think and went to investigate. I'd already found this on your shop door."

Bay took the scrap of paper with the brief, angry demand, "Where are you?" and signed D. Crow.

"Oh, shit."

Ignoring Duncan's low cough, Bay closed her eyes and waited for the world to right itself again. What else? she wondered. Adding job stress to an unhappy mix of hunger and the Darvocet and she was in dire need to get somewhere dark and private before she ruined Duncan's shoes with her undigested coffee.

"Are you okay?"

"No. I told this customer I'd be ready to repair his dragster this morning."

"As in racing car dragster? Bay, you're amazing."

"I can guarantee you that Doug Crow doesn't think so after hauling that long monster trailer over here only to have to take it home again, which I'm sure made him late for work."

"He'll understand once you explain things to him. In fact, I'll be happy to call him for you."

"Thanks, but he'll be wanting to know when I can do the work, so I might as well get it over with myself." Bay could see Jack approaching in her rearview mirror. The idea of being crowded by the two of them had her easing out of the truck. "Duncan, you know Detective Burke."

Ever the diplomat, Duncan reached out his hand. "Detective. I hope you can appreciate that I have a number of questions."

"It's Bay's business to decide whether to answer them—or not." Bending at the knees, Jack peered at her and carefully removed the sunglasses. "Just as I thought," he murmured. Plucking the keys from her hand, he placed them into Duncan's extended hand. "Make yourself useful."

Before Duncan could reply, Jack had Bay in his arms and was carrying her to the door.

"That's right," she said under her breath, "make things easier for me."

"Look who's talking."

Duncan did beat them to the door. Unlocking the

dead bolt, he thrust the door open…and the pencil went flying across the room.

It wasn't necessary to peek at Jack's profile, Bay could feel the tension increase in his rock-hard body, the arms around her flex. ''No, I don't want to borrow Bud,'' she drawled, hoping to lighten the mood a degree or two.

''One more word you're going back into my truck.'' Setting her on one of the two bar stools, he scowled at the phone that continued to emit the obnoxious tone it had started when Bay left yesterday. ''What's this?''

''Oh, now I'm allowed to speak?'' At his dangerous look, she added quickly, ''I left it that way…after the last call.''

''What do you mean?'' Duncan asked.

Jack replaced the receiver and vanished into the living room. Bay heard the TV go off and then he was heading down the hall.

''I don't like the feel of this at all.''

Placing the keys on the counter, Duncan shifted his hands to his hips. Like Jack he'd left his suit jacket hanging in his vehicle, but that's where any similarities between the men's attire ended. The price of Duncan's finely tailored silk undoubtedly had an extra zero behind it, and Bay took a wild guess that Jack would shave his head before wearing a pink shirt with his gray suit.

Sighing, Bay leaned an elbow on the counter so she could rest her head in her hand. The weight was growing all too heavy for her neck. ''I was mugged last night coming out of the mall. Detective Burke has been handling the case.''

''Bless your sweet heart.'' Duncan reached out and stroked the uninjured side of her face. ''But, darling, how can you bear it? *Him?*''

He hadn't made a sound; however, Bay could feel the electricity in the room increase and knew Jack had returned. ''No one knows me or my case better, Duncan.''

''You should have called *us*. Mother is going to fry her cellular chewing out the chief of police,'' he replied, rubbing the back of his neck.

''The media showed up at the hospital. I didn't want your family connected to any speculation or bad press.''

Duncan gave her a tolerant smile. ''If there's one thing we're expert at, it's handling the media.'' Then he frowned. ''Wait a minute. You said...you think the mugger knew who you were?''

''Without a doubt,'' Jack replied. ''By the way, where was your mother's chauffeur around nine o'clock?''

''I beg your pardon?'' Duncan stretched to maximize the spare inch he stood above Jack. ''Don't you have work to do, Detective?''

''I'm doing it, Mr. Ridgeway. Any other cop would ask you the same question.''

''*Any* other cop would know that we're Bay's strongest allies and friends. But then you have a history of accusing the wrong people, don't you?''

Bay sucked in a sharp breath. ''Duncan.'' She shot Jack an entreating look appealing to him not to lose his temper. "It was dark and no one was around when it happened. I was attacked from behind, so there isn't much that I could report."

"That was stated on the local news this morning," Jack told him. "I can't believe you missed it."

"Our church holds a prayer breakfast on Thursday mornings," Duncan replied coldly. His tone warmed when he added to Bay, "I'll go outside and call Mother. She doesn't need to hear this shocking news from strangers. I'll be right back and we'll see about getting you proper treatment."

Jack waited until the door closed behind him and murmured, "That's what's entertaining about the rich and powerful. They don't mind telling you to go fuck yourself, but they're so polite about it."

"Jack, please."

He immediately came to stand before her and gazed deeply into her eyes. "Thank you for that and for what you said before about knowing you. I can almost believe you don't hate me quite so much as you did."

"I stopped hating a long time ago."

"But have you forgiven?"

Mesmerized by his intense gaze, she couldn't think, let alone answer.

Drawing in a slow deep breath, Jack lightly cupped her chin in his hand. "I really do have to go."

"I know."

"I'm going to worry like hell."

"I'll be all right."

"I wish I could be sure of that...and that you'll be here when I get back."

"I will be. All I want to do is lie down and maybe, finally, sleep."

"Eat something first. Let Mr. Connected out there use his influence to get something delivered."

"Jack, he's really a sweet man."

His hand dropped away. "Oh, I know. Either that sweet man or his mother are one of the reasons I've been demoted."

15

In the silence that settled after his departure, Bay sat weak and trembling. Her skin still felt warm where Jack had touched her, and yet inside she was cold.

He was wrong, that's all.

Duncan returned, this time carrying a large rectangular gift box in gold brocade with an exquisite spray of silk gardenias fastened in the center of a huge gold ribbon bow. The foil sticker at the right bottom corner of the box indicated it was from one of Tyler's premiere dress shops. While beautiful, all Bay could think was that Jack had taken her purchases with him.

"What have you done?" she asked Duncan.

"I wish I'd had time, but it's not me, it's Mother. Another Sunday outfit, I suspect, although probably not for this Sunday. I always had a hunch she missed not having a daughter, clotheshorse that she is. She's enjoying the heck out of taking it out on you. I should have left it in the car, though. She sends her love and has given me direct orders to shuttle you to her posthaste."

Bay shook her head as much as the pain allowed. "I'm staying here."

"Don't be silly. I imagine she's already calling the

family physician to the estate. How bad is it under that bandage? Please tell me no additional stitches?"

"Seven."

He winced, began to reach for the bandage and withdrew. "Don't tell Mother that, she can't even bear to look at prime rib if it's too rare. Poor angel, let's get you into the car—"

"Duncan, I mean it. I'm through with being prodded and poked for a while. What I need is rest. Then I'll be fine."

"And you'll get that at our house."

"No."

"Bay, as much as I hate to admit it, if Burke was right about the perpetrator knowing you, he could find you here."

"I believe he's already been around."

"What?"

She hadn't wanted to disclose that yet, concerned that if too many people knew, then the wrong person knew. But under the circumstances, she felt it necessary and told him of the incidents. "The point is that he hasn't tried while I'm around. That makes me think he's either certain that I'd recognize him, or he's afraid that I could defend myself better here and he's smart enough not to risk that."

Duncan looked at her as though they'd just met.

"Sorry to burst the last of your illusions about me," she drawled. "I did warn you. Our backgrounds are worlds apart."

"Stop trying to scare me off. What upsets me is that the incident with the key caused you such unease. I know Elvin's swarthy looks and, er, colorful personality tends to make him seem more fitting as a pirate in a Gilbert and Sullivan operetta than Mother's majordomo. That said, he's been with Mother for years. She had him thoroughly checked out and while, sure, he had a skirmish or two in his youth, she would never have kept him around this long if he didn't live up to what she requires of him—dedication and responsibility. Do you think I could travel as much as I do without being confident that she was in good hands?''

Everything he said made sense; in fact, Bay began to wish she could turn back the clock, that she'd never challenged Elvin about that key. It certainly hadn't been his voice she'd heard last night, and—remembering the way he chewed on mint—not his hideous breath she'd been repulsed by. Nevertheless... ''Please don't take what I'm about to say as an outright rejection, but in response, I can only say that once upon a time, I would never have believed I would hear a jury say 'Guilty' about me. In other words, assurances aren't much different than fairy tales to me, Duncan...until proven otherwise.''

A flicker of amusement lit his blue-gray eyes and deepened his dimples. ''So it's performance that impresses you...that's a morsel of information to savor.''

There was something of the eternally mischievous boy in him. How different he was from Jack, who gave the impression that he'd been born old. ''I should report you to your mother.''

''Sugar, all she would say is, 'Thank you, Jesus, there's hope for him yet.'''

The man was simply too clever for her today. Not only were her thinking processes at a disadvantage, Bay couldn't believe he—as well as Madeleine and Martin Davis for that matter—could poke fun at themselves and their own as readily as they did. "I'll give you this, you do put a different face on religion than I'm used to seeing."

The light in his eyes went out completely. "If there's one thing *I*'ve learned, it's that God does have a sense of humor. Oh, yes, He does."

It should have been a reassuring observation, and yet, oddly, it wasn't. "Duncan...?"

In the next instant the smile was back, although this time it was rueful. Leaning against the counter, he folded his arms across his chest. "If I'd known you wanted your file because you were doing your own investigation, young lady, I would never have helped you get it."

"Don't tell me that Lyle Gessler didn't blab that I did everything except accuse him personally of being a liar when he came to report your news at Gatesville?"

"Ha! Lyle's problem is that he lacks Elvin's ability to turn the other cheek. Wish I could have seen his face when you challenged him. He can be a tad arrogant and does require occasional humbling. I've told Mother that I have my reservations about his abilities to keep up as the business grows—"

"And which of your businesses would that be?" Bay teased.

"I'll let you know when Mother runs out of ideas," Duncan said winking.

"It's good that she has you watching out for her." Bay had to cover her mouth against the yawn that no amount of good manners would repress.

Immediately contrite, Duncan drew her up from the stool. "I should be horsewhipped for rambling on. Go lie down. I'll be your sentry until you wake up. We can talk more then."

Bay was all for the lying down part; the rest was disconcerting. "You can't stay."

"Why not? Oh, don't tell me...you snore like an elephant after a thirty-hour labor? Dang, there go my visions of recreating *Sleeping Beauty.*"

"You're a busy man," she said dryly. "At least that's what you keep telling me."

"With a secretary who knows how to reschedule my appointments. I'll step outside again to call her so as not to disturb you. I'll also arrange for lunch to be delivered at half past noon."

Bay wanted to argue she simply didn't have the energy. Mouthing *thank you,* she retreated to the cool, shadowy seclusion of her bedroom. Slipping off her shoes, she crawled under the bedspread, sighed with relief and closed her eyes.

Good hands...good hands...

Frowning, she fell asleep.

16

9:45 a.m.

"Burke…in my office."

Jack had hoped Lieutenant Ed Gage would be tied up in a meeting or out of the building when he arrived at headquarters. After yesterday's ass chewing, the next millennium would be too soon for another run-in with the man who had his eye on the chief of police position.

If he received any sympathetic looks from the only other two detectives around at the moment, he didn't notice. Unable to put the past behind him, he'd become a pariah to his fellow cops and unless forced to work together on a larger case, they didn't want him tainting their chances for advancement.

Entering the corner office, he obeyed his superior officer's signal to shut the door. Jack thought the directive a joke. The guys outside had the hearing of the sharp-eared coyotes that pestered his stock at the ranch. Add Gage's stentorian baritone and no one missed much going on in here.

"Sir?" he asked keeping his face carefully blank.

Looking like the former marine he was, Gage stood behind his desk framed by his degrees, commendations and awards, and glared at Jack through narrowed eyes. "I just want to know one thing, Burke. Do you think I like to hear myself talk? I think you must, because I distinctly remember telling you yesterday that I did not want the chief chewing on my ass about the Ridgeways again, and yet how am I starting my day? By getting my ass chewed, an experience I'd gladly have shared with you had you been here on time."

"Sorry, sir. I was unavoidably delayed. But I'd like to correct one fact—I have not approached the Ridgeways."

The lieutenant's full lower lip curled. "Don't play games with me, mister. Their little friend, the one they got out of the pen, was assaulted last night at Broadway Square Mall. Are you going to tell me that you don't know anything about that?"

"She's not a Ridgeway." Yet, Jack thought grimly.

"I ought to drop-kick you straight out of this building via the roof. Don't you split hairs with me. Mrs. R. claims her and I don't care if that's as a lapdog, chambermaid, or long-lost daughter. The point is the Dragon Lady herself called breathing fire over your assignment to the case. I assured the chief, *I* did not do that. And do you know what he said, Burke? 'Who then? Or is he only taking direct instructions from Jesus H. Christ these days?'"

"I didn't go to the hospital in any official capacity, sir. I acted as a friend."

The proud man with the steel-wool hair cut into a

severe flattop snorted. ''She's more apt to turn your balls into car mirror ornaments than call you a friend.''

''Last night I received a call that Ms. Butler was at Mother Frances Hospital. It's my card she carried in her pocket, my number that was called for assistance in getting her released.''

''How'd it get there—with your home number apparently?''

''I gave it to her a few days ago when I went to apologize and wish her the best.''

The man with the acne-scarred face reared back as though dodging a red hornet. ''I don't want to hear that word, Burke. What happened, happened as a result of the best data we had at the time. Hell, you start apologizing and the next thing you have is reporters asking what other cases we've botched.''

''Who can fault them when the court concurs we've established one of such import?'' Jack watched the other cop's chest rise and fall with each stabilizing breath, but his coloring remained ruddy beneath his tan. Safe for the moment, he thought. Gage had to agree, or else justify denying Jack's request to review the latest edition of the English file, which Gage had kept in here for an unusually long time.

''You worry me, Detective. This department only succeeds when we're team players, not hotshots more interested in garnering press to promote our personal careers at the expense of the big picture.''

He should talk, Jack thought. ''Exactly what is the big picture...sir? My worry is that it has less and less to do with the truth. So does Ms. Butler. Yesterday, someone decided to tell her she didn't have the right to find out what that truth is. Have you been informed Ms. Butler's attacker delivered a message that I believe gives credence to her doubt about the latest turn in the English case?''

''No.''

''He said, 'Leave well enough alone.' That doesn't sound to me as if the testimony and conclusions drawn about English are conclusive...sir.''

17

1:00 p.m.

"No way."

Bay sat across the kitchen bar from Duncan and listened to how he'd resolved most of her headaches—at least for the next twenty-four hours. It was too good to be true. So was the enormous bouquet he'd had delivered while she'd slept, which almost blocked out her view of the kitchen door. She didn't know enough about flowers to recognize anything besides the carnations, roses and daisies; she could tell the breathtaking crystal vase alone must have cost a small fortune.

"It's true," Duncan said, stabbing another piece of beef with his fork. "You're getting the Nelson order and without Bruce stopping by to inspect the shop and interview you. When I told him that along with doing Mother's gate, you've been hired to redesign a famous racer's car repairs—"

Bay almost choked. "That's not exactly accurate. Redesign?"

"Sounds like it to me."

"Well, he's not famous."

"Did you not say the guy has won every race in his division in the tristate area?"

"Yes, but—"

"Then he's well-known."

"That's fudging."

"That's marketing. Anyway, Bruce wants you to do two of those plant cart gizmos for Celia's hothouse. Those hieroglyphics over there by the phone are the general measurements and such." Duncan nodded at the pad. "He'll leave the rest in your capable hands. No price ceiling."

"I won't overcharge him. Madeleine told me enough about what he's created for his wife to know matching that quality will be costly enough."

"Listen to you undermining my efforts. I can't wait to see it. Tell me, can you sign plant carts like a painting?"

"With an electric engraver, and it's not going to happen." Bay began to reach for the pad only to have Duncan shift it farther out of her reach.

"No work for you today, only play…and food. Eat."

She didn't know anything about eastern cuisine other than the spices were already warning they would hate her stomach. "I am, just slowly. I have to watch my lip and jaw," she said to avoid offending him. "What did Doug Crow say?"

"He's giving you season tickets to all of his races if you'll forgive him for being a pig this morning."

"Doug Crow is a weekend racer, not part of the big NHRA circuit."

"Oh, him. He says to get well and can you possibly have his car ready to race by a week from Saturday?"

"Poor Doug, I hope you didn't intimidate him too much. He seems a good guy, and a real up-and-comer from what I understand. Anyway, I can handle that schedule." Bay gave up on the meat and vegetables on her plate and concentrated on plain rice. "Thank you, Duncan. Joking aside, you've saved my business."

"It sounds like you're ready to hire some help."

"Hardly." She sensed he wanted to make her an offer and she didn't want to argue with either Ridgeway about loans or additional favors. "Did your secretary keep you out of hot water while you were playing my guy Friday?"

His dark-gold eyebrows twitched as he swallowed another bite. "I'm afraid she went home sick about an hour ago."

"I hope it's not serious."

"Sounds like that viral thing going around. Ordinarily, we could encourage her to take all the time she needs, but with vacations that leaves one gal holding the fort. There's no way around it, we have to send Holly over from the communications offices."

"But your mother said—" Bay touched her tongue to her stitches.

"That's all right. Your concern matches my own, particularly after the way she behaved last weekend."

"Then what are you doing here?"

"Trying to make a good impression on a new friend."

Bay put down her fork. "As soon as you finish

your lunch, you do what you have to do. I'm feeling much stronger.''

''Three hours of sleep after what you've been through is barely a nap. It doesn't begin to make up for the overall deficit. As for leaving you here by yourself—''

''Nag, nag, Mother.''

Duncan threw back his head and laughed. ''I'll get you for that.''

He left about twenty minutes later, warning he'd be in close touch and surprising her with a kiss on her uninjured cheek. ''In case this sweet understanding has an ulterior motive,'' he added once behind the wheel of his car, ''today doesn't qualify as our dinner date.''

Entertained as she was, Bay returned inside glad to have her privacy back. Old habits didn't just die hard, they became like an Egyptian curse to her. She guessed Duncan had gone through his own spasms, his tonic, to stay on the phone and conduct business the whole time she slept. Bay couldn't believe the food he'd ordered. Putting it down the garbage disposal would be an awful waste. Did raccoons have stronger stomachs than she did…?

The sound of a vehicle in her driveway had her returning to the door. Thinking Duncan had forgotten something, she opened up and came face-to-face with Jack.

''Yeah, I passed him,'' he said upon entering. ''No, he didn't see me. He was on the phone and checking his hair in the mirror. It's your eyes,'' he explained handing over her purchases. ''The harder you work on flat-lining your emotions, the more I know is going on. How are you?''

''Thrilled with the prospect of undergoing another interrogation or lecture.''

Until then Jack's focus had been on her; now he took in the flowers, the take-out boxes and the fancy dress box Bay had yet to open and was covering with the things he'd brought.

''I thought the earliest I'd hear from you was evening,'' she continued.

''I didn't call because I hoped you'd be sleeping.''

''I was.''

That didn't improve his mood. ''Do I want to ask when he returned?''

''No. He never left.''

Jack lingered by the door as though debating whether to leave or throw the crystal vase out. ''Nothing low-key about him, is there?''

''No one has ever given me flowers before,'' Bay said returning to stand before him. ''Please don't ask me to feel guilty for enjoying them.''

He shoved his hands into his pockets and narrowed his focus to only her and the hardness left his eyes. ''Can I start over?'' he asked gruffly. ''You look a lot better.''

A shoo-in for the title role in *Phantom of the Opera,* Bay thought, since the bandage had come loose from her temple when she woke and she'd left it off. But he wasn't exactly in prime shape himself. He looked like someone had kicked Bud and made him watch. She indicated the blue T-shirt she'd changed into and then her bruises. ‘‘I understand it fools the eye if you keep to one color scheme.’’

‘‘Stop.’’

‘‘I was about to make myself a sandwich. Should I make two?’’

Jack checked out one of the restaurant boxes. ‘‘Something wrong with this?’’

‘‘Not if your stomach is made of twelve-gauge steel.’’

‘‘A sandwich would be great.’’

‘‘All I can offer you to drink is the standard—coffee, water, juice or mouthwash.’’

Jack’s mouth curved into a downward smile. ‘‘I’d appreciate the coffee.’’

‘‘Have a seat.’’

He began rolling up his sleeves. ‘‘Let me wash up first.’’

After he got out of the way, she put on water for two cups of instant, put the restaurant fare into the sink and made duplicate sandwiches, not asking what he liked, rather using what she had. The whole time she was aware of his quiet scrutiny. Finally, she slid his plate in front of him.

‘‘Are you the type who needs to eat in peace, or are you going to tell me what’s happened?’’

‘‘I made things worse today.’’

Bay took her seat and wondered how things could get worse. ‘‘You said yesterday you got demoted.’’ The admission had troubled her ever since, as much for the news as for who he blamed.

‘‘They know down at the station that you don’t buy the Tarpley story.’’

"What's wrong with that?" Shrugging, she ripped open a bag of chips and placed it on the counter. "I haven't involved the press or embarrassed the Ridgeways in public."

"It still suggests you don't respect the police department's work."

"It's not their fault if Tarpley is lying."

"Martel supported Tarpley. He said Basque was there in Tyler at the time of Glenn's murder, so you see, you might as well be calling Martel, and, therefore, the whole force liars. Yeah, I know he's not even in the picture anymore. It doesn't matter, ranks close in times of trouble and there's this us-versus-them mentality. It can get rough, Bay."

Although she'd only taken a small bite of her sandwich, she had to chew a while to get it down. "They can't put me back in jail."

Jack's silent stare had her putting down the half-section of sandwich.

"They can?"

"Life could become sheer hell. They'll stop you for every traffic violation legitimate or otherwise. You'll come out of the mall, find your truck's taillight bashed and get pulled over as you drive to the auto parts store. Get enough of those before you can pay them all and you're hauled in."

"Arrested?" Bay didn't think she could deal with the humiliation of handcuffs again, let alone the trauma of being returned to a jail cell.

"And that's if this is only about their pride."

"I don't understand."

"If there's something else—something bigger and

uglier going on—then you could be framed the same way you were the first time around...or silenced permanently.''

Shivering as though someone had tampered with the thermostat again, Bay wrapped her hands around her mug to warm them. But she didn't pick it up. She couldn't find the strength.

Across the table Jack waited, his expression reflecting concern and compassion...and something else. Soul-deep shame.

''You've known something was wrong all along, haven't you?'' she asked slowly.

''It's why I've never put the case behind me. We remember the crime scenes, that's a fact of life with this job. You wouldn't get out of my head, either. I can see it like it's on Kodak paper, the way I first saw you huddled on the floor in the corner of your office. Everyone else on the scene thought you were giving an award-winning performance of a woman fighting to save herself from a death penalty conviction by grieving over the murder of her friend. When I looked into your eyes, I saw you'd experienced something unspeakable. Evil had stood within arm's reach of you.''

''Yes,'' Bay whispered.

''And as terrible as Glenn's death was, so was knowing you'd been spared for some reason.''

''Yes.'' For years she'd tried to form the thought herself and failed. Her eyes burned as she was thrust back to that ungodly night.

''You were spared because you were targeted to be used otherwise. But how could I convince a jury that my cop's instincts were as invaluable as my side arm?'' Jack continued. ''It's incredible. People gobble it up all the time in movies and books. On the evening news a guy getting his fifteen minutes of fame can talk about the inexplicable moment he was told to go left instead of right, and not only survived death himself, but saved others and he's called a hero. But hear the word *instinct* on a witness stand and like you said the D.A. does everything except call you a psychic hotline scam artist...and his accusation is backed with a fingerprint on a gun.''

''Or a lance.''

''Yeah, a lance...then comes the go-for-the-jugular question, *Don't you sometimes doubt that irrefutable inner voice yourself at times, Detective?''*

Jack closed his eyes. When he opened them again, Bay caught a glimpse of a man who'd spent years adrift in a sea of misery.

''You're no killer,'' he concluded. ''That was no act that had you shaking so bad it took two uniforms to get you to your feet and into a patrol car. For a few fateful seconds you'd shared the same breath of air with a monster...and from that moment he stole any hope of sanctuary from you.''

The tears pouring down Bay's cheeks went unchecked. All she could do was sit there as the tidal wave six years in the making washed away the protective crust she'd built over old wounds and emotions long since buried. At the same time she was buoyed by relief that someone finally comprehended what had happened—what was happening.

''Don't.'' Jack came around the counter and eased

her against him. ''The salt will sting like crazy in those scratches.''

''I'm fine. I just—I never realized.''

He kissed the top of her head. ''I wish I could have let you know I wanted to help, that I was trying. But the surveillance on mail—''

''Yes.''

It was the only thing she could say with her mind racing and her senses going haywire. All her life she'd been particular about who touched her. She understood the psychology behind that: the early loss of her mother, an emotionally cold, neglectful father and an environment that was great for job training, but terrible for relationships. Excuses, as far as she was concerned. Much like Jack described instinct, Bay opened herself to contact only when something deep inside her corresponded and since little did, intimacy became like an abusive relative, something to be avoided. She could go through the motions as others did—and had to a point—but finally refused to be that deceiving and hypocritical. Then here came Jack Burke, whose name was supposed to make her stomach burn and her hands clench. Her hands clenched all right; they gripped his forearms as he coaxed her head back urging her to look at him and held tight as he lowered his mouth to hers.

Tenderness and care had no business stirring such excitement, but after an initial caress of lips against lips, Bay opened to what Jack offered, and nothing had ever felt so right as their first, deep kiss. They could have been lovers reunited. An affirmation as well as an exploration, every cell in her body soon hummed with life. She grew warm and then warmer, until the burning in her stomach earned a new name—need—the one kind Bay couldn't let herself allow. Not yet.

She drew back. Jack came after her, then checked himself. His eyes registered comprehension and he started to pull away completely, but Bay wrapped her arms around him and hid her face against his chest. Immediately his arms enfolded her again.

"It's my fault." His lips and breath caressed the shell of her ear.

"Me. I chickened out. It's too soon and I look—"

"Like you." This time he did draw back some. "Bay, the bruises will fade. They make me ache and want to pulverize whoever did it, but you're still you. That's who I see. That's all I've ever seen. Those eyes, and what's in here." With the backs of his fingers he stroked the shallow spot between her breasts.

She couldn't think of anything to say in response and then the phone rang, and she lost her chance.

18

"Madeleine...hi."

Bay assumed this call would be coming, but Jack had managed to push it from her mind. As he returned to his seat on the other side of the counter, she watched his expression change, the worry become a hardness, like armor, hiding the man she'd responded to with such open desire.

"Darling, how are you feeling? You don't sound like yourself."

"I guess I haven't wakened fully."

"You're exhausted. Duncan tells me you only managed a tiny nap."

"Enough to get me through the rest of the day. Um, thank you for the box, I mean the gift. You really shouldn't have."

"He said you haven't opened it."

Bay wondered what Duncan didn't tell his mother. "The wrapping is so beautiful, I hate to ruin it."

Madeleine chuckled. "They do nice work, don't they? But go on. I'll hold."

Recognizing her determination, Bay decided it would take less energy to give in. Murmuring, "All right," she put down the phone, gave Jack a slight shake of her head and went to open the box. However, she really did regret sliding off the ribbon, once she lifted the lid, she understood Madeleine's amusement. She might as well have tried comparing plastic with pearls. Instinctively wiping her hands against her backside, she lifted out the daintiest pair of strappy white heels and an equally sexy bag on a fine gold chain. Then she reached for the white suit with the delicate seed pearl design on the left shoulder.

She could feel Jack's gaze and looked across the room almost hearing his thoughts. Yes, she would look like a bride in this.

Bay laid the suit back and returned to the phone. "It's...exquisite, but far too much. I can't accept this."

"Nonsense. I had such fun."

"I'm serious. You can't keep doing this."

"Why not? You need the wardrobe and I like to surprise you."

"You did that."

"You can wear it Sunday. Of course, I'll have Elvin pick you up because there's no way that truck is clean enough for—"

"Madeleine, I'm in no condition to be seen in public right now. You sit in the front row, for pity's sake. That video camera last week did everything except a cornea ID."

The older woman laughed again. "I'm so used to it, I hardly notice when it's on me."

"Well, let me tell you what the TV audience would notice, and it isn't your gorgeous outfit. Didn't Duncan share with you that I'm a wreck?"

"Oh, darling, you can't be that. What if I make it clear to the producers beforehand that they're only to get your good side and from a distance?"

"Madeleine, I'm firm on this."

"Then we'll see you at lunch."

Bay rubbed at the space between her eyebrows. She was getting another lesson on why her benefactress was so successful—she never gave up. She could only imagine what Jack was thinking. This conversation was all too easy to follow. "Thank you, but not lunch, either. I'd like some time to heal and to decide what I'm going to do."

"I knew it. You're scared. Duncan should never have left you out there by yourself. I don't know what got into him. Let me send Elvin over to pick you up and you spend the next few days here. We'll analyze the situation together."

"No, Madeleine. The gesture is gracious, the concern is sweet, but absolutely not."

"You're beginning to sound like a hermit."

What she wasn't and never would be was a social butterfly, not even of the aspiring variety. Not bothering to attempt explaining her creative nature, she focused on what she knew Madeleine could relate to. "I have projects waiting for me." Bay didn't dare look back at Jack, certain he could follow this conversation.

"I'm aware of that. We can work around your schedule. Elvin can drive you."

"You made a vehicle available to me so I can drive myself. I'm not coming."

"Bay." Madeleine sighed. "It's not the Elvin thing again? Duncan was supposed to explain."

"It has less to do with Elvin than you realize, and I'm not afraid to be here by myself. Right now it has to do with declaring boundaries."

That silenced Madeleine for a moment. "You think I'm being overbearing?" She made a brief, humorous sound. "This does make me feel like I have a daughter after all."

"Madeleine—" Bay moaned "—you could be the Department of Defense. All of it."

"In other words, because I don't know how to do things halfheartedly, I'm to be rejected outright."

"That's not what I said."

"If I find someone or something that inspires me, I feel obligated to do all I can to support them or it. I'll let you in on a secret, Bay. I'm not an exceptional woman. Don't try to argue, I know that's hard to believe considering my family pedigree, but as much as I adored my daddy, he didn't put a good deal of stock in females. It was he who pointed out to me that I had no notable talent, except for my ability to stand toe-to-toe to him without being crushed."

"So tell me what shrine I can go to and make an offer begging him to stop you from steamrollering over me," Bay drawled.

Madeleine laughed, albeit reluctantly. "I'm glad we're on the same side."

"Are you going to stop?"

"For the moment. Let me caution you of one thing and then I promise to let you go. Be careful of Jack

Burke. Duncan said he'll probably be back this afternoon fishing for information."

"I told him everything I know of the attack."

"About us, darling. You don't know how angry he's apt to be. We've taken steps to ensure he thinks twice before bothering you again, and I'm afraid that instead of getting the message, he's apt to bully you to get back at us."

"What steps? What have you done?"

"Used my assets, that's what they're there for. Detective Burke—not that he'll be able to call himself one much longer if I have any say—is going to understand he can't poke his nose where it's none of his business."

"Madeleine, I explained to Duncan how good he was to me after the attack."

"Making an impression in public. What else is new? Watch that man. He can't get over that he botched the biggest case of his life, and I suspect that if he senses it's over, he won't allow himself to go down alone. You know, darling, I wouldn't be surprised if he hired someone to hurt you just so he could come to your rescue."

"That's ridiculous. For what?"

"Why do people do anything mean-hearted? Jealousy, greed..."

Bay frowned, disappointed that Madeleine was jumping to such stark conclusions. "Whatever I thought of him before, I never saw him as that."

She heard a movement behind her and then Jack's hands settled on her shoulders. Warmth spread through her chest. He was filling in the holes in the one-sided dialogue and offering his emotional support. Bay covered his left hand with her own.

"I don't expect you to know all that's gone on, dear. Just watch yourself and let me know everything that happens."

Bay changed the subject to the Nelsons and how Duncan had locked in the contract for her. Safe ground until she could end the call.

Finally hanging up, she pressed her fingers to her eyes.

Jack massaged her shoulders gently, and kissed the back of her neck. "It's like trying to make sense of a blueprint when all of the dimensions are written in Chinese, isn't it? You might be able to tell what you're looking at, but you're not sure of the size of the beast."

With a breathless sound, Bay turned to face him. "That's it."

"You don't have to look so surprised."

"Impressed."

"You would have come up with the same analogy if you weren't constantly having to fight Mrs. R. as she tries to turn you into an eighteen-year-old version of the daughter she never had."

"Are you trying for a grand slam?" Bay groaned and shook her head slowly. "She's wonderful. They're both terrific to me."

"They're suffocating you."

"God, yes. And, yet...they're like the family I never had."

"Do you think Duncan Ridgeway wants you to think of him as your brother?"

Bay looked from the flowers to the gift box and frowned up at him. "Stop. You're scaring me."

"How do you think I feel?"

"Like a guy who's leading four to zip."

"Yeah, but it's only the top of the first inning."

Bay shook off the shiver brought on by his dark suppositions and slipped around him to give herself space to think. "No. I'm not Duncan's type."

"Looks as if he already has his mama's approval, though."

She turned her back on the box. "That's going back. If she won't take it, I'll bring it directly to the store and insist they credit her account. As for Duncan, I'm a novelty to him. Believe me, any interest he thinks he feels will wear off, and so will any approval by Madeleine after another few conversations like this one. He needs someone who is willing to put his schedule first and be an asset with the socializing, the politics...that's not me."

"Is that why you bought that sexy outfit yesterday? To dissuade his attention?"

"It's a simple black dress appropriate for funerals as much as anything."

"Uh-huh, and instead of listening to the eulogy, every red-blooded male would be wondering what they'd find if they untied that sash at your waist."

"Duncan convinced his mother to give me my file," Bay said, an edge entering her voice. "There are things missing out of it. I thought having dinner with him would give me an opportunity to talk to privately and get his help in finding out why."

"You don't need to dangle sugar in front of him

to do that." At her confused and increasingly offended look, he murmured, "Keep your eyes on the blueprint."

She paced from the pantry door to the entry into the living room. "I can't make myself see what you're seeing."

"You said it. You don't want to." Jack pointed to the phone. "I heard you trying to defend me without ticking her off. To keep her from coming after me more than she has. Why do you think she's doing that in the first place, Bay?"

"To punish you for hurting me."

"That's what she wants you to believe. What do you see? What do you know?"

She couldn't see anything anymore; the picture kept changing and her throbbing head was messing with her stomach again. "I have to lie down."

For a moment Jack looked as though he wanted to push on but, in the next, he came to her and enfolded her against him. "Don't shut me out."

"I don't want to."

"You feel it, too, what's between us whenever we're this close?"

Not only did she feel safe in his arms, he made her ache with a hunger foreign to her. "Sex would only complicate things," she said to herself as much as him.

Jack kissed her temple, the side of her neck. "It wouldn't be just sex and you know it. That's what scares you most." And then he took her mouth again, ever careful of causing pain, but driving her with breathtaking speed to where they'd left off before.

Increasingly dizzy, Bay gripped his shirt, too aware her heart was pounding as hard and fast as his. Then she felt his body growing harder, and he shifted her, trapped her in the corner of the cabinets again and thrust himself against her until she moaned into his mouth and arched to get at more of him.

The next thing she knew she was alone listening to the door shut softly behind him. Dazed, his parting words reverberated through her.

"If you kiss me back like that again, I won't give a damn how complicated it makes things, we're going to find the closest flat surface and get so hot you'll be willing to swear to anything, even that you forgive me."

19

The rest of the afternoon evolved into an exercise in answering machine discipline.

Wanting only to curl up under the bedspread and hide, Bay first forced herself to clean up in the kitchen. Duncan would give her some space hoping she would get in another nap she thought, finally wiping out the steel sink. As for Jack, surely he had to go back to the station and, considering what he'd alluded to, she doubted he would call her from there. She did need to block out the world for a while, but she didn't get halfway down the hall before the phone began ringing....

"Bay? Duncan. Catching more Zs? Hope things are quieter there than they are here. I'll check with you later. In the meantime if you need anything, I left my card by your phone. Give me a buzz when you get up again so I know you're all right...."

"It's me," came a deeper, immediately recognizable voice. "Listen...I'm thinking you might have forgotten to lock up after I left. You don't have to pick up if you don't want to, but check the door....

* * *

"All right," Jack said less patiently. "I do want to know you're okay. Pick up. Bay...?

"Pick up. You know I'll have to drive over there if you don't."

The warning launched Bay out of her nest in the corner of the couch to snatch up the kitchen extension. "Don't threaten me, Jack."

"Don't make me crazy worrying about you."

"I was trying to rest."

"You can't sleep any more than I can work."

Bay replaced the receiver in the cradle because she couldn't disagree with him and wouldn't admit that.

"Bay? Duncan. Guess you're not up yet. Listen, I have to dash out of town. Things I thought were set on the East Coast are unraveling a bit. When it rains it pours and all that. Tell you about it when I get back. Anyway, you have the number at the house—use it. Better yet, please reconsider Mother's offer. Yes, she told me she talked to you, too. We're here to help, honey."

"Bay, it's Jack. Don't hang up. I've just left the station for the day, do you need anything? Okay, so maybe you can sleep, but wake up now and pick up so I know you're all right...Bay. Pick up, woman, or I'll be guilty of breaking and entering in about seven minutes."

Bay reached for the bedroom extension. "Try it and I'll dial 911."

"That's better. Where are you? You sound muffled."

"Under the bedspread. It's the darkest place in the house."

"Are you feeling worse? Need me to take you back to Emergency?"

"Headache. I took something. Just waited too long."

"You also barely got half of that sandwich down. Your body is crying out for help."

"Only my eardrums."

"I think you should let me in and we'll try the soup route again. Have any canned stuff in your cupboard?"

"Go home to that miniature moose and practice on him."

"Not until I'm convinced you're able to hold your own."

"Against what? You, the Ridgeways and the other two-thirds of the northern hemisphere? Jack, I don't want to talk to you right now."

"That much I'm grasping. I still want to listen until I'm convinced you're not hiding something medical or otherwise threatening."

"What do you need me to do, recite the alphabet backward for you? I'd have to get a pen and paper first. As for the 'otherwise,' if you're referring to Duncan, he's left town on a business emergency. So much for your concerns about me getting swept off my feet."

"He might be the patient type—like me." After a

long pause he continued, "Maybe that could have been left unsaid."

"All I'm asking for is some time and room. Until a few days ago I had nothing but that. Now everyone is eating my clock by telling me what they want me to do."

"There's one difference. I'm not trying to cover my ass."

20

Angry enough with himself to kick out his own windshield, Jack crossed the Loop and headed down Airport Drive. It wasn't his intention to add to Bay's stress, but having held her and kissed her, he was realizing that he couldn't go back to the way things had been—of at least pretending a professional impartiality. Could be he'd upset her enough to report him; nevertheless, going home and leaving her out here without some kind of protection wasn't something he could do. The news about Duncan Ridgeway convinced him. Maybe Slick's explanation was bona fide, but equally likely the guy was buying himself a dose of Bay's "time and space"...or an alibi.

As he approached her place, Jack pulled over to the service lane. Traffic was at its heaviest, but he could see over most of it. No other vehicles were up at the shop or house; in fact, the place looked locked up tight for the night. Satisfied he had a small window of time, he merged back into traffic.

Bud was sitting by the turn to the garage waiting for him as though he'd received a call in advance. Barking, he loped down to meet him, happily jumping over the side and into the bed of the truck for a quick ride. The greeting brought Simon from the barn, slapping his gloves against his thigh.

Jack didn't trigger the garage door opener, but parked out on the concrete slab. As he climbed out, Bud stretched his neck for a face-to-face greeting. "No wet kisses, you big washrag," Jack said, taking hold of the animal's great head and massaging him affectionately.

"Whassup?" Simon asked upon reaching him.

"I'll be pulling an all-nighter. Just need to get a change of clothes, then I'm out of here."

"After last night?" The hired hand shook his head in sympathy.

"How'd it go today?"

"Fine. Could use some rain."

"You'll be saying that every day until September. I'll ring you in the morning, but if you need anything, buzz my pager."

"How many times since I been here I bother you?"

"That's why I'm reminding you."

Simon took off his straw hat and wiped his sweat-and-dust-caked brow with an equally dirty forearm. "This about the little scrapper?"

"Yeah."

Minutes later he was back in the truck and headed down the driveway again, a dejected Bud in his rear-view mirror dropping to his belly and laying his head on his paws. The sight tore at Jack, but then so did a lot of things these days.

While collecting his stuff, he'd been debating where he could have the best view of her property and yet be out of sight of traffic. Parking behind her shop would be ideal. Proximity-wise—he could cut off anyone pulling in—but even if she didn't hear him arriving, she was bound to spot him by the time he left in the morning. Then wouldn't there be hell to pay…a double dose if they got wind of his unauthorized trespassing down at the station.

Jack's second choice was a dirt driveway across the highway slightly catty-corner from hers. The lack of a mailbox out front and the overgrown woods creating a tunnel-like effect beyond the highway easement suggested he wouldn't have to worry about traffic. Nevertheless, when he got to the spot, he drove down a ways to be sure he wouldn't get a back window riddled with buckshot after dark. Not surprisingly, about a hundred yards down he came upon a huge sweet gum that had come out of the ground roots and all and fallen across the entire width of the drive. It had been there a few years, since it was a while ago that the water table was so high as to compromise the tree's shallow root system.

Confident he had his spot, he backed up until he had room to make a three-point-turn and eased toward the road to where he could see Bay's place and still be hidden from highway traffic. Avoiding a middle-of-the-night encounter with a patrol unit was the best way to avoid the lieutenant demanding his badge come morning.

Killing the engine, Jack slid his seat back for maximum leg room. Completely removing his tie, he hung it on the clothes hanger holding tomorrow's suit, then he settled in for the long night.

* * *

It was almost midnight—he'd checked a few minutes ago to stave off another wave of sleepiness—and traffic was virtually nonexistent when the dark SUV on his side hit its brakes and slowed to a crawl as it passed Bay's. Almost out of sight, it cut a U-turn and started back.

Jack sat up, instantly alert.

The vehicle stayed in the service lane and stopped at her driveway. Without taking his eyes off the SUV, he unsnapped his holster strap and checked to make sure his flashlight was on the console where he'd placed it earlier. Suddenly the interior lights came on in the SUV and Jack saw a man and woman. They could have been him and Bay, except that the woman's hair was shoulder length.

Lost, he thought as he watched them peering at a sheet of paper.

After several seconds, the man turned off the light and cut another U-turn on the empty highway. For the briefest instant lights skimmed Jack's truck, but he'd already ducked, even though he figured he was far enough in the woods not to catch their interest. To be sure about his hunch, he keyed the engine and followed the vehicle.

Sure enough, the SUV slowed again about a quarter mile down the road in front of a house that had a small tin tool shed to the left of the house. Easing by, Jack drove a short piece and made his own turn. As he passed the place again, he saw the couple being met at the door by a man in a robe who hugged them before ushering them inside.

"At least that's one happy ending tonight," he murmured. Yawning, he returned to his post.

21

Friday, June 7, 2001
5:55 a.m.

Bay had just put water on for her second mug of coffee when she remembered it was trash pickup day. The truck came early and she hurried outside to roll the vinyl can on the two-wheeled trolley down to the edge of the driveway. That's when her heart made a little skip.

That pickup truck across the street...she'd never seen it there before. Actually, she'd never paid much attention to that driveway. No one lived there that she knew; however, the white, late-model pickup truck reminded her of...

Her heart beginning to pound, she walked along the curb to get a better look. Twilight could be deceptive, but, yes, she could even make out the license, not that it helped her. What did help was the clearer view of the man slumped with his head against the driver's window.

Checking to make sure no vehicles were close, she jogged across the highway. By the time she'd reached the other side, his eyes were open as if he'd sensed her approach. Bay would have snickered at his expression...if she hadn't been so ticked.

Starting up the engine, he rolled down the power window.

"I can't wait to hear this," she drawled, her hands on her hips.

His sleep-heavy eyes skimmed over her black T-shirt and jeans. "What's to tell? You wouldn't come home with me and I sure wasn't leaving you out here by yourself."

She couldn't believe it; he'd camped out here all night? No need to ask, he was wearing what she last saw him in, and there was another suit in a similar shade of gray hanging off the gun rack. What did he plan to do, change in the rest room at the station? That would go over well with his superiors.

"You're nuts, Burke." But Bay's indignation was already moderating. "You might as well come over to inhale some coffee and wash up. I don't want you causing an accident falling asleep behind the wheel or scaring mothers dropping off their kids at the day care down the street." With those burning eyes and a night's growth of near-black beard, he looked like a guy coming down from a drug-induced high or one who'd stepped permanently into the twilight zone.

"That's a deal. Hop in, I'll drive you over."

Pretending she didn't hear him, she ran back across the street. She needed a moment to settle the butterflies in her stomach, as well as to think about her unwise impulse to do some caretaking.

By the time she was at her door, he had his clothes

and shaving kit, and was right behind her. She stepped aside to let him pass and closed up behind them.

"I really appreciate this." He stopped in the middle of the room as though it was his first time inside. "And your understanding."

"I realize your intentions were decent. Did you see anything?"

"Thought something was going down around midnight, but they turned out to be lost travelers belonging to your neighbors down the road a piece."

She frowned slightly. By that hour she was definitely out of it. "I don't know that I would have heard anyone if they had tried to break in."

"Exactly."

He glanced around and Bay understood he was feeling self-conscious. Considering their last few conversations, she couldn't blame him.

"If you'd like to shower, use the master bath with the separate stall. It's the only one stocked, anyway. I'll work on food."

"I hate to put you through any more trouble, but I wouldn't turn it down."

In other words, he'd missed dinner. She suspected that what he had here yesterday was it. "And you give me a hard time," she muttered to herself as she reached for the refrigerator door.

By the time he returned, she'd made a hash of potatoes, bacon, green peppers, onions and tomatoes, sautéed and mixed into scrambled eggs. Framing it with toast, she set the heaping plate at the table where she'd placed cutlery and a napkin. "Do you want jam?" she asked returning for the coffee.

"Sure. That would complete the smorgasbord."

That stopped her. "It may not be pretty—I grew up in a house where it was everyone for himself—but it will get you through the morning."

"That's what I meant. It looks great." Jack smiled when she brought the remainders in a pan and settled beside him. "My mother used to do that. She would go through all of this trouble for us and then scrape and lick bowls and call it her dinner."

"No need to dirty another plate." Bay watched him take a mouthful and close his eyes in pleasure. Ironically, the unveiled moment exposed his fatigue even more. "How are you going to get through the day as tired as you are?"

"Mind over matter. I've done stakeouts before. They wear you down after two or three days, but it's part of the job."

"Not this time. You were warned away from me."

"I was speaking in the general sense."

"You aren't planning to park out there again?"

"If that's what it takes, until we get a break."

Bay scooped up a bite from the pan. "And your explanation to your boss when you fall out of your chair during your morning briefing?"

"That I was up all night with a sick heifer."

"Good for one night, then what?"

"I have lots of heifers."

"Very funny. What if I tell you that I sleep with a large kitchen knife under my pillow? Will you go home then?"

"Exactly how much rest do you think I'd get visualizing you waiting until someone is close before you can defend yourself?"

"I'm stronger than I look. At the trial, you had to agree that the years spent in my profession made my size pretty much irrelevant."

Jack put down his fork. "Do you really want to rehash that again? There's a difference between being competent in your workplace, and being caught off guard in your bed and someone is bearing down on you—hell, Bay. I don't want to have this conversation."

Neither did Bay, really, and she carried the empty pan to the sink and ran water into it. She'd just been working her way up to what she needed to say. "There's something you should know before you go in today. Aside from planning to return Madeleine's latest gift, I've, um, I've decided to move."

The return to the table was one of the longest journeys of her life, maybe relative to the walk to Glenn's grave if she'd been allowed to make it. Less sleep-heavy, Jack's eyes still sent her pulse skittering and had her wrapping her hands around her coffee mug so as not to fidget under his scrutiny.

"Don't do any mental high fives yet. Not only don't I know where I'm going to end up, you and I need to talk."

"True. Go ahead."

Finally ready to listen, she experienced a moment of such dread, she almost chickened out. "You've skimmed the periphery of why you were demoted," she began slowly. ''Why you think the Ridgeways dislike you?''

''Get the intensity right, sweetheart. *Hate.* If they had their way, I'd be history, just like Razor Basque.''

Despite Madeleine's impassioned outburst about Jack, Bay thought that was going a bit far. ''Why is that? Mind you, I'm only quoting, but Madeleine says you're jealous of the church's success.''

''Perfect strategy. If I am, in any way, shape or form, critical then I'm what...an atheist, agnostic, unchristian? In the Bible Belt that makes me a first-string quarterback for Satan.''

''It doesn't help to exaggerate.''

''Sorry. I've been dealing with this for some time and it never ceases to grate on me. They get to hop in front of virtually any camera and spew all the garbage they want. Me, I don't dare whisper their name in public without the threat of a subpoena.''

''But have you?''

''Spoken about them? Inside the department, in confidence to my sergeant, then to my lieutenant.''

Bay tried for a soft whistle despite her lip. ''That's a serious finger-point.''

''And I have the damaged career to prove it.'' Jack put down his fork. ''You think I want to threaten something if it's as positive as Mission of Mercy's core idea? People need centering, a strong faith foundation and to see that a small grassroots effort can make a difference. The problem is, opportunists know how to use goodwill to their own benefit, too.''

''I can't stand it,'' Bay groaned. ''Give me the bad news. Who all's guilty of what?''

"I don't know. It's like I'm working on a puzzle and I don't have the picture on the top of the box to work from, so I don't know what fits where. But I'll tell you what, if things ever start to domino, a good chunk of this county's powerful and affluent would be scurrying for cover to avoid implication."

She would have preferred he hedge. No, Bay amended with brutal honesty, she wanted him to lie. This shouldn't be happening. She'd been cleared. From here on, there should be nothing before her but good news and great projects. A life.

Feeling the weight of a hand on her forearm, she looked up.

"I've been building a file," Jack insisted, dead serious. "It began as a new reconstruction of your case. It's turned into... Well, you'll have to see it to believe it."

"Will I get to?"

"Do you understand that once that happens, things could get even rougher for you?"

"They were bound to anyway, since I'm not about to give up on getting answers about Glenn."

"And what if suddenly I'm not around to watch over you?"

Visions of his arrest or worse had Bay's mouth growing dry. "You're not supposed to scare an ally, Burke. That's the bad guys' modus operandi or whatever you call it."

"Some fear is a healthy thing. It'll keep you from doing something reckless."

"When do I see what you have?" she asked again.

Jack looked down at his hand still holding her.

22

After Jack left, Bay remained in the house, as he suggested, giving herself a little additional recovery time. For the rest of the morning she caught up with phone work, ultimately calling the Nelsons to thank them for their order and to review the dimensions and mobility requirements of the two carts.

"Pardon? Sure aluminum weighs less," she said, frowning at Bruce's last-minute suggestion, "and we can do that. But you said Mrs. Nelson wants the entire thing green like the fiberglass grating I'm recommending. Iron handles paint a lot better, and once I add the industrial quality wheels, she won't have any problem with maneuverability. Inevitably, though, she'll bump it against things and that paint will scratch. Let me suggest that if you're willing to do this kind of custom work, I'd recommend a nice satin-finished stainless. It'll give the carts the look of quality I think you're wanting and show wear less."

Once she had his consent, she hung up and drafted a design for the carts. Satisfied with the results, she called in the order for the fiberglass. Then she called Mike Martel to check his stock on the stainless and ask him who he used these days for wheels.

It was approaching noon when she finished, and she knew there was no putting off this next, less pleasant part of her day. Printing a note for the shop door for Doug Crow in case he succeeded in leaving work earlier than he'd said when they talked on the phone, she headed into town, Madeleine's beautiful box beside her on the passenger seat. Never more circumspect of traffic laws, she made it without even seeing a patrol car.

Vivacious was located on South Broadway, past the mall, in one of the trendier shopping strips. Upon seeing the stylish brick exterior with the brass gas lamps gracing either side of the leaded-glass double doors, Bay wished she'd changed into one of her dresses. Then again, she thought dejectedly, one look at her face and no one in the store would be paying attention to what she was wearing.

"Can I help you?"

As soon as she spotted the breathtaking redhead with jade-green eyes emerging from the fitting room on the left, Bay knew luck was operating in forked-tail mode. While she knew they had to be close in age, the woman's presence, complimented by a snazzy green suit, lent her a sophistication that left Bay feeling about twelve. In return, the woman sized her up, leaving Bay surprised at having been not ordered out on the spot. It was, of course, the box that triggered her curiosity.

Steeling herself, Bay turned to face the woman. "I believe you can."

The salesclerk's step barely faltered, but as she

drew closer, she remained focused on the box. "I remember that. I wrapped it myself."

"You did a beautiful job."

"Is there a problem?"

"None." Bay placed it on the checkout counter in the middle of the store. "Will you adjust Mrs. Madeleine Ridgeway's account accordingly?"

"The outfit was for you. Was the size wrong? Six, wasn't it?" With a sweeping glance at Bay, she lifted a finely plucked eyebrow the color of toasted cinnamon.

"I didn't look, but that would be correct."

"Yes, of course, that shade of white might not be the best for your fair coloring. I could recommend some blush that would—"

"You don't understand. I simply can't accept it."

She might as well have declared she'd found a mustard smudge on the skirt.

"Don't you know Candace thinks you really do have a head injury?"

Bay groaned inwardly and glanced over to see Holly Kirkland exiting the dressing room, a peach-colored sheath draped over her arm. This was all she needed, Holly running to inform Madeleine before Bay could explain herself.

"Hello, Holly. I'll bet that looks terrific on you."

Ignoring the compliment, Holly's eyes widened. "Good grief, I'd heard you'd fallen, but I didn't realize—"

Fallen? Who was describing it like that? "I was attacked."

As the younger woman digested that, Bay glanced

at the box again remembering the white suit Holly had worn last Sunday and an uneasy feeling swept over her. Surely Madeleine hadn't purchased this one to taunt Holly?

"Weren't you at the mall?"

"Leaving it."

"You were mugged."

"Well, no. I guess it was more personal than that." She didn't want to be having this conversation in front of this salesclerk who was bound to share it word for word with Madeleine, not to mention everyone else who came into the store. She said to the woman, "I appreciate your time, and the suit is lovely. If you'll see Mrs. Ridgeway's account is adjusted...?"

"Right away."

"Thank you."

Murmuring goodbye to both women, Bay left the store. She wasn't halfway to the truck before Holly came hurrying after her.

"Bay—wait." Looking a little surprised at herself, Holly crossed her arms under her breasts as she stopped before her. "What do you mean by personal? Do you mean a hate-crime thing or did you know the person?"

"Neither. But the man had a message for me." Bay shared it and watched Holly's tawny complexion grow pale.

"What do you suppose he meant by that?"

Obviously Madeleine and Duncan hadn't shared the warning, either. "I guess that I'm on the right track. Since my release, I've been trying to resolve

some questions I have about that and Glenn's death,''
she explained.

''You have?'' Holly seemed genuinely dumbfounded. After a second she murmured, ''I hope you feel better soon.''

Intrigued, Bay watched her return to the store. Wait until Jack heard this, she thought.

23

"I can't believe it."

Bay winced upon hearing Madeleine's voice. She'd intended to call her as soon as she got home, then was delayed when Doug arrived with his dragster. Seeing her injuries, he'd wanted to stay and help her attach the panels, and it took her some convincing to assure him that she would work better on her own and at her own pace. She'd heard the phone ring twice, but had avoided answering until Doug left.

"Hi Madeleine. I was tied up with a customer, sorry to have missed your earlier call."

"Never mind that. How could you do it, Bay?"

"I take it you mean returning the suit and all? I told you it was too much."

"If it gives me pleasure, I see nothing wrong with it."

"But there are two peoples' perspectives involved here," Bay reminded her gently. "Besides, you know that whole look isn't me. Candace seemed to agree. Did she happen to share that with you?"

"She did not. I'll speak to her about that next time I'm in. I am not amused when people undermine my wishes."

"Oh, now hold on a second. We're talking about an outfit, not a vote on some congressional bill. And at what point do *my* feelings and opinions matter here?"

"You have a limited wardrobe," Madeleine said with slightly less chill in her voice.

"It's perfect for my work, thanks to you. What's more, you agreed I could repay you for everything. That suit was practically couture. I can't afford anything like that."

"There are functions I want you to attend. In cases like that, I don't expect, nor will I accept reimbursement."

Here we go again, Bay thought.

"I'm in no shape to participate in any social outings and won't be for some time. I can't tell you how difficult it was for me just to slip into Vivacious this morning."

"Don't be silly. In a few more days, those stitches will come out and then makeup will take care of the rest."

How did she know? She hadn't seen her yet. A bit put off at the dismissive tone, Bay said, "Even if I didn't disagree, you're forgetting my work. I'm booked solid for the time being."

"That's wonderful, but you don't work evenings and weekends."

"I don't?"

"Now don't go getting stubborn on me. I'm not trying to arrange your schedule for you, I'm concerned about your health and welfare," Madeleine replied quickly. "I suppose it won't be the end of the world if you miss showing your support at the ladies devotional group's box lunch sale at Bergfeld Park next Wednesday—even though common sense tells me you're human and eat lunch like the rest of us. I do want you to mark your calendar for next Friday. Duncan and I have a table reserved at the Chamber of Commerce awards banquet and you must join us.''

''Thank you, but I won't be able to make it.''

''You can't afford not to. Everyone who is anyone in the city will be there. It will present a splendid opportunity for me to boast about you.''

''Madeleine—'' Bay took a calming breath ''—I'm only beginning to regain my footing, professionally as well as personally. This attack has set me back. Injuries aside, I couldn't attend something so public with any sense of confidence.''

''Nonsense. You have to put the past—all of it—behind you. What's done is done. You have to move forward.''

''Is that why you told Holly that I'd only fallen?''

Madeleine hesitated. ''Candace didn't tell me that Holly was there.''

''That's not the issue,'' Bay said with a sinking feeling. ''You're suggesting something different than what happened. I didn't fall because I was clumsy and lost my balance. I was attacked.''

''I never said—'' Madeleine gasped. ''I don't deserve that. Duncan and I begged you to come stay with us, which speaks for itself as to our faith in and commitment to you. Holly must have misunderstood or confused things. You know she's had her problems, too.''

Pushed by emotions she didn't like, Bay knew she needed to get off the phone. "Madeleine, I see my customer is here to pick up an item. I have to go."

"Of course, dear, but I think we need to sit down and have an honest talk. I feel you're being influenced by something I don't understand, and it concerns me. Call me when you have a free moment and we'll arrange that."

Not able to actually agree, Bay simply said, "I'll talk to you later."

It was a relief to have Doug's car to focus on. Bay spent the rest of the afternoon fitting and securing the steel panels to the dragster. She lost track of time as she had to make adjustment after adjustment and wasn't surprised when Jack phoned saying it was after five and he would be late.

"I still have one panel to go. Take your time," she told him knowing she needed as much extra time as she could get.

But she did end up needing a second pair of hands, so she called Doug, who'd promised to keep his distance unless she said otherwise. His quick arrival provided the first bit of amusement she'd had all day.

"Were you sitting in the car with one hand on the ignition and the other on your cellular?" she drawled.

"Close to it," he said with a sheepish grin.

Seeing his eyes shine as he looked at the nearly completed dragster, Bay was determined to get things right for him. Even so, it was another hour before she fastened the last rivet. Jack was pulling in when Doug was shaking her hand for the second time.

"I guess you'll be driving over to Hallsville first thing in the morning," she said to the young racer. She handed him his receipt and pocketed the cash.

"You bet."

"Not going to wait until she's painted?"

"Pretty as she looks now, I might just leave her. Blind the competition, too," he said, beaming.

"By midday that same sun will blind you," she said, pointing inches beyond the windshield where she suspected he would get the worst glare. "Anyway, let me know if the aerodynamic changes we tried help your time."

"Sure thing. Howdy," Doug said to Jack as he joined them.

Bay made the introductions and the men shook hands.

"Nice machine you have there," Jack said.

"Good thing you didn't see it when I first brought it in."

Declining Bay's suggestion that he take the old panels with him, Doug insisted she keep whatever they would bring in scrap. Then Doug asked if he could give her a hug.

Knowing it was enthusiasm and nothing more, Bay extended her arms. Afterward, the three of them loaded the dragster back on its trailer and Doug eased the lengthy rig onto the highway.

"Lady, you are a pro," Jack drawled.

Aware of flaws his inexperienced eye wouldn't catch, Bay shrugged. "It's not bad for the short time we had. I only hope he doesn't have a wreck soon.

As much as I appreciate the cash, that kind of work wears you down.''

''Damn,'' Jack said, noticing the bloody slice across her left palm. ''Why don't you wear gloves?''

''Impractical. Sometimes there's not enough room to get my fingers into tight spots, and sheet metal is nothing more than a big razor blade. I got off pretty clean.''

''Right,'' Jack drawled looking unconvinced. ''Go on up to the house and take care of that and I'll lock up for you.''

''Give me five minutes to shower and change and I'll be ready to follow you.''

''Uh-uh. I'll drive you back.''

Too hot and sweaty to stand there and argue with him, Bay jogged to the house. Maybe he was right, she allowed. Reminding him that she was determined to maintain her independence was one thing, but as late as it was, she wouldn't relish coming back here by herself.

It was closer to ten minutes before she joined him in the kitchen. Jack had been frowning at the bouquet again, and she saw the bitterness beneath the fatigue. Then he spotted her and his eyes warmed.

''How's the head, any lingering pain or dizziness? I can already tell from that job you did that there's nothing wrong with your vision.''

''I'm glad I didn't have to wear a welding hood today, but I'm fine. I'll be glad to get these nasty stitches out of my lip, though.''

''Me, too,'' Jack murmured, his gaze on her mouth.

She could almost hear the rest of his thought and

felt a heat spread through her. "You know, we could hold off on this until tomorrow. You look like you've put in a long day yourself."

"All I would do is go home and fantasize beating a certain lieutenant to a pulp and end up drinking too much beer again."

But his flat belly belied that statement. "Want to talk about it?"

"There's nothing to say. Gage assigned me to the dead files—cases that haven't been resolved and probably never will be. When I finally get a possible glimmer on one, a possible clue that was passed on too quickly, he won't allow me to pursue it. He gives it to the new guy in the department. Don't think I care about the recognition the guy'll get if he has a breakthrough," he added. "I care about him suddenly being seen as an expert and believing it himself to where he gets reckless and messes up a future case."

"Sounds like Lieutenant Gage wants you to quit."

"Gage wants me off the planet." Jack nodded to the door. "You set? Get your pencil."

Jack Burke would be a formidable enemy and undoubtedly made a fine detective, Bay thought as she followed him outside, carefully positioning the pencil as usual.

With new respect, she hesitated after only a few steps. "Maybe you should check my refrigerator and take whatever you think we could use for dinner. I'm starving."

"About time. I picked up a pizza on my way here."

It smelled heavenly and before fastening her seat

belt, Bay couldn't resist reaching for the box. Setting it on her lap, she lifted the lid and moaned in pleasure. "How did you know the Supreme was my favorite?"

"Because of the kind of breakfast you made me. Hey," Jack said as she scooped up a slice and took a bite. "Not fair."

"Okay, okay, here."

She brought the pizza to his mouth, offering him the second bite. After a startled glance, he took everything up to the tips of her fingers. As his teeth grazed her, Bay couldn't contain the slight reflexive start.

Swallowing, he said, "It's okay. It's the same for me."

"What?"

"The awareness. Sexual chemistry. I didn't believe it could happen this fast."

Bay couldn't believe it was happening at all. She'd ended her virginity at the ripe old age of twenty-two when, tired of wondering what all of the fuss was about, she accepted an invitation to go out for a drink with a guy she knew at the welding supply store. Three beers and a few body-grinding dances later, she'd convinced herself she liked him enough to go to his apartment. Admittedly reckless, it wasn't the worst experience in her life; what disappointed her was that she'd felt next to nothing.

"I wasn't flirting."

"I know. If you were, we'd be making an illegal U-turn back to your place."

"Here, eat so you won't make me change my mind about going with you," she said, offering him another bite. No matter what she felt, it would be a feat to convince herself his provocative comments weren't more about getting his mind off the day's frustrations. "I was going to hold off telling you until later," she said to change the subject, "but Madeleine and I came close to having a serious argument today."

"You returned the clothes?"

"And Holly Kirkland was in the dressing room at the time. Guess what Madeleine told her had happened to me?"

"Whatever it was, you don't sound like you're pleased."

"She said I fell. Fell like some clumsy ox." Bay was indignant. "Why not acknowledge the truth that I'd been assaulted?"

"Good question. Did you ask her?"

"She tried to avoid addressing that. She was agitated that the salesclerk who informed her that I'd been in the store hadn't told her about Holly."

"Interesting. You did well, Butler. That's one lady who's hard to rattle."

Bay knew that. She also knew how she'd felt listening to Madeleine avoid explaining her behavior.

Her mood must have transmitted itself to Jack. He was soon casting her a sidelong look and demanding, "What?"

"I thought when I got out that my biggest challenge would be to avoid the media and the negative reactions from people with a long memory." She met Jack's next glance. "I didn't expect to doubt the one I called friend."

He turned into his driveway. "So where does that leave me?"

24

Jack waited for Bay's answer knowing he was a fool to ask. Aside from her, he had the longest memory of all, but he sure as hell wasn't the one person she trusted...yet.

As he pulled up before the garage, he pressed the door opener and it lifted. Once he parked and killed the engine, he turned to her for an answer.

"Well?"

"I guess you're the man with the answers."

Not all of them, but Jack would settle for that.

"Come on inside before Bud smells that pizza and tries to cheat you out of it."

He hit the remote again and took the box from her. He noticed she didn't get out of the truck until the garage door was completely closed.

In the kitchen he put the box on the counter, one eye checking his answering machine. Zero messages—good news as far as he was concerned. He would have liked nothing better than to spend the rest of the evening sitting across from Bay and simply shooting the breeze and looking at her. But that wasn't why she agreed to come.

"What do you say we eat before we dig into the file?"

"Yeah, less chance of incriminating tomato sauce on the pages," she drawled.

Jack slung his jacket over a leather-backed chair. "Beer? There's no other way to eat pizza."

"Okay."

She'd reverted to shyness again and he hated that. He liked having her here, and wanted her to feel comfortable.

Transferring the box to the glass-topped table, Jack took two Miller Lites from the refrigerator and tore several sheets of paper towels from the roll by the sink. "Sit," he said, pulling out a chair for himself. She settled in the chair beside him.

"Where is your dog?" Bay asked.

"With Simon, or exploring. He'll get here in his own time and let you know he wants in, so you better eat up." Jack popped the tab on his beer, then remembered his manners. "Would you prefer a glass?"

"I'm not sure I should have this. I haven't had one in a while." She popped the tab on hers and took the first swallow, only to frown and quickly press a paper towel to her mouth. "What I need is a baby bottle."

Jack grimaced, thinking about the spicy pizza on that lip. "I should have picked up chicken."

"No way. That's the one thing they served plenty of in prison. Besides, pizza is a treat for me." At his questioning look, she shrugged. "I'm not splurging on luxuries. Too much equipment to buy. Just don't watch, and I'll try not to make too much of a mess."

They each devoured a full slice and were on to their second before they spoke again.

"This isn't the table that your mother had here, is it?" Bay asked out of the blue.

Both detective and man were intrigued. "How'd you know that?"

"A woman would want wood in this kitchen."

Jack glanced around at the rich maple cupboards, the built-in hutch his father made for his mother the year before he died. The honey tones complimenting the lattice-and-ivy-vine wallpaper, the copper molds she'd never thought to take with her because they seemed made for the place. "The house she moved into when she remarried had a circular breakfast nook like this one, and she asked if she could take it with her. Couldn't argue since she was giving me the house. I sent Simon out to find something to fill the space and this is what he came home with."

"You didn't care?"

Those were complicated times and Jack had barely come to terms with his own grief when his mother made her announcement about remarrying. She could have emptied the place if she'd wanted. After that there'd been Bay and the trial. He realized he'd been going through the motions of living here for too long and not really paying attention.

"I guess I didn't, not really. Was there something you particularly liked or were attached to, living in the trailer?"

Bay uttered a brief sound that was close to a laugh. "Attached to? No. But I liked that I never had to worry about my father bringing anyone home. That would have been totally humiliating. Women must have figured out fast that as good as he was at his work, he was awful as marriage material.''

''You were so young, I'd have thought having a new mother would have made things easier for you somehow. Chances are you would have gotten into a real house.''

After blotting her mouth, Bay folded and refolded her napkin. ''Could be. I honestly don't remember. Maybe I'm just too pragmatic to dream.''

''You're an artist, you can't be a total pragmatist.''

''You think all artists are dreamers? I don't think so. I think some are simply scientists experimenting with facts—math and psychics and whatnot—and sometimes they find a happy coincidence.'' Bay reached for another slice of pizza. ''Eat up and let's get to work, or neither one of us will be worth squat in the morning.''

Jack would have preferred to get more information from her, and yet he knew she was right. He could afford to miss some sleep considering his limited activity in the department, but she worked around dangerous equipment. It would probably finish him off if he was responsible for her getting maimed—or worse.

Minutes later when she backed away from the table, there was a bang in the next room that gave her a start.

''What did I tell you?'' Jack rose and closed the lid of the box containing two more slices of pizza and moved it to the higher kitchen counter. Then he extended his hand to Bay. ''Come on. Trust me.''

She did place her hand in his, but with evident

reluctance. When he drew her to the French doors in the den and she saw that Bud was on his hind legs peering inside as though searching for his dinner, she hung back.

"I suppose it would be mean of me to ask you to feed him outside?"

"He's already eaten. He just wants to say hello."

The instant the door was cracked, Bud threw his weight against it and burst inside. He yelped and leaped against Bay. Fortunately, Jack anticipated that and helped block him, at the same time slipping an arm around her waist.

"Sit. Be a good boy." To Bay, Jack said, "Go ahead and give him a pat or two. He's only welcoming you back."

The dog was pressing his big head against her as though either hiding or using her as a towel. Belatedly, Jack realized how that was adding unwanted pressure on her bruised ribs and spleen.

"Okay, Bud, enough. C'mon, I'll give you a bone."

At the word, the dog charged to the kitchen. There, Jack took a steak bone from the refrigerator. Tossing it in the microwave for a few seconds, he removed the wrapper and led the excited animal back to the French doors where he tossed it out into the yard. With an ecstatic yelp, Bud gave chase.

"That'll keep him busy for a while. Your ribs okay?"

"Sure. Thanks."

She was ready to get down to the grim stuff. For his part, Jack, who had waited for years to share this with her, wanted to hold off a bit longer. But delaying things would only make it tougher for her.

"Come on into the study. Some of the material is in hard copy and some on computer disk."

He led her to the room that he'd turned into an office-library. In the middle was a partner's desk—an antique from a law office—and lining the walls was a hodgepodge of bookcases and file cabinets. Everything was loaded with books, newspapers, magazines and files, with more stacked on the floor.

Bay hesitated in the doorway. "Is this all about the Ridgeways?"

"No. A lot of it is about your case, the Mission of Mercy and other churches or religious sects that have a history of tainted pasts."

Bay shot him a grim look. "This isn't a one-night study, is it?"

"You'll get the gist of things fast enough. As I told you, though, I don't have all of the answers yet."

"But you're drawing conclusions, I can see that. All right, where do I start?"

Jack indicated a file set out on the desk. Bay sat and began to read.

He had practically memorized the articles. The top one was a profile done by *Texas Monthly* barely a year ago, a human interest story of how Martin Davis established the Mission of Mercy Church. While comparatively complimentary about all he'd achieved in this East Texas community, it pointed to enough unknowns and shadowy situations to suggest Davis was a man with a past worthy of deeper study.

The article began with Davis's birth...or rather rebirth. Claiming to have been struck by lightning—an interesting way, the reporter pointed out, to connect himself not only to a military hero but also to an apostle—he'd wakened in the rain-soaked yard of a run-down church. Carrying no ID and swearing he had no recollection of who he was or where he belonged, he whispered a single name to the man who found him, "Martin Davis," insisting it was the only thing that kept floating up from the black sea his mind had become. To Minister John Davis, it was a sign, for Martin had been his beloved late wife's maiden name. Rescued by the aging minister, soon "Martin Davis" ingratiated himself to the devout man's congregation, as well. Tutored by his adoptive father, he proved a quick study and to Minister Davis's great joy began filling in for the weakening preacher at Sunday services. After suffering a mild stroke, the childless widower officially made Martin his heir. Weeks later, he experienced another stroke and died, and Martin Davis inherited the modest home on a valuable piece of property, and was asked to take on the leadership of the church he was credited with reviving. He humbly accepted even though he openly reminded them that, to his knowledge, he lacked any accreditation from a seminary or, for that matter, any school of higher learning.

Then a spare three months after John Davis's death, Martin Davis married Odessa Adams and announced he'd been "called by the Lord to move on." Selling everything he'd inherited from John Davis, he drove himself and his worshipful bride around the country waiting for the next "signal from Above," subsequently landing in Texas and a spot of land outside the city limits of Tyler. It was there, he reported, that the Lord told him to begin spreading the Word.

Parking his car and pitching a tent, he could be seen day after day standing in the field and preaching to the squirrels and birds and the devoted Odessa, as though they were a congregation of hundreds. Curious, drivers began to pull over, intrigued by the man who was testifying when they drove to work and still at it when they drove home. Inevitably, he caused a few too many fender benders and the police tried to make him stop. It earned him exactly the kind of media attention he'd been waiting for. He received an offer to be the assistant at a downtown church, along with another offer from a wealthy businessman to use a vacant building. Davis rejected both, insisting that he was obligated to follow his Master's bidding. That brave declaration was witnessed by Madeleine Ridgeway, newly widowed and deeply moved by the man's dedication. In the name of her late, beloved husband, she became a vocal supporter of Davis and used her influence to help him establish Mission of Mercy, now a multimillion dollar business with a national broadcasting audience and an international ministry.

Bay looked up after finishing the article. "Good grief."

Running his tongue over the inside of his cheek, Jack asked innocently, "Don't tell me you don't believe in miracles?"

"I have to, I'm sitting here. But...well, the lightning I can buy, but amnesia and the Martin Davis thing? Give me a break."

"That's why they're called *miracles,*" Jack drawled.

Bay sent him a dark look before flipping through several other pages. "He never recovered his memory?"

"Nice way to get rid of your past, eh? You'll find one article in there describing how Odessa tried to defend him from a skeptical reporter, proudly claiming he bears a scar above his heart from the strike. Eventually another reporter, who'd apparently read that article, tracked down a doctor in Iowa, who asked not to be identified, but acknowledged he believes Davis is the guy he once treated for a knife wound in the same area. A guy who vanished from the emergency room when he heard the police were coming to interview him."

"Iowa. Was that where Davis's first church was? I don't remember seeing—"

"No, you didn't miss it. He's never divulged that information and still won't today. His excuse is that the media has become like the tabloids—interested only in scandal—and that he values his former congregation's privacy too much to expose them to such harassment and mean-spiritedness."

"Uh-huh. But once the TV stations got wind of this, surely they showed his picture all over. Good heavens, it's a novel enough story to have gotten national attention."

"From the looks of things, it did. Apparently though, the right person or people didn't see it. Oh, and he later claimed the police did a missing persons search and came up dry. Nobody was looking for a

Martin Davis—or rather, a John Doe fitting his description, and he didn't appear to have a criminal record.''

''Yeah, but did they check the mental hospitals?''

Jack smiled. ''Good point. You know he could just simply be a guy from Nowheresville who got up one morning, looked at his life and decided he was tired of being invisible.''

''Fine. It still makes him a liar and cheat. He deceived John Davis—''

''A defense lawyer would say he told Mr. Davis what he wanted to hear.'' When she groaned, he nodded to the rest of the stack. ''Keep going. Want another beer?'' When she declined, he added, ''How about a cup of coffee?''

''That I'll take. Thanks.''

As he went to the kitchen to prepare the coffee, Jack thought of the next few stories she would read. They were shorter pieces from the Tyler paper where the dispute over the property occurred.

When Martin Davis learned the property consisted of a mere three acres—which Madeleine Ridgeway quickly purchased, awarding Davis a hundred-year lease—he researched the connecting properties and learned the land on the north, some seven acres, was all that was left of Otto Mossberg's family farm. Mossberg all but threw Davis out of his house calling him a quack. Even Madeleine Ridgeway with her charm and conviction couldn't soften the old immigrant. He declared, ''I'll park a trailer on the property and open a massage parlor and tattoo studio before letting that snake-oil salesman have the place.''

Mossberg's concern, however, was that he'd just been diagnosed with cancer. What's more, he was the last living member of his family, save a few distant relations he disliked almost as much as he did Davis. Like an answer to a prayer, along came clean-cut, low-key Stephen Crandall, who said he wanted to build an assisted living center on the land. Otto sold with great relief under the stipulation that he would have one of the rooms rent-free. He died a few weeks later during surgery without knowing Crandall was the nephew of Madeleine's late husband's business associate. And in one of Texas's underreported real estate flip-flop deals, Martin Davis had his property.

When Jack returned, Bay was standing by the window watching the last birds seek cover as darkness fell. He set her mug on the blotter beside the file.

"You okay?"

"They cheated that poor old man."

"Some would say they were simply being astute businesspeople. He had no heirs, and the land would have gone to some charity that would probably have sold it anyway, then spent the bulk of the revenue on administrative expenses. That's if those distant relations weren't the money-hungry kind and hired a lawyer to fight for their rightful share as blood kin."

"You're defending Davis and Madeleine."

"Playing devil's advocate."

As she returned to the desk and sat down, Jack went to the window and closed the miniblinds. He heard her flip through a few more pages.

"They approach fund-raising like it was a political campaign," she mused half to herself.

"It works. Look at everyone in those pictures." Davis made sure he was shot posing with the Who's Who in the area—Tyler's former mayor, the current mayor, Smith County's D.A., the chief of police and numerous financial powerbrokers, business leaders and socialites. There were even those taken with celebrities who passed through to perform at local theaters, to speak at the area colleges, or to play in charity golf tournaments. "Who's going to point fingers and call Mission of Mercy or Davis a fraud after rushing to be photographed with him, especially when there are probably records of donations to go with those pictures?"

"And directing it all is Madeleine Ridgeway," Bay whispered.

Jack stepped behind her chair. Placing his mug beside hers, he gently massaged her shoulders. "I know this is disappointing."

"That she's made some decisions I see as unethical? I'm not naive, Jack. Since my return, I've had a clearer perspective of how Madeleine believes in bottom-line results. It's part of the reason I told you that I had to sign back the property. I can't in good conscience question or criticize her if she's basically financing my existence. What I'm having a bigger problem digesting is that she can even buy into something so...so..."

"Theatrical and hyped."

"I know she doesn't shirk from public attention and seems to like her role as Davis's sometime cohost on TV. Still...it must be the orphanages and schools that allow her to stomach this packaging of God."

Jack stilled his hands. "Now that's naive."

She glanced back at him. "What am I missing?"

"Read on."

"I will, but you tell me your side first."

"Added celebrity and the satisfaction of doing good works, is that what you think the Ridgeways are about? They're powerbrokers, Bay, no different than the banking Shylocks who tried to rape the government treasury and the railroad tycoons who first wiped out the buffalo and then the Native Americans. Were they the devil incarnate? Hardly. Who's going to deny that our financial institutions and the railroad are a major part of what makes this country great? But at what cost? Was their way the only way it could be done, was it the best way? Hell no, and those are the questions the Ridgeways and Davis, et al. need to answer."

"You don't think they take in enough money to do all they're doing?" Bay asked slowly. "They have something going every day—church garage sales, bake sales, some ladies' box lunch thing Madeleine told me about, the Moms for MOM—Get it? Mission of Mercy?—walkathon coming up to promote mothers doing more for the mission programs. They make good money and entertain in helpful ways."

"Bay, that's camouflage. You can't bring in the big bucks with piddly nonsense like that. Look, the church has roughly one thousand members at this stage, including children, right? If every one of them put ten dollars in the offering basket every Sunday—and you know that's a high-end estimate—you have ten grand a week, about forty a month, maybe a half million a year. That's barely enough to run the TV station, including salaries. Check them out if you can. A sure sign the pay stinks is the high employee turnover rate. Yet I understand the waiting list here is almost half of what the mailing list is. Then there's Davis's two homes—neither of which have a mortgage—the matching BMWs he and Odessa drive. Do I need to go on?''

Although she was frowning, Bay replied, ''KWRD brings in donations. I heard Madeleine talking to Martin Davis about the percentage of increase during lunch last week.''

''Much of which goes right back out in new products—tapes, self-help books and whatnot.''

''So what are you saying? There are no schools in Colombia and Mexico and the other places?''

''Oh, they're real all right.''

''Then...?'' Her frown deepened. ''Where's the extra money coming from, Jack?''

''Keep reading, because when you finish, I think you'll come to the same conclusion I have...you'll begin to understand why your friend needed to die.''

25

"All right, leave."

Bay felt Jack's surprise in the subtle movement of his hands on her shoulders. In the next instant he was sitting on the edge of the desk searching her face.

"I won't get through this file with you waiting for me to comment on every article."

"I'm sorry for phrasing that the way I did."

"You should be. I know you were speaking objectively, but...damn it, Jack. Do you really believe Glenn's death is connected to the Ridgeways, to the church?"

"I hope I'm wrong. Unfortunately, I also know the statistics. You heard them at the trial, they helped work against you. You weren't being robbed, you weren't being blackmailed."

"Maybe Madeleine's people are right after all. Maybe Glenn had succumbed to a gambling weakness he tried to hide from me," she began.

"*Who* says that?" Jack tapped the pile of articles. "These people, Bay. These people whose biggest concern is to draw attention away from themselves...and if you have trouble believing that, go stand in front of a mirror."

With that he left and Bay sat there feeling she'd just been flattened by a cold wave. But she deserved it. Taking a bolstering sip of her coffee, she moved on to the next story...and then the next. Jack had done an amazing job collecting these pieces. The entire history of Mission of Mercy—the public side—was here: the groundbreaking, the fundraisers, the launch of KWRD. The famous faces at the dedication were a coup—state representatives, a judge—but Bay's attention was caught by the guests from south of the border. Not the doctor from the small orphanage in Mexico or the mayor of a Colombian village hoping to benefit from the church's outreach programs. It was a bull-faced man standing way in the back who was in the process of turning his face away from the camera when the photo was taken. He didn't belong there; she couldn't say why, she just knew it and set that page aside.

She moved on to articles covering complaints such as a building contractor Martin Davis says donated a portion of his services and the man denying it, a nearby coffeehouse unhappy with the relentless bell ringing that interfered with their performers, a pine tree on church property falling during high winds on the dry cleaners on the north boundary that not only caused a power outage and cost the business most of a day's work, but severely burned an employee. The church had called that incident an "act of God." The business owners said it was reckless endangerment. Whether or not they believed they were guilty, over and over the church paid up to silence negative publicity. Then, a year after Bay's incarceration, they experienced tax compliance problems with the IRS. Mission of Mercy was growing and expanding its interests so fast they were suspected of acquiring more than passive income, they were receiving significant unrelated business income.

What had happened? Bay searched for more articles related to the situation, but found nothing except for a small, three-inch, single-column piece, buried between ads in the business section announcing the IRS had "resolved with satisfaction" their investigation. The filing was dated just sixteen months ago. Incredible, Bay thought. How much had it cost Mission of Mercy in accountant fees to fight this, and did "satisfaction" mean it had cost the church a settlement? If so, Madeleine, Duncan and Martin Davis appeared no worse for wear. Jack was right, there had to be an enormous amount of money in play here.

She then came upon a *Houston Chronicle* article from earlier in the year announcing the sale of real estate for a new branch of the church to be opened in the prestigious River Oaks section. Good heavens, she thought, they were franchising.

The coffee mug was empty and her eyes were burning when Jack returned with another mug. "Want a refill?"

She almost turned him down but then extended her hand, realizing she wasn't likely to sleep anyway with all this new and troubling data churning in her mind. To her surprise, Jack took hold of her hand and lifted it to his lips.

"I apologize for what I said earlier." He placed

the mug in her hand. "I shouldn't get impatient because you don't immediately see what I see."

Not accustomed to romantic gestures, Bay delayed her reply to fully appreciate what felt like a baby bird fluttering in her chest. "I'm sure it doesn't help that I act like someone with PMS, one minute defending Madeleine and the next— But you're right, Jack. There's big money here."

"So much they need to expand to another city," he said, noting where she'd gotten to in her reading. "Wonder what kind of message from upstairs Davis received about that?"

Taking a sip of her coffee, Bay pushed the photo she'd held out toward him. "I found this interesting. It's an old photo, I know, but they really pushed for publicity shots that included international dignitaries and staff. After a while though, there's nothing, not even photographs of buildings to show what they've accomplished. Just pictures of kids."

"I noticed that, too. Probably because it's those small faces that bring in donations, not images of the fat cats. As for the buildings, it could be a security thing. If these images get shown back in the homeland, it might compromise the school or orphanage's security." Settling down on the left side of the desk, Jack's eyes narrowed as he studied the photo more closely. "Don't you know the guy trying to hide in back gave the photographer hell for that shot?"

"Who is he?"

"No doubt a bodyguard for the Colombian VIP."

"At a church event?"

"From what I understand, things are rougher down

there than ever. Who's to say a kidnapping or hit couldn't be ordered to take place up here?''

''And ruin one of Madeleine's events?'' Bay drawled. ''They wouldn't dare. Did you ever find out how much they had to pay to appease the IRS? I guess it would take knowing someone on the inside.''

''Specifically, a gal I dated in high school. It would mean her job if anyone found out.''

''Oh. Sorry.'' Bay frowned as she sipped at the hot coffee. It had less to do with the steaming brew than the images of Jack, even a young Jack, with other women.

''That's not what I meant. Just don't you make the mistake of sharing what you know. It cost the church coffers almost a half million.''

Bay was glad she'd already swallowed. ''Five hundred— That's usually pennies on a dollar of what's really owed, isn't it?'' Yet the church planned to open a sister branch in Houston. She set down her mug. ''I've always thought Madeleine's wealth came from the family business. There's probably more to it than that, isn't there?''

''That's what I'm thinking.''

Chances are, not all of that wealth was legal, either. If Madeleine was willing to destroy Jack and take on the IRS, what else was she capable of?

Something in her expression must have transmitted itself to Jack because he reached over and closed the file. ''You've had enough for one night.''

Knowing he was right, she stood and winced at her protesting muscles. ''Yeah, you'd better get me back. Tomorrow's going to be a huge day.''

"What's on your mind now?"

"Moving. Immediately. I intended to do it slowly so as not to make Madeleine feel I was ungrateful for all she'd done for me—"

"I thought we'd had this conversation before?"

"Hear me out. What I'm telling you is that I understand momentum is working against me. But what else is new? I'll see what I can figure out in the morning."

"Stay here."

Bay didn't wear a watch and tried to check the time on Jack's. "Is it that late? You should have stopped me sooner, so I wouldn't cost you—"

"No, I mean move in here."

Standing so close to him kicked her pulse into a crazy rhythm that affected her ability to breathe normally. "Gee, Burke, no one's asked me to shack up with them before."

"Their loss. That's not what I'm suggesting either…yet. I'm offering you an option. Sanctuary."

God, she didn't want to fall for this man. "You know I can't do that."

"No, I don't. There's plenty of room—hell, play musical bedrooms or sleep on the couch if it turns you on. The barn is available, too, so you won't have a problem with work space. Did you know I have a welding machine out there?"

"I'm not surprised. Lots of farmers and ranchers try to be self-sufficient and save on repairs. Do you use it or does Simon?"

"Both of us. We're nowhere near your class, though."

The uninjured side of her mouth curved. "Stop trying to butter me up. The answer stays the same. I'm thinking of going to speak to Mike Martel again. I know he'd let me subcontract out of his shop, but he also has a small RV parked inside the shop that he might let me rent temporarily."

"No way. Bay, that's not the best part of town during the day, at night they have break-ins and drive-by shootings...."

"I'll be inside."

"You'll be a good fifteen minutes farther away than you are now. Why not set up shop here?"

"Can you imagine Madeleine's reaction? She's already after your hide, she'll go for the jugular next. Do you think I need to add that to my conscience?" She laid a hand on his chest, willing him to understand. "I've spent the last six years being watched and told what I can and can't do. Madeleine doesn't realize she's almost as bad as the prison guards. I won't go from being monitored by her to being monitored by you."

"I don't want to police you, I want to keep you alive." As her lips curved, Jack drew her around the edge of the desk and between his legs. "You almost smiled. I want to see the day when it's the real thing. I dream about it. I want it as much as I want to kiss you again."

To stop the words and keep him from stealing her heart completely, Bay wrapped her arms around his neck, shades of her childhood get-it-over-with technique. But when he drew her so close their hearts vibrated from the other's beat, she knew she wasn't only graduating, she was transcending to a plain unexplored.

First his breath caressed her, then his lips. Patiently, his fingers traced, his palms soothed. She found herself reaching for that deeper kiss and holding her breath until his fingers reached the outer swell of her breasts.

He made her forget what she looked like, encouraged her to lower her defenses and just be. Shifting, he perfected the fit of their hips and she could feel how, like her, he was as caught up in the magic between them.

On a sigh, he rested his forehead against hers. ''At least stay with me tonight. I won't ask for anything other than to hold you. I swear.''

The skeptic in her would have groaned at the corny line, but the lonely woman and damaged girl decided to trust. She really was exhausted and knew she would never be able to sleep peacefully in her house again.

Jack led her to the master bedroom, indicated where he kept his T-shirts, neatly folded in an antique armoire, and went outside to check things one last time. Yawning, Bay barely took note of anything else; the king-size bed with the forest-green sheets was calling to her.

It couldn't have been five minutes before Jack returned, but when he did, she was so comfortable, she'd almost drifted off to sleep. The sound of him moving around the dark room, clothes rustling as he undressed was strangely soothing. To her surprise, so was the shift of the mattress and his warm length sliding in behind her.

"God, you feel good," he murmured, wrapping one arm around her to tuck her closer. "Okay?"

"Mm."

He kissed her on the nape. "Thank you for this."

His tenderness made her want to cry. With her own words locked in her throat, she could only share what she was feeling by taking his hand and moving it to cover her left breast.

An explosion shattered the night's serenity. Bay bolted upright, trying to determine where the noise had come from. A strong arm pulled her down.

"Jack...?"

"That's a gunshot. Get down behind the bed and keep away from the windows. I'll be back as soon as I can."

She did as he directed, barely catching a glimpse of him grabbing his gun and vanishing down the hall wearing only his shorts. Gunfire... Bay touched her injured face. What had she done now to bring this on?

This time it seemed forever until Jack returned. When he did, he immediately grabbed a pair of jeans off a chair and tugged them on, then came around to lift her to her feet.

"You okay?" he asked, smoothing a hand over her hair.

"Never mind me, are you okay? What happened?"

"Someone shot through the office window. The shattering you heard was the result of a bullet ending up in one of my framed certificates in the opposite wall. I've called the sheriff's department and someone should be here in a minute.''

''Not the police?''

''I'm outside the city limits, thank goodness.''

''You don't want them to know?''

''Sweetheart, it could be someone from the department who did this. But I'm going to tell the deputy it was probably some drunk shooting at a deer in my pasture. This way I've covered my ass by reporting the disturbance and he's done his job in case someone else heard this.'' He pulled her close for a brief, fierce hug. ''Thank God you weren't sitting at the desk when it happened. What I need you to do is to climb back into bed and stay as quiet as you can. I'm not going to mention you if I don't have to.''

''Are Simon and Bud all right?''

''They're fine. Simon was at the back door with his shotgun the moment I unlocked it and Bud was right at his side. He stays close to us when there's shooting. Gotta go.'' He pressed a kiss between her eyebrows and left again.

For close to an hour Bay did as Jack asked, trying to hear as much as she could.

''Good thing you don't use this as a bedroom,'' a tenor voice said. ''Those miniblinds messed up the trajectory of that bullet and somebody coulda been hurt.''

''Yeah, as you can see I had been working in here, but I'd just turned in,'' Jack replied.

''Let's see if we can find— Here's the bullet. Whatcha think, Detective?''

"Something in the .30 caliber range. My guess is a .308 or 30-06."

"Sounds like a deer hunter to me. Course, the coyotes've been bad this year and somebody coulda thought they were doing you a favor. This wall sure is a mess. At least you can get away with putting a piece of duct tape over that hole in the window till you have time to replace it. Sorry you had the scare, though."

"As long as no one was hurt."

Jack and the deputy went back outside and Bay used the opportunity to sneak down the hall to see the damage herself. The light remained on and a cautious peek around the corner indicated they hadn't left the miniblinds pulled up. But she jumped when she stepped on something cool and hard instead of carpet. Glass.

From outside came the sound of a vehicle driving away. Relieved, Bay used the opportunity to peer around the edge of the blinds and check the bullet hole. It looked deceptively small and the outside floodlights gave it a slight starlike quality.

"I didn't figure you'd behave."

Bay started and spun around. He'd moved far too quietly for a man his size. "I heard you go back outside."

"You could have cut your foot on the glass. No, leave it," Jack said when she crossed the room and bent to clean it up. "I want you to try to get some rest. I'm going to your place to see if everything's all right."

"I'll come with you." Bay followed him back to

the master bedroom and headed for the bathroom where she'd left her things.

"No."

His firm rejection had her retracing her steps.

"I'm not going to be able to rest knowing you may be in danger."

"Bay, this is what I do."

The simple reply was more than an assurance, it was an indication of what she would be dealing with if she became his lover—a fact of life she'd better get used to fast. She rushed to him.

Jack's embrace welcomed her, but his sigh voiced relief. "I half expected you to back away from me."

"Let Simon go with you. If Bud is outside—"

"Simon stays here."

"Maybe if you let the dog inside with me…?"

Jack's chest shook briefly from a silent laugh. "And I'd come home to the bedroom door scratched free of paint from Bud trying to check on you. No, Simon will keep watch with Bud outside, though I think the excitement is over."

"How do you—what do you believe this is all about?"

"We'll talk when I get back. You'd better give me your key."

26

Waiting this time was worse but thankfully Jack was back in less time than it took to deal with the deputy. Bay had taken up watch on the couch to wait for him, but sprang up when she heard Bud bark. Crossing the room, she saw headlights through the formal dining room window. Moments later the garage door lifted. Wanting to yank open the utility door to see for herself that he was all right, she hesitated at the sound of voices—he was speaking with Simon. Too self-conscious to be seen underdressed again, she endured another minute or two of waiting. Finally, though, the connecting door to the garage opened.

"I need a beer," Jack said heading straight to the refrigerator. "Want one?"

"No, thanks. Are you okay?"

"Fine. As far as I can tell your place wasn't touched. You had a couple hang-up calls, though, and Ridgeway phoned. He'll be back in town first thing in the morning and wants to know if you'd like him to bring dinner over. He left a number for you."

While he paused to take a long swallow of his beer, Bay considered his news—the hang-ups and Duncan's call. "Do you think whoever shot through your window knew I was here?"

"That's one possibility. Another is that I've pissed off the lieutenant for the last time. Considering his mood when I challenged him today—" Jack checked his watch and grimaced "—yesterday. If I'm right, then we do have to look into getting you situated elsewhere."

"Jack, I'm not afraid of a bunch of bullies. I've dealt with them before."

"Don't remind me. Come here."

He set the beer on the counter as Bay slipped her arms inside his unbuttoned shirt and around his waist, gravitating to his warmth and strength. As he enfolded her, she pressed a kiss to his breastbone, then lifted her head for the kiss she knew was coming. There was a little desperation in this one, but he was ever mindful of her injuries.

"I needed that more than I needed the beer," he said thickly.

"Me, too, especially when I get the feeling you're not telling me something."

"What you're picking up on is frustration because I just don't know. Hell, it *could* have been some fool varmint hunting from his truck on his way home from a club. The farther you get away from town, the more often nutty stuff like that happens. On the other hand, is it just a coincidence that we've both been paid night visits? Maybe from here on I'll handle both sides of this investigation and you keep your distance from me."

"Sell that plan to someone else."

"Bay, think."

"I am. What if Madeleine does know I'm here? Those hang-ups? What if she sent Elvin down here to try to scare me away from you? You're playing right into her hands."

"Then stay put in that house and let her believe she's succeeded."

"That's no longer an option. I should never have accepted her offer in the first place."

"Well, if you think she's hot at me, she'll be even hotter if she finds out we're a team."

A team. Bay smiled.

"Damn it, don't do that now. It's not fair."

"Can't help it, I like that you think we are. And I don't care if she knows. Isn't there strength in numbers?"

Jack groaned and framed her face with his hands. "At what point do you think it'll dawn on her that she made a mistake in getting you out of prison? Have you thought about that? Have you thought that you might end up being more trouble to her, or whatever this enterprise is, than you're worth? You still don't know why she arranged for you to be released. They could have a plan for you that hasn't even begun yet. Right now my hunch is that you become Mrs. Duncan Ridgeway, which would permanently silence you. Remember, a wife can't testify against her husband."

"That's crazy. And do you think I could sleep in your bed and even consider going to dinner with him, let alone what you're suggesting?"

"It's the only reason I haven't totally lost my mind.

But what will you say if he asks why you're turning him down?''

''I'm seeing someone else.''

Jack's intense gaze held hers. ''Is it serious?''

''I didn't want it to be...I can't seem to help myself.''

''Stop trying,'' he murmured a second before claiming her mouth again.

This kiss had Bay rising on tiptoe, erasing any doubts she had about wanting something more intimate with him. As good as it felt being in his arms, it couldn't assuage a deeper hunger.

Jack raised his head slightly and asked, ''Are you sure?''

''Yes.''

He turned out the lights and, taking her hand, led her down the hall, pausing at the office. When he turned on that light and saw she'd cleaned up the glass, he backed her against the wall. ''There's a price for disobeying orders.''

''I'm not afraid.''

''I'm so glad.''

After another kiss, he led her the rest of the way to his room and in the glow from the night-light in the bathroom they undressed each other. He made her forget her lack of experience and her inner critic that worked overtime about her doubtful sex appeal. The way he touched her left her feeling sleek and special; she, in turn, learned that exploring his body was an unbelievable turn-on.

Urging her against the pillows, Jack brushed his lips across her ribs. ''I'm going to be too heavy.''

"You won't."

"You're adorable. I could just...absorb you."

But she did the absorbing, taking him inside her in a slow, yet smooth movement that made her breath hitch in surprise and pleasure. Better yet was seeing similar emotions play on his face and feel the growing tension in his body as he began moving inside her. He made her grateful she'd never known this kind of intimate connection before—she learned from him that this genuine caring and sharing was possible.

Wanting to be closer to him, she wrapped her legs around his waist. With a husky murmur of approval, Jack sat up taking her with him, and settling her on his lap.

"I love you," he rasped burying his face in the curve of her neck and shoulder.

The declaration struck her with the velocity of the gunshot hitting the house. Wanting to stay in the moment, to savor and analyze, to give him a response worthy of such an admission, she was thrust beyond reason. All she could do was whisper his name.

It must have been enough...he didn't let her go.

27

Saturday, June 8, 2001

Martel's wasn't working a crew that weekend, but when he received Bay's call, Mike Martel agreed to meet her at the shop. With reluctance Jack had dropped her off at the house and let her take her soon-to-be-ex-truck to the meeting. However, he'd warned that if he didn't hear from her within a reasonable time, he would be all over Martel like a swarm of those killer bees beginning to migrate into the Rio Grande Valley.

As he'd indicated in their initial meeting, Mike was receptive to Bay's offer to work out of his building for a percentage, and to help him out when he needed an extra hand. She didn't have to explain much. Wincing at her injuries, he'd simply asked, "Does what happened have something to do with this?"

"I think so." She apologized for not being able to tell him more, but assured him she hadn't broken any law, and felt compelled to add, "I do need to warn you about something. This arrangement might cost me some of my contracts. Even if it doesn't, my, um, protection from the press may vanish and I might become fair game again. That could become disruptive to your business and I'd understand if you needed to call off our agreement.''

''Hell, I'd love an opportunity to tell a reporter what is and isn't news,'' Martel drawled, handing over a set of keys to her. ''Listen, kiddo, my kids are out of college and my wife has the touch at Bingo and at playing the slots in Shreveport. I'm not worried about business. You just start eating double cheeseburgers, 'cause I know you can weld, and I have a feeling you're a woman of your word. You'll be worth your weight in gold to me.''

For the rest of the morning, Bay and Jack worked on moving her projects from the shop on Airline Drive to Martel's. As well, they moved her personal belongings out of the house. On the last trip, he picked up lunch and they ate in the RV. Afterward, he presented her with a cellular phone. Touched as she was, she had difficulty accepting it.

Jack sighed. ''The phone's in your name, even though the billing address is mine. You can change it at any time. As much as I'd like to offer, I won't bug you about accepting my financial help—unless you ask for it.''

Relieved, Bay accepted the phone with gratitude.

''Speaking of finances—what the hell are you going to do for transportation?''

Bay indicated one of the keys on the set Mike had given her. ''I'm sort of renting the blue half-ton outside.'' She couldn't blame Jack for making a face; it was no gift, which was why Mike wouldn't take any money from her. He said if she'd pay for the gas and keep it clean, it would be payment enough to him. Bay figured it would take her until she dropped from exhaustion tonight to get the thing presentable again.

"Mrs. R. will try to make you keep the truck she gave you."

"I couldn't, not now." She nodded to the phone. "Show me how to work that thing. I'd better get the rest of this move done or I'll lose my nerve."

"Fat chance," Jack muttered, flipping open the phone.

The first call she made was to Duncan to tell him she wouldn't be available for dinner. As it happened he was in his mother's office and it didn't surprise Bay when Madeleine took control of the phone.

"What's going on, Bay? Yesterday the suit, today I hear the word moving?"

"I do need to talk to you. Can you squeeze me into your schedule?"

"I suppose if I want to be kept informed, I'd better. Come over as soon as you can."

Disconnecting, Bay met Jack's concerned gaze. "That was fun."

"I wish I could do this for you."

"You'd better not be here if someone agrees to drive me back. If they don't offer, though—"

"Oh, I'll be close from the time you leave here until you get back."

"My own personal shadow." She went to him. He hadn't said anything, but since they'd made love, she knew he'd been aware of a remoteness in her, although she'd been trying to hide it. She wanted to spare him her doubts about the wisdom of their getting involved, and her inability to believe he could love her, let alone fall in love in just over a week.

Jack's embrace was easy, relaxed, a complete contradiction to the watchfulness and concern in his gaze. "Like the idea of that?"

She lifted her left eyebrow. "I'm an ex-con, what do you think?" As soon as she saw his disappointment, she regretted the reply. "It doesn't feel that way with you."

"That's because I don't see you the way you describe yourself."

Yes, she thought, he was a romantic, while she was a cynic. Some combination. She touched the soft hairs in the V of his plaid shirt. It brought back images of last night and his hurt this morning when she'd slipped out of bed as he'd reached for her.

"You've been so patient."

"I'm learning the fastest way to chase you away is to crowd you."

But it was costing him. She couldn't bring herself to think about how much. "You deserve better...there's also all of your responsibilities back at the ranch."

"Simon can cope for a while. Everything else revolves around you. If you're not okay, then there's not much point to the rest."

Her heart did one of those crazy little flip-flops. "Maybe could you kiss me so I could believe that for a little while?"

He locked her to him in a way that made it blatantly obvious how quickly he responded to her. Then he transmitted with his lips and tongue what she had felt last night. For a few moments, Bay gave him all of herself—her concentration, her heart, her trust.

"Jesus," he rasped, finally forcing himself away from her. "You'd better get going or Madeleine Ridgeway will still be waiting when the moon rises."

Weak-kneed, Bay gripped the table to steady herself and fumbled with her keys and phone. She was amazed that she made it down the expanded metal stairs without falling on her face. She could swear the concrete floor of the shop had turned to melting rubber.

"Bay."

Jack slammed the RV door and checked the lock before turning to her. She didn't look anywhere but his dark, intense eyes.

"Get this done with as little conversation as possible. There'll be less chance of making any serious mistakes that way. If you sense anything wrong, get out."

"I will."

The midday heat was enough to steal the air from her lungs, but Bay was grateful that it required conscious effort to breathe. Regardless of the air conditioning in the truck, she wasn't thrilled that she would be perspiring by the time she reached the Ridgeway estate. So much for maintaining her confidence, she thought.

Aware of Jack following discreetly, Bay made her way down Broadway beyond the southernmost intersection of the Loop. When she turned into the estate,

Jack continued on past and she knew he would wait for her.

Duncan's car was parked under the portico just behind his mother's. To Bay it was symbolic of his ongoing role as Crown Prince to Madeleine's Queen. She parked behind the Jaguar, taking no pleasure in seeing that Elvin was outside polishing the windows and chrome on the Town Car. It was the first time she had seen him in a plain T-shirt and jeans. The clothes suited his rough-and-tumble features the way his improvised chauffeur's uniform never would. Still, Bay couldn't argue that he maintained the Ridgeway image well.

"Hey." He nodded to the truck. "She looks dusty. How many miles've you put on her already? Pull it up into the shade and I'll make sure everything's topped off."

"No rush. You'll have plenty of time tomorrow or the day after."

Leaving him to wonder about what that meant, she rang the doorbell.

The petite Lulu answered the door, bobbing her head and leading Bay to Madeleine's office. Now that she knew more, Bay could only imagine how many siblings and cousins Lucia had back home in South America who dreamed of having their relative's job...and what Lulu would say in response.

Spotting her first, Duncan came around the glass desk, his hands extended. "Here you are, and looking so much better."

"You're a terrible liar," Bay replied, "but a sweet one."

''Oh, I can see you're still not resting as much as you should. The swelling's gone down, though, and the bruising—''

''Is criminal.'' Madeleine brushed him aside and embraced Bay. ''Darling, I had no idea until Duncan told me. You poor child, come sit down. Do you need a drink, maybe a stiff Scotch, or would you prefer some herbal tea?''

The choices were more laughable than appealing. ''Neither, thanks. Believe it or not, I'm feeling almost myself.''

''You didn't sound it on the phone,'' Duncan said.

''There's a lot going on.'' She included Madeleine in her glance. ''I don't know how else to tell you other than to blurt it out. I've moved.'' She handed Madeleine the envelope that she had initially presented to her. ''That's the deed signed back to you, the title to the truck and all of the keys. I want you to know I really do appreciate everything you did and intended to do, but—''

''No.'' Madeleine tried to hand the envelope back. ''I won't take it.''

''You don't have a choice.''

While it was his mother who looked stung, it was Duncan who asked, ''Why, Bay?''

''I've been trying to explain. It's necessary for me to do things in my own way at my own pace. I don't mean to seem ungrateful, and I assure you it has nothing to do with stubbornness, it's simply the way I feel I can transmit some integrity to my work.''

''Heaven save me from that word. You know, sweetie, you're not the first creative person I've dealt with and they all chant that word like some mantra. Will you please explain to me what keeping a roof over your head has to do with integrity?''

Duncan coughed and turned away.

Bay gave her a mildly reproving look, but decided to be kind and not remind her of the most recent outfit. ''The appropriate church clothes?''

''Did you expect me to let you attend services in coveralls?''

''I *hoped* to be allowed to decide for myself if I wanted to attend services at all and, if so, where.''

''If you've converted to another religion, just say so.''

''Then what? Will you and Martin hold a prayer breakfast to save my soul?''

Laughing outright, Duncan ignored his mother's irritated look. ''I do think you've met your match.''

Madeleine made a slow journey around her office, touching a glass figurine here, a plush chair there. When she stood behind her desk, she gripped the back of the leather chair. ''Is it permissible to ask where you propose to work, let alone sleep?''

''I've made arrangements with Mike Martel.''

The name caused a most unusual reaction. For once Madeleine didn't know how to respond.

''Martel, that's a coincidence. Isn't he...? Duncan, that's the policeman's name.''

''A distant relation,'' Bay said, hoping to cut that discussion short. ''Mike Martel's welding shop is on the north side of the Loop. It's a good-size business with room for someone with a schedule like mine and he has terrific equipment. He's letting me subcontract there."

"You have your own shop."

"With virtually nothing in it. I need the equipment."

"I told you, we'll get it for you."

"You can't be my bank, Madeleine, and I can't allow myself to get that deep in debt."

"So you're rejecting me entirely? I admire your levelheadedness, Bay, but this...this reasoning escapes me."

Duncan eased down on one of the arms of the leather chairs. "It sounds like you've done your research and feel comfortable with this."

"For goodness' sake, whose side are you on?" Madeleine snapped. "And how many times have I told you if you're going to sit in that chair, sit *in* it."

Duncan didn't budge, but he winked at Bay. "My only question is how will you get to work?"

"Not a problem. I'm staying in Mike's RV inside the shop."

"Oh, for pity's sake. Come full circle, haven't we?"

"Mother."

Duncan's terse warning was the first time Bay had ever heard him speak to his mother with anything other than admiration and affection. It sunk in with Madeleine, too, if belatedly, and she covered her face with her hands.

"Yes, yes, that was an abominable thing to say. I apologize. You see how you've shaken me? The Queen of Control has lost it."

Bay found it hard to speak. ''The arrangements may not be ideal, but they'll do. Oh, and to answer your question, Duncan, I'm renting Mike's extra truck until I can afford my own.''

''Martel's...that's not in the best neighborhood.''

''Duncan, I'm not a concierge at a five-star hotel. My profession, out of necessity, tends to be located in the industrial section of town. But if it's any consolation, Mike has a full crew working during the day, and an excellent alarm system to keep me company at night.''

Duncan turned to his mother. ''If this is what she wants, it sounds fine to me.''

Madeleine ignored him, her gaze fixed somewhere across the room. ''Elvin worked so hard to fix up that house.''

''It won't be wasted if you decide to put it on the market. It's a terrific location, Madeleine.''

''Not good enough apparently. What about the welding machine and all of the stock?''

''I've moved the stock—perhaps prematurely you may say. The next owner might want to buy the welder.''

''Is this a total break? Am I never going to see you again?''

''Of course not. I mean—'' Bay thought of Jack's warning ''—look, I accept this as my fault. I should have stood my ground in the beginning and then we wouldn't be having this difficulty.''

The approach had a soothing effect on Madeleine. ''I'm not upset with you, darling. I'm venting over the past that has made you so cautious and wary.''

"I can't deny my lessons have left me with a few hard edges, but I believe they've served me well enough."

"You remind me so much of myself. All right then, Ms. Independence, have it your way. Do I still get my gate?"

"If you still want it. I half expected you to cancel and tell Mr. Nelson and anyone else that might be interested to take their business elsewhere."

"Ha. I should make you sweat." Madeleine came over and hugged her. "My problem is I care about you too much. Get healed fast. I'll be back to harassing you soon enough."

Bay endured the embrace as long as she could before easing free and backing to the door. "I won't take any more of your time. I still have a lot to get organized."

Duncan followed her into the foyer. "Do you need a ride?"

"Why, yes, if you wouldn't mind? I was going to ask Elvin."

"He always gets the fun chores. I'll be happy to take you…where?"

"Martel's."

Once outside Duncan hailed Elvin. "You'll want to get the keys to the truck from Mother. Put it back in the garage."

Elvin stood there openmouthed, window cleaner in one hand and paper towels in another.

"Flies, Elvin," Duncan drawled, opening the passenger door on the Jaguar for Bay.

When he settled in on his side, he chuckled. "He'll

rush inside and ask Mother what's up. He's a worse gossip than some of the gals in the office."

"I don't mind his knowing."

"No, of course, not. But it's the principle," he said easing around the Town Car to the street. "He won't do anything on my say-so. He always has to get Mother's blessing."

Filing away that tidbit of information, Bay looked around wondering if Jack could see them. "It's not a bad thing that he's devoted to her, I guess."

"At least he's that. If you don't mind my being nosy, will you tell me how you decided on Martel's? Did you already know them? Professionally, I mean?"

Not wanting to lie, she said, "He knew our business better than I knew his."

"Small world, huh? I mean being related to that cop who was so instrumental in you getting back your freedom."

"I don't believe they're close. They could well be strangers with a name in common."

"They don't visit and such?"

"I don't have that impression." Bay shifted to look out the sideview mirror, but the angle favored Duncan's view not hers. "When I asked if they happened to be related, Mike changed the subject rather quickly. Typical extended family reaction, I guess."

"I hope it's simply due to different lifestyles and interests than bad feelings. I'll always be grateful to Nicholas, regardless. Are we still going to have that dinner when you're feeling up to it?"

So this was why he'd wanted to be alone with her,

Bay thought. How to answer...? "Duncan, I should warn you, your mother may still end up angry with me. You, too, for that matter. I'm not going back to the church."

"Ah. I suppose I should have seen that coming. Still, it's not what I asked."

She didn't understand his persistence, unless she'd missed some signal between mother and son that it would be his job to keep an eye on her. "Could we take it one day at a time? I really do have to focus on my career right now and, having glimpsed your demanding schedule, even synchronizing our schedules sounds more trouble than you might find worthwhile."

"That's why I like you—the trappings don't lure you. You know Mother's done her share of matchmaking. And I'm tired of realizing those stars in a woman's eyes are really dollar signs. Today you genuinely proved you could care less about the money, and you have no idea how rare that is. I don't want to lose you, Bay, even if it means we'll never be more than friends. The world can be a lonely place at times."

She studied his profile and saw the melancholy that underscored his words. "Yes, it can."

"Then we'll work from that angle. And, as your friend, I want you to know if Mother becomes a handful, I'll be happy to run interference for you."

"You helped a great deal today. I think you sat on that chair arm just to take some of the heat off me."

He laughed as he pulled into the shop's parking lot. "And was instantly reduced to being a twelve-year-old. Now when I get home, she'll want to talk about the expected profit-and-loss reports on the family warehouse business. It's a wonder I can remember when to suck my thumb and when to reach for my calculator. Would you like me to come in with you while you check around?''

''Far be it from me to delay the cross-examination any more than I already have. No, I'm fine, really, and I do have to get to work. There's a lot to arrange so I can be out of everyone else's way by Monday. Thank you, Duncan,'' she added softly. ''You've been an awfully nice surprise.''

''I like the sound of that. All right, scram, cutie, so I can leave seeing you safely locked inside.''

Bay waved from the shop door before closing it behind her, then stood listening for the sound of the Jag's powerful engine as it pulled away. She stood there a good minute before reopening the door to wait for Jack. She'd almost decided he was following Duncan back to the estate when he pulled in.

''You thought he might circle back,'' she said as he entered the shop.

''If he was at all suspicious of you, he would have.'' Unsmiling, he searched her face. ''How did it go?''

''Madeleine got a bit testy. Duncan seems okay with it.''

''Good cop, bad cop.''

She hadn't thought of it that way. ''I suppose that's one point of view.''

''What's yours?''

''You won't like it.''

''Is that the good news?''

''I think he may be sincere in his support of me doing things my way.''

She waited, but Jack's expression remained unchanged, which gave her a clue that he was doing a slow burn inside.

''You fell for that golden-boy charm again. All he has to do is say, 'I'm here for you,' and you lose your perspective.''

''And you're sounding like a man who's spent the last half hour getting as overheated as his truck.''

''Well put,'' Jack murmured, sliding an arm around her waist and tugging her close. ''Kiss me and remember what real heat is.''

Her soft laugh became a moan of pleasure as he exposed her to the passion simmering below his dry wit. Even though she knew he was fighting an internal battle with his jealousy, he made her want to forget about everything and invite him into that RV in the darkest corner of the shop.

''That's better,'' he murmured, brushing her damp hair from her stitched brow. ''Now tell me everything. Sometimes what isn't said is as important as what is.''

''I need something wet and cold if I'm going to do that.''

There was a soda machine in the break room and Jack slipped in enough change for both of them, then let her choose. She punched the bottled water button and so did he. After downing almost half of the bottle she repeated the conversation as best as she could remember it.

"No casual comments as you left like, 'What did you do last night?'" he asked when she was done.

"Wouldn't that be a dead giveaway?"

"The problem with real life is that criminals have to think on their feet 24/7. They make mistakes."

"Not this time they didn't...if they had anything to do with that."

"It's a lawyer's job to tell a jury everyone's innocent until proven guilty. The rest of us have to assume someone's lying through their teeth or hiding something." Jack finished his water and tossed the bottle in the trash. "I have to get out of here before Martel arrives."

"It's his day off."

"If he doesn't show just to check up on you under the pretense of offering to help or that he forgot to show you something, then he's either a lousy businessman who doesn't care about his property, or someone to watch like the others."

Bay knew that; she was just tired of thinking that way. When Jack took hold of her chin and forced her to look at him, she saw apology in his eyes.

"Come to the ranch with me. Take a break. We both need it. I'll get you back here first thing in the morning or we can park that rusting rat nest you'll be driving in the garage for the night so no one knows for sure where you are."

Her head said to stay put and get caught up. Her heart wanted Jack—wanted a reprieve. She tossed her empty bottle in the trash.

"Let's go."

28

Monday, June 10, 2001

"Bay—telephone."

Damn, she thought, about to drop her welding hood. She was at exactly the spot on the gate she'd been the night Glenn died, and she wasn't in any mood for interruptions. She wanted to get this over with.

Glancing over her shoulder she saw Larry at the break room door, his golden-red curls soaking wet, as though he'd just stuck his head under a faucet. Even with the fans running, the shop had to be close to three digits, not much cooler than outside.

"Can you take a message?"

"I tried. Told her you was welding, but she said she wasn't callin' back."

Madeleine. Easing the welding hood past her bandage, she set it down and shut off the welder. The rest of the weekend had been quiet as far as the Ridgeways were concerned, so it came as no surprise that something was about to begin cooking again.

"Thanks. Looking good over there," she said as

she passed a young man. He'd just finished heliarc welding and looked as drained as if he'd run a marathon. Punching the blinking light, she picked up the receiver. "Butler."

"This is Holly."

Ever since their brief, interesting exchange outside the dress shop, the younger woman had been in Bay's thoughts. "How did you track me down?"

"I only have a moment. You took too long getting to the phone. I want to see you."

She sure had a winning way about her Bay thought, plucking the rag from her back pocket. Checking for a clean spot, she wiped at the trickle she felt at her throat. "You obviously know where I am."

"I can't be seen there. We break for lunch in forty minutes. Meet me—"

"Hold on. I'm not taking lunch today. I'm at a critical stage on a project." A UFO would have to beam her up before she stopped again. It wasn't a power play; she had to finish getting the *Maiden* set for painting tomorrow so she could work on the Nelsons' carts while she waited for the paint to dry properly. "What about later?"

"Five-thirty. You know the grocery store on the east side of the Loop from where you are?"

"Vaguely. I haven't been over that way since I've been back."

"It's still there. Five-thirty. You remember what I'm driving?"

Most cars looked alike to her, and she was guilty of muttering, "Bubble cars," when passing them on the Loop; however, she figured the teal-green color would set Holly's apart. "I'll be driving a light-blue Chevy pickup with the rusting hood."

Holly hung up without comment.

"Yeah, it left me speechless, too," Bay drawled replacing her handset. Shaking her head, she went back to her workbench.

What on earth was that all about? For someone wanting to talk, Holly had been rather rude...or was she just anxious? Maybe she'd been concerned about getting caught making a personal call. Bay could imagine what Jack was going to say. *She hates your guts and you went to meet her without telling me or anyone?*

Thinking of Jack made her wistful. The weekend hadn't turned out the way he'd obviously hoped because she'd started her period. If he'd been disappointed, though, he never let on. With Bud in the back of the truck, he gave her a tour of his land and stock, then insisted she nap. Later he grilled steaks, after which she did more reading—until fatigue caught up with her again. The next thing she knew it was daylight and she was alone, curled into a tight ball beneath the blanket.

Remembering how sweet he'd been made her yearn to hear his voice again. She pulled out her small phone and punched in his pager number. Less than a minute later he phoned.

"Hey, you."

He made the casual greeting sound like a caress. "Sorry to bother you at the office."

"Everything all right?"

"I'm not sure." Briefly, she told him about the call and arranged meeting.

"Do you think she's stable?" Jack asked.

"I don't know, but if she wanted to hurt me, why choose such a public place?"

"The same reason other people take their guns to work and start blasting anyone in their line of fire." He sighed. "I can tell you're going to do this regardless. I should be able to get out of here on time to cruise by, then meet you at the shop afterward."

"You'll be careful not to let her spot you?"

"No sweat. Later."

Bay winced at his abrupt disconnect, but knew someone must have come by, no doubt that lieutenant who was making his life such a trial these days. Sighing, she pocketed her phone thinking what she would have liked to say. She missed him, and he'd been right yesterday when she'd insisted on returning here to work. She would have slept better at his ranch. If he asked again, she wanted to be done with her work so she could accept.

Good intentions and a steady pace didn't get Bay out of the shop on time and it was exactly five-thirty when she locked up. The rest of the crew left in a mass exodus at the stroke of five. Mike had gone hours earlier to take his ten-year-old daughter to a semi-pro ball game where her oldest stepbrother would be playing first base. Mike had apologized for asking her to take phone messages, explaining it was all the kid wanted for her birthday.

"No problem. Are you taking a camera?" Bay asked.

"Intended to, but my older daughter dropped it in the pool over the weekend."

"Stop and buy one of those disposable ones. It sounds like you have a case of serious hero worship there and your kid will appreciate the effort."

Thinking of how he'd smacked his head before thanking her brought a fleeting smile to her lips as she raced around the northeast curve of the Loop. But for the rest of the trip she prayed she wouldn't cross the path of a patrol car, and also that Holly would wait for her.

The sporty little car was there; however, her relief was short-lived. There was no sign of Jack.

Parking on the passenger side, Bay switched from truck to car...belatedly noticing that the engine was idling, thanks to the heavy equipment that had been thrumming in her ears all day. Glenn had been right, she thought, we're all doomed to be deaf before we're totally gray.

"You are a glutton for punishment."

Bay saw that Holly's focus was on the truck. It gave her a moment to admire her royal-purple suit. The woman left her looking like a soiled paper napkin on a table of clean linens.

"What can I say? The price was right."

Holly shut off the ignition. "You're doing a lot of that."

"Being a smart-ass? My first cellmate said it was a poor man's Kevlar."

Grimacing, Holly murmured, "Good point. But I

was actually referring to your, um, downsizing—your rejection of Madeleine's invitation to be the Crown Princess. Mind my asking why? The Queen B was committed to making things pretty comfy for you."

"You want me to say something critical so you can run back and report me? Anything Madeleine needs to know, I've said to her face."

As she reached for the door handle, Holly touched her other arm. "What I'm trying to say is...I envy you for being the quicker study."

"Blows to the head will do that to me. One good whack and I generally say to myself, 'Butler, this isn't working.'"

"You don't look as bad as you did on Friday."

"Keep it up and I might have to add you to my will."

Unperturbed, Holly asked, "Any luck yet in finding out who hurt you?"

"Not yet. Hints, intelligent guesses and anonymous calls would be gratefully accepted, though."

"First tell me if this is for real, you moving out of that place and into that dump up the highway?"

"Excuse me but that RV is a palace compared to what I grew up in." Suddenly Bay realized why Holly couldn't stop doubting her honesty. "You're scary, lady. Are you telling me you could never give up a job if it wasn't right for you, or you wouldn't walk away from a position because you knew you were in over your head, that your only escape would be another promotion? There is a serious flaw with that way of life."

Holly shifted her gaze to her lap. It was then that

Bay noticed Glenn's engagement ring on her right hand. She continued to wear it like a widow would wear her wedding ring.

"I guess I deserve that," Holly said slowly. "And I owe you an apology. I had to be certain, can you understand?"

"Yeah, well, your idea of certain felt like vengefulness to me. Your character assassination helped steal years from me. All I can say to you is that you followed directions well. What's worse is you believed everything you said."

Holly bit at her artfully painted lower lip. "That's the thing. I didn't. Bay, Glenn thought you all but walked on water. Every other word out of his mouth was 'Bay this' and 'Bay that'...I couldn't compete with that."

Bay couldn't believe what she was hearing. "You didn't need to. He loved you."

"Yes. I realize that now. There never was anything between you two."

How could anyone this gorgeous be so insecure? "We were able to see things in metal, we understood how the weather made our work easier or harder, we could recognize what was imported and what was domestic stock without seeing the shipping labels or test reports. That's all. Outside of the shop, we were oil and vinegar."

"The D.A. said you were having an affair, using Glenn and me to get closer to the Ridgeways."

"The D.A. *alleged* that and you chose to believe it. It was, and is, a lie."

"Yeah. I just...why did they have to dirty his reputation to save you? The whole story that got you out—''

''Is a lie. I agree. What was I supposed to do, stay in there and try to argue from behind bars?''

''Then you are trying to make it right?''

Something about her weary, fatalistic tone gave Bay a feeling of unease. ''What do you want from me, Holly?''

The younger woman sat staring at the steering wheel as though it were a seer's crystal ball. ''Nothing. It's time to pay up, that's all. Maybe I can give you room.''

''Room for what? You're not making sense.''

''That's okay.''

''Wait a minute. If you know something, you need to talk to the right people. Don't go doing something—''

''Get out, please.''

''Let's work together. Compare notes.''

''Get out!''

29

Bay was leaning against the pickup when Jack drove into the space where Holly had been parked. Staying out of sight hadn't been a problem since the grocery store was crowded with people hurrying from work to grab something for dinner, but not being able to see everything going on in the coupe put his nerves on edge. Once he saw Bay's expression, the knot in his gut grew tighter.

"You okay?" he demanded before he'd finished climbing out of the truck. He gripped her arms to reassure her. She looked ready to slide to the ground. "Bay, what happened?"

"She knows."

"Knows what?" But as he spoke, Jack glanced around and saw they were attracting too much attention. "We have to move, sweetheart. Bay—" He gave her a shake.

"Hey, mister! Get your hands off her."

The stranger's voice got through to Bay and she glanced over her shoulder at the young man who obviously thought Jack was manhandling her. His eyes widened in shock when he saw her face.

"Holy shit...did he do that to you? Officer!"

There was a uniformed cop leaving the market with a deli bag tucked in the curve of his arm. Noticing the teen's distress, he came over, his expression darkening when he saw Bay.

Crap, Jack thought and flashed his badge. "Detective Jack Burke."

The uniformed cop stopped and Jack could see the relief on his face. But then a touch of wariness returned.

"Everything all right here, Detective?"

"I've just been given some bad news about a mutual friend," Bay said before he could reply. "We—were in an accident together."

"I see. I mean, sorry about that. Anything I can do? An escort to the—someplace?"

"Thank you so much, but I think we'll be all right. I'll follow Jack."

The patrolman nodded. "Y'all be careful on the roads."

"Thank you, Officer," Bay murmured.

As soon as the two were out of earshot, Jack pressed a kiss to Bay's forehead. "Bless your quick mind."

"Let's get out of here before someone comes along that does recognize one of us. Can I go to the ranch with you?"

His heart lifted. "What do you think? Do we need to stop at Martel's first?"

"For a minute. Thanks."

It was close to ten by the time she grabbed a change of clothes, checked the office answering machine, inspected the windows and other exits and finally reset the alarm. Jack stayed in the background observing how quickly she'd learned as much as she had about the building and security procedure.

As she resettled in the truck, he noted she remained pale, stronger than when he had first reached her, yet still tense.

"I have to know," he told her. "Did she threaten you?"

"No. It wasn't anything like that."

Jack slid her a sidelong glance. "Start talking whenever you're ready."

"I blew it," she cried. "I didn't handle this well at all. You know what I said about her initial call. Well, I should have pulled new information out of her. I didn't, not anything you'd find worthwhile."

"Let me be the judge of that."

"I didn't, Jack. All I can say is that she's on edge and planning to do something. I don't like it."

"Do something against you?"

"She apologized to me, if you can believe that. No, she has information about…I don't know who. It's evident she's put something together, I could read between the lines. Madeleine and Duncan have been calling her a basket case and alluding to her drinking, but I think a good part of that is a con. I think she's shaken now. What she knows must be scaring her."

"Did you offer to get her help?"

"That's when she ordered me out of the car. She says it's her turn to pay up, whatever that means. Pay for what? I'm thinking she's let herself become an unwitting participant in something."

"Easy enough in her vulnerable condition. As

shaky as she is, though, it would make better sense to get rid of her.''

Bay wrapped her arms around herself. ''I hope you mean relocation and not something else. Madeleine did see that she was moved out of the church administration office.''

''And over into communications. Some punishment.''

''That's how Madeleine says she likes to operate—'friends close, and enemies closer.'''

''Pretty risky.'' Jack wondered if he was completely off that, despite some borderline business practices, Mission of Mercy was clean. ''All we can do is hope Holly will reconsider and ask for help when it counts.''

''That's it? Jack, that's not good enough.''

''You said it yourself—you have virtually nothing.''

''I can get back over there and be around if and when she needs help.''

Traffic was heavy even on Airline Drive and Jack could only glance away from the road for a second, but he didn't like the determined gleam he saw in her eyes. ''Do not suggest moving back into that house.''

''No. But I need to get over to the estate and get invited to some church function. How else will we know what Holly's up to?''

''By the four-alarm fire sirens sure to sound.''

''You don't mean that. You won't leave her out there alone.''

He was tempted. Sure, he was glad Holly Kirkland had smartened up; nevertheless, he wasn't about to let Bay jeopardize her safety for a woman who'd wanted to find a way to justify the death penalty for Bay. Not proud of his bitterness, he wasn't going to pretend any real concern for Holly until she was willing to work inside the parameters of the law.

"Let's throw some ideas around during dinner, okay?" It was as near to acquiescence as he was willing to get for the moment.

She cast him a grateful look. "In that case I'll cook."

30

Tuesday, June 11, 2001
10:45 a.m.

''Is this some kind of a joke?''

Clipboard in one hand and tape measure in the other, Bay took her time acknowledging Elvin. ''Morning. It's going to be another scorcher, isn't it?''

Madeleine's chauffeur passed her to check Bay's rusting pickup parked right outside the front gates of the estate. ''You'll have to move this rust bucket over where the pines will hide it. Mrs. R. doesn't want anything unsightly around the property. What are you doing here anyway?''

''Checking the hinging on this gate to see what I'll need.''

''Well, move the truck. You should know by now how she is.''

Pleased, Bay did as he directed. She no longer felt comfortable being here but, with Elvin's blessing, she was one step closer to having free movement around the place.

As she walked back up the driveway, Bay drew the Martel cap lower over her eyes. If he hadn't noticed the logo already, the movement would draw his attention and she wanted to see his reaction.

"Have to be careful about sun on the wounds," she said when he did a double take.

Amused, she watched him try two or three expressions before settling on indifference. As chauffeur, Elvin knew almost as much about the Ridgeway goings on as Madeleine and Duncan, and likely knew the importance of the name Martel to the family.

"If you're going to visit, Elvin, grab the end of this tape." He was hanging around and Bay suspected he intended to fish for information himself.

"What for?"

"I want to do some measuring."

"You already did that last week."

"Yeah, and some yahoo spilled coffee all over my notes this morning. It's just as well, though. With this drought, I have to know how your ground's holding up under the weight of this flimsy gate. What I'll be installing will be significantly heavier. If there's not enough concrete on those corner posts, the gates will sag with time and drag on the driveway."

"Of course there's enough support." Elvin pointed out the length of the fence. "The whole thing is sitting on a pad of concrete all the way around the estate. You think the guy who had this contract before you didn't know what he was doing? I don't know why we have to take down a perfectly good gate."

"Because Madeleine wants something that's one-of-a-kind to make a statement, the way the house makes a statement and the way she does. I thought you knew that.''

''It was just an opinion,'' he conceded.

''Would you mind holding to the same mark as you did the first time, I have two different readings.''

''I'm starting to sweat like a pig and we're leaving for Austin in less than a half hour. Do what you've gotta do. I'm getting into the shade before I have to go change shirts.''

''You mean Madeleine won't be available for a final consultation today? I need to check her appointments so I can block off this area for a few hours one day next week.''

''It ain't happening today.''

''What about Duncan?'' she called after him.

''Try him at the studio,'' Elvin said over his shoulder.

Glancing at her watch, Bay delayed her measuring and sketching for another fifteen minutes and then left for Mission of Mercy before Madeleine appeared.

The Jaguar was parked under a colonnade at the main entrance of the KWRD offices. Bay parked beyond it, out of view of the glass entryway.

''Can I help you?'' the middle-aged receptionist asked. She reminded Bay of Odessa with her big hair and a face free of makeup, but without the beatific smile.

''I've come from the Ridgeway estate to see Duncan. Would you tell him Bay Butler would like a moment of his time?''

''Do you have an appointment?''

The woman continued to frown as she studied her

appointment book for a long time. Bay figured it was because she didn't want to be caught staring. Personally, she'd been pleased with how fast she was healing. If all continued to go well, she planned to remove the stitches in her lip by herself tomorrow. This woman was acting as though she was either a freak or a frump.

"I don't need an appointment," she said with stiff politeness. "Would you ring him, please?"

"He'll only just be getting out of a meeting. He usually likes to return phone calls between appointments."

"And his mother is paying me by the hour."

"Bay." Holly appeared on the other side of the reception desk. "I didn't realize you were scheduled to be here today."

"I wasn't, but I'm installing the new gate at the house over the next several days and with Madeleine on her way out of town, I was told to check convenient dates with Duncan."

"They've finished a taping and he'll be heading for his office. Come with me. It's all right, Naomi," she said to the receptionist.

Holly took Bay's arm and led her down the hall. As soon as they were out of sight from the front desk, Holly paused and whispered, "Are you checking up on me?"

"I wasn't planning to come here until I discovered I couldn't see Madeleine. Do you think I like being stared at?"

"Naomi makes a face if a delivery person has a Band-Aid. I meant it yesterday, you do look better."

"Thanks. This lighting sure likes you."

"Madeleine's idea. She insists on pink bulbs wherever she walks. Haven't you noticed them at the mansion?" As they passed an office she glanced inside. Seeing it was empty, she continued, "I know I left abruptly yesterday. I admit I was somewhat stressed."

"That much was evident."

"Get Duncan to invite you to Sunday brunch this weekend."

"Pardon?" The way Holly jumped from one subject to another caused Bay not to worry about substance abuse, but her mental health overall.

"Sunday lunch. I may need you to keep attention off me for a few minutes."

"What are you planning?"

"Bay." Duncan stopped in the middle of the intersecting hallways. "What a nice surprise."

"I found her being grilled by Naomi," Holly said. "She said she needs to talk to you." She tapped the cassette she was holding against her left palm. "I have to get this transcript into the computer. Excuse me."

"Thanks, Holly," Bay called after her.

"Come to my office." Looking sincerely pleased, Duncan led her down the hallway. "I hope this is pleasure and not business. My ego needs stroking this morning. I was filling in for Mother on the morning show and literally forgot a guest's name."

"With your schedule, I'm surprised you remember your own name. You're still heading the board of the family business, aren't you? I mean on top of your work here?"

"A typical figurehead with minimal power. Mother handpicked a good team to do the hard work there."

"You're being modest, I'm sure."

He certainly rated a plush office. Bay liked the camel-blue-and-cream color scheme and the welcoming living room ambiance. But when he beckoned her to sit on one of the two peacock print couches, she hesitated.

"Oh, I don't want to take that much of your time. Naomi said you'd be busy answering phone calls before your next appointment."

He shook his head. "Too many people think they know what I'm going to do before I do it. Nothing would give me more pleasure than to help you if I can."

While thinking about the message in that statement, Bay explained what she needed and why. "I suppose it's too much to hope you know your mother's schedule as well as your own?"

"Let me try. I'm out of town starting tomorrow through Friday. Mother returns tomorrow and is here all week. She has things scheduled at the house, but I don't see a problem with your going ahead and doing what you need to. Worse comes to worst, everyone can use the service gate for a few days."

"You think your mother will ask guests to use a side entrance?"

"She'll agree unless the Queen of England or Sean Connery show up. She thinks he's the one man she could have been happy with aside from my father."

Laughing softly, Bay replied, "I'll consider myself forewarned. This is what I propose, then...." She went on to outline her plan to install the gates starting Thursday, doing the brass wrapping on Friday and, if necessary, on Saturday. "Whether we run into trouble on Thursday will determine how long we run into Saturday. On top of that, no one but me has done this kind of wrapping before."

"Sounds perfect. We can toast the results on Sunday. Don't say you won't come to lunch. Mother won't let me live it down if I don't invite you."

Bay wanted to decline out of guilt and because she didn't know what Holly was up to. In the end, though, she nodded. "I may be ready to party a little by then."

"After waiting all this time? I would think so."

It shouldn't be this easy, Bay thought. This time success left a bad taste in her mouth.

31

Sunday, June 16, 2001

"I'd like to propose a toast."

Everyone focused on Madeleine, who rose from her chair at the head of the table and raised her champagne glass. One by one the guests reached for theirs, and as Duncan met Bay's questioning glance, he winked.

"I trust all of you noticed the striking improvement to the front of the estate as you arrived," Madeleine began. "When I saw the design several years ago in its minimal form, I recognized instantly that it belonged here. It's no secret that it was a difficult journey to fulfill that vision, but today I'd like you all to join me in saluting its creator. Bay, you are an inspiration to me and I hope that this marks not only the beginning of a fruitful artist-patron relationship between us but an endless friendship."

"Amen," Duncan murmured before sipping his champagne. As the other guests added their congratulations, Bay looked across the table and met Holly's gaze before the younger woman downed her champagne in one long gulp. If this was an act, she hoped Holly could pull it off drunk because she'd already downed two glasses earlier.

"Here we go again," Duncan said quietly.

Bay saw he'd waited for the woman sitting on his right, the chairman of the Moms for MOM group, to enter a conversation between the choir director on her right and Odessa on Bay's left before issuing his own reaction to Holly. "Would you like me to try to talk to her?"

"It's hopeless. Besides she's liable to create a worse scene."

His expression warmed as he looked at her. "Have I told you how much I like that dress?"

"Twice. You're going to embarrass me." But when she'd checked herself in the bathroom mirror, she'd wished Jack could see her. The black dress that he hadn't been happy with really was flattering and with her face almost healed, except for the slight scar at her right temple, she thought she looked okay. "I saw you on TV last night. I didn't realize you sang."

"Turning the tables, eh? If you heard me, you know I *don't* sing."

"I thought you did well." The gospel number was a duet with Madeleine's guest of honor, Maria Alvaredo, sitting at the other end of the table. "I'm sorry I missed her at services this morning. Did you two repeat that performance for the congregation?"

"Once is quite enough. So tell me, what's next on your work schedule?"

"Mike asked for my help on a tricky tank fabrication for Flowers Bakery, since his most experienced man is on vacation. Cylindrical forms are easy enough once you get the formula down, but on this unit you have to get the diverter valves and vent socks perfectly placed or you'll have ingredients going all over the place.'' Bay grimaced. ''Boring details, sorry.''

''On the contrary, I'm realizing how much you have to know about other people's businesses in order to create what they need.''

''Speaking of which, you probably know your mother wants to talk about a sculpture for the entryway of the church?''

''Sounds like a good idea. That sign is informative and the flowerbed is attractive, but something that would become like a corporate logo would allow us to use it on our stationery and at our satellite locations. Did she tell you about our Houston location?''

''My goodness, you are growing,'' Bay said, unable to stomach the idea of lying to him.

''Hopefully not too fast, though no one is worried but me. Martin is training a young man. He's been down there holding services in an elementary school auditorium. We weren't ready to risk the expense of a building until he had a congregation of three hundred. He's got almost five hundred members! It'll end up larger than us. I teased Martin that he may have to switch locations.''

''Oh, we'd never leave Tyler,'' Odessa said. ''As good as the Lord was to lead us here and provide this comfortable life and loving friends, it would break our hearts to leave. Martin is right, though, Duncan. Y'all have to train a substitute preacher for when he has to travel more and minister to his ministers.''

To Bay's surprise, Duncan wasn't enthusiastic about that. In fact he took his time replying.

''It's something he'll have to take up with the elders and trustees.''

A slightly awkward silence followed and Bay was relieved when Lulu arrived with their main course, pecan-crusted catfish, garlic potatoes and grilled vegetables. Bay couldn't believe the size of her filet.

''I think it came off of a whale, not a catfish.''

Duncan chuckled. ''The guy who supplies us with these raises them on a farm near Jacksonville. He—''

A crash at the other end of the table drew everyone's attention. Holly was on her feet, while a shaken Lulu was desperately trying to pick up a plate while helping Holly wipe mashed potatoes and slices of zucchini and carrots off her blue silk dress. In a flurry of cries, chatter and apologies the maid and the guests sorted out the mess.

''It's my fault,'' Holly assured her. ''No, no, not to worry about the dress. It'll wash out. I'll just go rinse it off. You take care of everyone else.''

As she left, Madeleine said to Lulu, ''When you have things back under control, dear, you might bring Ms. Kirkland a glass of unsweetened tea to help balance her sugar level.''

Bay didn't realize she'd made a sound until she felt Duncan lay a calming hand over hers.

''She means well.''

''If Holly isn't back in five minutes, I'm going to

check on her. I think we've made progress in our relationship,'' she added softly. ''Maybe I can help.''

''Then you'd better eat. The downside of that crust is that it gets mushy once it's cold.''

It was difficult to do justice to the tasty meal, and it was almost a relief to be asked a question, since then Bay could give up the pretense of trying to eat. Finally, however, she put down her fork and removed her napkin from her lap.

''Something isn't right. I'm going to go check on her,'' she told Duncan.

As she passed Madeleine, she caught her mouthed *Thank you.* She couldn't do more than nod, afraid her guilt would betray her somehow.

''Some spy you'd make,'' she muttered to herself out in the hallway.

She knew there was a bathroom at the rear of the house near the sunroom to service guests using the pool, and she checked there first. Having no luck there or at the sunroom bar, she all but ran for Madeleine's office. There she found Holly stuffing something into her tiny clutch bag.

''Holly, are you crazy? Get out of here.''

''I'm done. Are they getting suspicious?''

''No, they're pretending everything is perfect and that it's entirely normal to have a ten-thousand dollar rug drenched with garlic and fish.''

''Pocket change to that witch. With a little luck, though, soon she'll be staring at a concrete floor.'' Holly came around the desk. ''Thanks for watching my back.''

''Holly, you have to leave. Not only does Madeleine have a mean glint in her eye when she looks at you, I can't bear the thought of you sitting in the dining room with something incriminating in your purse. I'll say the stain only got worse with water and that you didn't want to upset Lulu. There's some bottled water over there,'' Bay said nodding to the sideboard. ''You don't want Elvin to contradict us.''

''Good point. I'm sick of their vacuous conversation anyway.''

Bay escorted Holly outside where Elvin immediately came to attention.

''What's up?'' he asked frowning at Holly's dress. ''Lunch can't be over already?''

''Another genius,'' Holly muttered.

''Hush. There was an accident and Holly's too uncomfortable to sit in these wet things,'' Bay replied as they passed him.

''Clumsy drunk,'' he said as though not caring if they heard or not.

Although Holly snickered, Bay was furious. ''I should report him.''

''Don't waste your breath. Madeleine won't care and Duncan always yields to whatever Mommy wants.''

''Will you be able to drive?'' Bay asked as they reached Holly's car.

''Sure. But listen, do what you can to get him inside for a minute.''

''Holly, enough already.''

''He'll try to stop me on my way out and demand to check my purse.''

''Why would he do that?''

"Because once he caught me lifting a small figurine. Oh, don't look at me that way. I know it was wrong, but I was so damned angry at her, I wanted to make her as crazy as she's made me."

"Didn't it cross your mind that she might blame Lulu or one of the other employees?"

"Yes, that's why I figured out a better way to hurt her. Go on now. I'm fine."

As Bay returned to Elvin she nodded inside. "I'm going to check the bathroom and make sure there isn't water everywhere. Would you go tell Madeleine that Holly has gone home?"

Although he said nothing, he did follow her inside. Bay took her time returning to the dining room, needing a moment or two to compose herself. She gambled that by the time she returned, the dinner plates would have been removed. She didn't think she could get down another bite.

Duncan rose when she approached her seat and assisted her, discreetly touching her shoulder and whispering, "Thank you," before resuming his seat.

"It's probably best that she left," she murmured.

"For the last time if I have anything to say about it."

It was a relief to get out of there herself. Depressed and restless, she wanted to go talk to Holly and find out more about the risk she'd taken that had compromised Bay, as much as herself. She resisted, however, knowing that would be an invitation to trouble. If Madeleine noticed something missing, Bay wanted to be as far away from the scene as possible. When she stopped at the light at Airline Drive, she felt a strong pull in the opposite direction and yielded to it.

Jack happened to be returning from the back acreage when she arrived. The welcoming smile that spread over his face made her glad she'd followed her stronger impulse.

"Look at you."

"I know I should have called first."

"Stop. You know if I had my way, you'd be here all the time. Pull the truck inside the garage and tell me how it went. What's under that pretty smile or were you hoping I wouldn't notice?"

Not surprised he did, Bay did as directed, although she wasn't sure yet about staying. Hiding her presence seemed to be working, though. Things had gotten extremely quiet all around—Jack's superior officers hadn't harassed him all week and she hadn't received any other hang-up calls or warnings.

"Holly had a plan all right, she caused another scene, and I caught her taking some papers out of Madeleine's office."

"Did she get away with it?"

"Listen to you—it's stolen property, Jack. You know the law better than me, but my hunch is the material would be useless in court. And think if she'd been caught. She specifically asked me to be there for her without warning me what she was up to. She wasn't thinking that she was putting my neck in a noose along with hers."

"At least she didn't tell you why. What was it she took?"

"It's something incriminating to Madeleine, otherwise why bother?"

"I want to hold you, but I'm a mess." Arms akimbo he displayed the dust and grime from his morning's work. "Come inside and give me a minute to rinse this off and change."

When he returned, his hair still wet and his shirt unbuttoned, he swept her into his arms and kissed her fully on the mouth. Until today he'd been only tender, protective and careful of her injuries, but there was an undercurrent of hunger in him now that told her what he'd been suppressing.

"I've been thinking about what you said," he told her. "Do you want me to go talk to her?"

"Could you?"

"From the sound of things, she needs reining in. Do you have her address?"

"It's in the phone book. Look under H. G. Kirkland." Bay ran her hand over the button seam of his shirt. "Jack, thank you. I know I sound paranoid, but I have a bad feeling about this. Shall I go with you?"

"No, you stay here. I don't plan on being more than an hour and I'm guessing you'd like to get your hands on more of my files."

Bay couldn't deny that. She'd been so enthralled with the Mission of Mercy history he'd collected, she hadn't had a chance to read her own file yet. "Don't worry. I'll take it to your bedroom."

"If you want to get comfortable, feel free to raid my closet. The thought of that will get me home all the faster."

32

Jack drove to South Broadway and then east to an older neighborhood of brick homes nestled under great canopies of black oaks, Southern magnolias and pines. It was his understanding from Bay that Holly had received the house as a gift from her parents, who had retired and relocated to be closer to the rest of the family in Georgia.

Finding the house was no problem; it was on a corner, a well-tended white brick in the standard ranch style, slightly more colorful than those around it. There were plenty of flowers and yard ornaments and a lively wind sock that made Jack imagine a person who enjoyed life and who looked at things in a positive way, not exactly how he and Bay saw Holly. But then all he was learning about the comely Ms. Kirkland spoke of contradiction: a tragic figure who continued to mourn the love she'd lost and, at the same time, a vibrant woman who was seeking revenge for not being embraced by an otherwise supportive, affluent family. Jack relished this opportunity to clear up some questions nagging him and to draw his own conclusions.

While he heard music inside, the latest from Faith

Hill, Holly took her time answering the doorbell. Dressed in a short white robe with her hair swept casually on top of her head, she looked at once messy and inviting. Uncertain as to what—if anything—she wore under the robe, Jack made an immediate decision to hold their conversation right here, even if invited inside. The glass of white wine in her hand supported that decision. He and Bay had enough problems without Holly adding assault charges into the mix if she disliked the questions he was about to pose.

"Well, well," she murmured, her full mouth curving with amusement.

"Afternoon, Holly. A mutual friend sent me."

"Now who could that be?" Her dark eyes lit with mischief. "Not either of the Ridgeways, I'll bet."

"She's worried about you, about that stunt you pulled a couple of hours ago."

After a brief look of surprise, she grew speculative. "So you're still in touch with Bay? Yeah, I heard you helped her after that mugging."

"Miracles happen."

"I'll say. Considering the bad blood between—" Holly shrugged and took a sip of her wine. "Then who am I to talk? Your *friend* has a bigger heart than me, Detective. But tell her thanks for the concern and that I'm just peachy, about to unwind in my hot tub. Is that all you needed?"

"A little reassurance would be nice."

"About?"

"What you took from the Ridgeway estate today. If it's supposed to be used as evidence of some kind, you blew it. No judge will let you submit stolen property into court.''

Beginning to look like she was enjoying herself, Holly leaned one shoulder against the doorjamb. ''You think I want to hang around for a trial? At the least it'll expose them for the hypocrites and cheats they are. If I'm really lucky, the full truth will come out and shut down that whole circus once and for all. Either way, I've done all I can and I'm getting on with my life.''

Jack tried to figure out what she actually had. ''It's interesting that you're so eager to bite the hand that generously supported you through some rough times.''

Holly's expression darkened with hatred. ''*Generous?* You have no idea, Detective. I've paid a high price for the privilege of seeing those sanctimonious monsters day after day, year in and year out.''

''Fair enough. This information sounds pretty explosive. Can I see it?''

''Sorry. It's no longer in my possession. And don't bother threatening me with a search warrant. You don't need the added humiliation on your already tarnished career.''

Jack felt his pulse quicken. ''You've given it to someone else.'' When she failed to comment one way or another, his frustration got the best of him. ''Holly, you're playing a dangerous game. You know the Ridgeways are powerful and highly connected.''

''Oh, they know their share of bottom dwellers, too,'' she replied bitterly. ''That's why I've been eager to finish up. Tomorrow I'm calling a Realtor and putting this place on the market. That's not public information, okay? It'll get around fast enough as it is. I'm pricing it right and the market is hot. Either way, I'm leaving before the wrong people hear."

"I hope you succeed. But what are you going to do if you're needed to testify—provided anything you know is admissible?"

"Don't fish, Detective, you'll find out everything you need to know soon enough. As for testifying, you can forget it. All anyone needs to know is that it was provided by an anonymous whistle-blower."

Jack shook his head seeing nothing but problems for this young woman. "You don't think your sudden departure will be a clue as to the person's identity?"

"That can't be helped, which is why I'm putting myself out of reach. I plan to take a nice long vacation—out of the country."

Jack decided to take another tack. "What about Bay? Has it crossed your mind that in helping you, she's made herself vulnerable? They may blame all of this on her."

"Impossible. She never had the access. You're right about her being in danger, though. Like me, she trusted the wrong people. The difference is I didn't go telling the wrong people I intended to clear Glenn's name. I'm sorry about the troubles she's had. We all have our job to do, though. I trust you'll watch over her."

"Damn straight."

Holly nodded slowly. "I thought as much. Does our fair damsel know you're in love with her?"

"I don't think that's any of your business, considering what you're doing to her."

"I was wrong about her, I admit it, but you'll soon see I've made amends. Now here's one more gift. Keep her away from Duncan until this breaks wide open. He'll steal her from you, and don't think he can't—and, no, that's not petty jealousy. Yes, I was fooled for a while and had my head turned. Fortunately, I wisened up. But Bay doesn't have the view I do and once the Queen Bitch thinks she's hooked, she'll ring those wedding bells so fast, Bay will think her arrest and conviction happened in slow motion. Now go away, Detective, because I still have a lot of packing to do."

"Wait a minute. Hey!"

Jack had had doors shut in his face before, but he'd never wanted to kick any of them open this badly. Holly Kirkland was right to call Madeleine Ridgeway a bitch and, as far as he was concerned, she was a Grade A variety herself.

Swearing, Jack spun around and slammed his palm against the small porch. Maybe what Holly was doing could end up helping Bay somehow; however, she obviously wasn't doing it for that reason or to make amends as she'd claimed. This was all about resolving some personal vendetta, and anyone who got in her way was fair game.

Furious and heartsick, Jack hurried to his truck. He relished the day that Holly would be out of their lives. Permanently. For the moment, though, the most important thing was to keep Bay safe.

33

Monday, June 17, 2001
9:15 a.m.

"Bay...honey, I have bad news. Holly's dead."

It took Bay several seconds to recognize Duncan's voice. The awful announcement stopped everything for her. She stood in Mike's office where they'd been discussing the bakery project and knew she had to say something, only her mind and body refused to cooperate.

"Bay. Are you there? God, I'm sorry to have to tell you this way."

"When?" she whispered. "How?"

"It looks like she drowned. I've only just arrived. Elvin called me right after dialing 911."

"Elvin?" Bay's heart lurched anew. "What on earth was he doing there?"

"Mother sent him. Holly didn't report for work this morning. We had a taping at seven. When she didn't show...considering how she behaved yesterday... hell, you know we feel it's our job to keep an eye on her. Her family's all in Georgia and she's scared away anyone who ever tried to be her friend.''

''She was in a swimming pool?''

''Hot tub. Look, I have to go. There's no one else to see to things until the family can be notified and take over.''

''I'll be right there.''

She heard his sigh of relief.

''Are you sure you're up to it? It would help me a ton but, honey, the press is already arriving. I hate putting you through that.''

''You don't think they'll be looking for me anyway for some kind of statement? See you in...fifteen minutes.''

''I'll tell the police to let you pass. Thank you, Bay. I don't know that I can do this by myself.''

''I'm on my way.''

Bay couldn't believe it. Vibrant, beautiful Holly. Drowned in a hot tub of all things on the eve before she was leaving? Ridiculous.

''Bad news?'' Mike asked as she slowly hung up the phone.

''Someone I knew just died. I'm sorry, I have to go.''

''Yeah. Jeez...what can I do?''

She didn't answer, she was dialing Jack's office number. It rang and rang but no one picked up. She then messaged his pager. He answered when she was already heading around the Loop.

''I just heard myself,'' he said when he heard her voice. ''Who called you?''

''Duncan.''

"Why am I not surprised?"

Bay let that one pass. Although he had taken Holly's warning from yesterday more seriously than she did, now wasn't the time to worry about Duncan's intentions one way or another. "Jack, it's impossible. You said she was drinking, but did she seem so far gone she could pass out?"

"Not at the time. Personally, I can't believe she'd let herself get so soused she would risk missing a flight or something."

"Jack, Elvin found her." She told him what Duncan had said. A chill overcame her and she gripped the steering wheel more tightly to fight a shiver. Yesterday, they'd discussed the possible information Holly might have had and its ramifications. She recognized that there was danger, but not this...and what of Holly's data? What if she didn't pass it on? Could that be the real reason Elvin had been sent over there?

"I'll let you know what I find out," Jack said.

"No need. I'm on my way there, too."

"The hell you are. Bay, don't."

"I already told Duncan that I'm coming. He's asked for my help."

"I'm sure. He doesn't give a damn that the place will be swarming with cops as well as the media."

"It'll be all right, Jack. That can't matter right now. My God, she's dead and you want me to worry about myself?"

"She sure didn't."

"I'll see you there," she murmured and disconnected.

Bay drove the rest of the way in a blur. It was

impossible to get closer than a block away. Police and media were there in droves. Jack apparently hadn't arrived yet and Bay saw no one she recognized, except the press and several of them recognized her as she made her way through the crowd of media.

"Bay Butler! Can we get a comment? Why are you here? Who contacted you?"

Experiencing a moment of panic, Bay almost lost her nerve. What saved her was the mental image of the video cameras catching her fleeing the scene. What a fiasco the media could make of that.

She swallowed and struggled for a helpful reply. "I'm here as a friend. Excuse me, please."

"Holly Kirkland testified against you, how can you call her a friend?"

"That was a misunderstanding and it was all cleared up."

"When was the last time you saw her?"

"Yesterday. We had lunch together."

"Here?"

"No. At the Ridgeways'."

Grateful to have reached the police tape, she ducked under it only to be stopped by a uniformed officer. "Is Duncan Ridgeway still inside? He called me."

"You can wait by his car, ma'am."

"I'd prefer to be away from those cameras," she said, hoping to gain his sympathy. This was a young officer who hadn't been on the force during her trial.

"Sorry, ma'am. They don't need help contaminating the crime scene."

Crime scene! Although she had her own suspicions,

hearing the officer say the actual words made it all too real. Shaken, she crossed the lawn to the driveway.

The Jaguar was parked to the right of the Lincoln. Elvin was leaning against Madeleine's vehicle puffing on a cigarette. She didn't want to talk to him and debated trying to get into the house despite the officer's warning but decided against it.

"I didn't know you smoked," Bay said, approaching Elvin.

"Quit ten years ago, but if you saw what I saw, you'd be wanting one, too."

"The hot tub."

"Like I told the cops, I rang the front door and when nobody answered, I looked and saw through the window that her car was in the garage, so I went around back and over the chain-link fence to see if she was in the kitchen. That's when I heard the tub running." He took another puff and shook his head. "That hair. I always told her it was gonna get her into trouble someday. Course, that's because she was always touching it and using it to flirt and all." He dropped the butt of the cigarette and crushed it out with his shoe. "Must've gotten caught in the turbo something or other."

"Does Madeleine know?"

"Yeah. Mr. R. told her. I need to get over there, but he's called Pastor Davis and her doctor to stay with her for now."

"I take it you already made your statement? Can't you go?"

"I'm not leaving Mr. R."

"How long has Duncan been in there?"

"Fifteen, twenty minutes. Since he called you."

Duncan emerged from the house before Bay could ask Elvin anything else. She was amazed at his pasty coloring and shell-shocked expression. Was he reeling simply because he'd never seen a dead body before, or had their past relationship meant more than he'd admitted?

He reached for her and hugged her close. She was stunned to feel him trembling and despite her wariness of him, found herself rubbing his back in reassurance. All the while her thoughts spun. *"What is the truth? What is the lie?"*

"Thank you for coming," he rasped.

"I'm so sorry, Duncan. Have you been able to get hold of her family?"

"Yes. God, it was terrible. She was too young for this. The waste..."

"Can we go?" Elvin asked.

The condescension in his tone didn't slip by Duncan any more than it did Bay. While she was trying to decide what to say, he was drawing Elvin close to the garage, which hid them from some of the press.

"They're changing the scope of this case."

"Don't let them spook you," Elvin replied, though he didn't make eye contact with either of them. "They treat everything that isn't a clear-cut heart attack as a crime scene."

"Okay, Mr. Expert, then let's just say they definitely don't think this was a heart attack...or a drowning from alcohol consumption."

The tension between the men had Bay wishing Jack would get here. He would know how to handle this.

"I told you," Elvin replied, barely civil. "I could smell the stuff as though she was floating in a distillery."

"A toxicology test during the autopsy will confirm her alcohol consumption."

"What, she couldn't drop the bottle?"

"Then what, it went down the drain?" Duncan snapped. "There isn't one in the tub."

Elvin's face grew bright-red. "Maybe she put it in the trash. Exactly what are you suggesting, *sir?*"

Before Duncan could reply, Bay heard someone cry out behind her, "That's him! Police, stop that man!"

Everyone turned, including Jack, who'd been coming across the lawn. Bay looked back across the street at Holly's neighbor and couldn't believe what she saw. The woman was definitely pointing—at Jack! Elvin started choking on his cigarette. Glancing his way, Bay glimpsed his face before he turned completely away. The bastard was laughing.

"Sir—Detective!"

Jack paused to wait for the uniformed cop jogging toward him. "Yes?"

"Ask him, officer," the elderly woman called. "He was here yesterday and he was mad when he left. He hit that post on the porch, I saw him. His fingerprints'll still be there, I betcha."

Bay felt herself die a little, while Duncan grew alert.

"What's this? You were here yesterday, Burke?"

"What if I was?"

While the cop at the street went to talk to Holly's neighbor, Duncan signaled the uniformed cop at the doorway. "Would you please tell Detective Stevens that he needs to speak to Detective Burke and get his statement, as well."

"What are you trying to pull?" Jack demanded.

"Don't pretend you don't know. They're telling me Holly didn't just drown. She was murdered."

34

"No!" Bay didn't realize she'd cried out until she met Jack's cautionary look. "I don't understand. Duncan, we all saw her at the house. I'm not saying she was drunk, but they do warn the combination of alcohol and warm water can be dangerous." It was a weak recovery at best.

"Well, I saw the body they removed from the tub," Duncan said. "If you simply drown there's no bruising. Even her nails were ripped to shreds from fighting for her life."

Bay waited for Elvin to respond but suddenly he'd grown mute.

"Isn't that to be expected?" she continued. "Elvin said her hair got caught. She would have roused enough to realize what was happening and fought to break free."

"Maybe. It doesn't explain the bruise on her forehead, which is not that different from yours, Bay. Was she supposed to have done that to herself?" Duncan turned to Jack. "Why did you do it, Burke? She had her problems, sure, but she was a decent human being with a full life ahead of her. Wasn't what you did to Bay bad enough?"

Sensing Jack about to erupt at that outrageous accusation, Bay stepped between them. "Duncan, stop. Jack had nothing to do with my injury and you know it."

"But he made sure you went to prison."

"Step aside, Bay," Jack said easing her out of harm's way. "I've listened to his run-on mouth long enough." Then the storm door opened. "Get out of here," he said to Bay under his breath. "I don't want them to put you through the wringer, too."

"I can't do that."

As he swore under his breath, Detective Lyon Stevens motioned for Jack to join them inside. She knew it would be the last she saw of him for a good while.

The calls grew louder from the press and Bay could only cross her arms and turn her back to them. "This is insane," she said to no one in particular.

"Honey, go to the house." Duncan came to her and tried to put his arm around her. "I know Mother would welcome your company. You always seem to lift her spirits."

Suspecting he knew exactly how consoling that would look on video, Bay stepped away. "I'm sorry, it's so hot, I don't know how you can stand it in those long sleeves."

"All the more reason to go to our place."

"I meant what I said, I'm staying here."

"Why are you doing this to yourself?"

"You called me, remember?"

He closed his eyes and nodded.

The door opened again and the body was wheeled out. Bay got through the moment by observing everyone else's reactions to the gurney rolling by. Elvin continued to lean against the Lincoln and stare at some place beyond the toes of his black loafers. Duncan seemed to be reliving the moment when he'd found her in the tub, then he abruptly turned his back to the scene. The crowd grew hushed and, aside from the sounds of traffic from Broadway, all Bay heard was the clicking of cameras.

It was another several minutes before Jack emerged. This time two uniformed policemen escorted him. While he wasn't handcuffed, the expression on his face said he might as well be.

While he briefly met her anxious gaze, he didn't risk any comment. That told her how concerned he was.

Thinking it might now be time to go, Detective Stevens stepped outside again. "Ms. Butler? A moment of your time please?"

She'd never seen this man before but he stared at her as though he knew her inside and out. He simply extended his left hand out to her and opened the storm door with his right. It was enough. Like a child trying to make herself the smallest of targets, she wrapped her arms tighter around herself and rushed past him into the house.

The whitewashed, textured walls and bright kitchen lights at the other end of the narrow foyer didn't ease the heavy atmosphere inside the house. In the same way the half-dozen people moving about didn't relieve the ominous quiet. Bay knew what they were doing. She'd watched them take samples at her old shop and understood they were as indifferent to her as she was dismayed by their presence. She turned her back to them, and that's when she had her first glimpse of Holly's home. The old gold-and-black Spanish-style couch and green recliner set around a pressed-wood coffee table in the small formal living room had her grimacing. It was truly an awful mix and didn't strike her as Holly's taste at all.

"Something wrong?"

"No. I was just—I guess she inherited her parents' furniture."

"This is your first time in the house?"

"Yes."

"By the way, I'm Lyon Stevens. Am I correct in understanding that you saw Ms. Kirkland yesterday, as well?"

"Yes."

"What time would that be?"

"After church—I didn't attend—to about one-thirty. Holly left early."

"Why?"

"She felt uncomfortable after spilling food on her dress."

"I mean, why didn't you attend services with the others?"

Bay frowned, already sensing he wasn't going to make this fast or easy on her. She wished she knew whether it was because of her own past or had Jack disclosed their relationship? "It wasn't because of Holly. I didn't want to go."

"You're not religious?"

"I don't think my religious or spiritual beliefs are any of your business, Detective. As for doing anything because someone says it's what's done, yeah, I have a problem with that.''

''Do you then like to do the opposite out of spite?''

Detective Stevens didn't budge from the doorway and he completely blocked her view of the outside. She couldn't tell if Jack or even Duncan were still there. ''I do what feels right for me.''

''Would you consider yourself a friend of Ms. Kirkland's?''

''You know we weren't. Holly testified against me at my trial.''

''Do you hate her for it?''

''I didn't send her a Hallmark card.''

''Do you hate her?''

Bay exhaled, tired of what no longer mattered—what hadn't mattered for years. ''I don't know that I wouldn't have felt the same way if I'd been in her place.''

''So you're not religious or spiritual and yet you found the compassion to forgive her?''

''If you're going to answer my questions for me, Detective, I think I'd like to leave now.'' He compressed his lips and Bay decided it might be as close to a smile as the man ever came. ''We were both badly wounded by Glenn's death. We had come to that understanding.''

''She said that to you?'' When Bay nodded, he asked, ''When?''

''As late as this week.''

''That's disturbing, don't you think? The very week the woman makes peace with her archenemy, she drowns under highly suspicious circumstances. Nice, tidy closure for you.''

''Closure is psychobabble.''

''Another rejected concept. You're a tiny bit antisocial.''

''No, particular.''

Stevens stood there for a good fifteen seconds studying her. Finally he said, ''Me, too. All right, give me a recap of your last observations of Ms. Kirkland. What was her mood? Did she seem more or less high-strung than usual?''

''Holly wasn't high-strung, she was a little spoiled, and deeply hurt. She was also damned angry.''

''Was the accident at the lunch table alcohol related?''

''I think it was convenient for her to let others think that. I also think Holly could outdrink a trawler full of Russian sailors.''

''And yet you helped her to her car.''

Thank you, Elvin, Bay thought. Of course, she wasn't surprised he would be the one to draw her into this if only to get attention off himself. ''I told you, we'd developed a truce and I felt the need to warn her that she was risking her job.''

''You said she remained angry about Glenn's murder. Why would she be taking that anger out on the people who employed and helped her?''

''You don't read the paper?''

''Humor me.''

''They came to the conclusion that Glenn was heavily into gambling. To Holly that was the equivalent of saying he was responsible for his own murder."

"What do you say?"

"I was assaulted a few weeks ago for what I thought. I guess compared to Holly, I can consider myself lucky."

"I'm sorry you experienced that. Believe me, I'm going to be looking into it, as well. But I also think you know more than you're telling me. What's your relationship with Jack?"

"He's been a good friend."

"You're very closemouthed about your friends... even the unlikely ones."

"They tend to be the keepers."

"Just friends?"

"You're arresting him. Ask him yourself."

"He's not under arrest, but he did see Ms. Kirkland even after you did. They had a heated discussion."

About to challenge the word *heated,* Bay recognized the trap and remained silent. When she could control the shaking in her voice she said, "If there's nothing else, Detective...?"

"Thank you for your cooperation."

Not at all convinced he would let her pass, Bay eased by the man who was every bit as large as Jack and outweighed him by a good thirty pounds. Outside, she saw the crowd had only grown, but the ambulance and the Town Car were gone. There was also no sign of Jack, but Duncan sat in his Jaguar. When he spotted her, he motioned her over to the passenger seat. It meant getting past the press, and for that reason alone she was willing to deal with any questions he might have.

"Thanks," she said ducking in beside him. "I thought for sure you'd have been gone by now."

"Stevens is tough. I was afraid he was going to try to bully you into going downtown, too."

"That would have been a trick. Someone would have had to plant my fingerprints or DNA here along with that booze to justify that."

"If it's all the same to you, when I drop you off at your car, I'd like you to follow me to the house. No one will harass you there and I know Mother will be comforted by your company."

"I can't, Duncan. I have to get back. Even if I didn't, my hiding out at your place wouldn't improve the gossip mill. Tell your mother I'll be in touch with her tomorrow. Maybe we'll know more by then."

"You're probably right," he said pulling alongside her truck. "God, it's not even eleven and I'm ready for a drink myself."

Since she knew exactly what he meant, she could only say, "Take care."

Emerging from the sports car, she heard the reporters closing in behind her. She barely got her door locked when they were at her window and, when they refused to get out of the way, she had to drive up on the curb and onto a neighbor's lawn to avoid hitting someone. Duncan had already vanished down Broadway.

On the bright side, she noticed Jack's truck was gone. She hoped it was a sign that he wouldn't be held. Or could it be that Stevens had given instructions to have his vehicle impounded?

"Stop," she moaned.

From fighting her own negativity, she moved on to worrying about being followed. Driving with her attention split between the rearview mirror and the road, she was slow in spotting a teenager in a souped-up pickup who ran a red light and cut her off. Braking hard, everything in the cab went flying, the clipboard and pencils on the seat, her bottle of water...and then something hit her heel. Since it didn't hurt and her light was still green, she continued forward, but she leaned over to push the thing back under the seat. Feeling a packet of some kind, she couldn't help but glance down.

Her foot slipped off the accelerator. Where had that come from?

Straightening, she saw she'd now become a traffic hazard, and all around cars honked as she veered out of her lane. Knowing she would have no peace until she discovered what it was, she turned right into the lot of a shopping center, making sure none of the media spotted her.

Once again she reached for the packet. It was letter-size, a brown mailing envelope about an inch thick. In the address area was scrawled a hasty "Bay." A clip held it shut.

Bending the prongs on the clasp, she opened the envelope and looked inside. She saw some folded papers that reminded her of those she'd seen Holly stuffing into her purse yesterday. There was also a stack of other documents. The whole thing was held together by a rubber band and what appeared to be a handwritten note on yellow-lined paper was stuck on top.

Dear God, she thought, now she knew why Holly had wanted her to get invited for lunch, and why she directed her to get Elvin away from the front of the house.

Convinced the material was damaging, or worse, she knew better than to try to read any of it in public. Her heart pounding, she set the envelope on the seat beside her and drove back onto Broadway.

What to do and where to go? She had two blocks to settle the debate. To return to the shop would cost her time; there would be little privacy until this afternoon, and too many people might see her put the envelope in the RV. She could leave it in the truck, but decided that option was unacceptable.

She phoned Mike and apologized for the delay in getting back to the shop, gave him a brief and vague rundown of the growing seriousness of the situation, then asked if she could keep the truck for the rest of the day. To her relief he assured her there was no problem and wished her luck. Luck... Holly was dead, Jack was gone and she could only guess what kind of a time bomb was on the seat beside her. She wasn't feeling all that lucky, but she did know, however, where she could feel protected.

Hurrying around the Loop, she drove to Jack's ranch. Common sense told her that he would have called her if he'd gotten out; nevertheless, she was hoping she would see him as she pulled into the driveway. Simon and Bud coming out of the trailer was a decent consolation. A glance at her clock reminded her that it was now noon.

"You're early today, miss."

"I'm sorry to interrupt your private time, Simon. There's been bad news." Bay reached outside to reassure Bud by scratching his broad head the way Jack had taught her. "You haven't by chance heard from Jack?"

"No. Didn't expect to until this evening. What's happened?"

"The young woman he went to see yesterday? She's dead, and the police have taken him in for questioning." She explained why and assured Simon, "I don't think there's any way they can keep him, but..."

Simon immediately took over. Motioning her to wait a moment, he disappeared around the back of the house, and shortly the garage door started rising.

"Park in here and stay inside," he told her. "I'll be close until we hear from Jack. Lock the back door. I have a key if there's an emergency."

"Try real hard not to scare me, Simon."

"Jack's orders, miss. You see me out there with the shotgun, you don't worry. Just let me know what you hear."

Thanking him, she did as directed and closed up behind herself. Once inside, she went to the double French doors and locked them. It was reassuring to be here, surrounded by Jack's presence, but she knew she wouldn't know real peace until he returned. To keep herself preoccupied, she settled at the dinette table and finally pulled everything out of the envelope.

Holly's note was written in red ink, her penmanship as neat and flowing as anyone would expect from seeing her. How could that lovely creature be gone? Glenn and Holly both dead. With burning eyes, she read...

> Bay, by the time you find this, I'll be out of reach. My job is done, the rest is up to you and Jack Burke, if he's who you claim he is.
>
> This is by no means all of the existing evidence. The lie that is Mission of Mercy, Martin Davis, and most especially, the Ridgeways, goes back to Glenn's death; I'm convinced of that. But while I long had my suspicions that something was wrong, saw that our receivables were growing in increments not supported by our membership, it wasn't until two years ago that I succeeded in locating proof. If you find trustworthy legal assistance, get hold of Madeleine's laptop fast. There you'll discover all of the files and codes. Those codes will explain where the exorbitant funds really came from—and how they are dispersed. The codes are also used to identify fictitious account names that were a guise to make the receivables look legitimate. As well, there is an accounting of payments to the principles.
>
> Madeleine's downfall in the end—aside from her inability to forget or get over the guilt of you—is her insistence to know the full scope of

her power in a few clicks of a keyboard. If the laptop vanishes, there must be diskettes in a safety vault somewhere.

As for those principles, you'll note those lists are incomplete. This has been the most painstaking and dangerous process for me and I'm still building as I write this. No doubt you will be shocked at some of the more prominent names. But even I can't prepare you for the blow that will come from seeing three others.

I can't stress enough, choose your confidants with care. The city's leadership is contaminated and I can't tell you how deeply it goes. To be safe, seek guidance from the outside.

In the end, you'll wonder why I didn't do more, and sooner. The answer is simple and complex. I was afraid, I grew confused, I dwelt too long in the safety zone of denial. Through it all, the mystery behind Glenn's death remains that—a mystery—but I know he must have somehow, inadvertently, become aware of at least a portion of this, and that one of the three names cited in your own court files is, indeed, his murderer. Understand that Glenn's killer remains free. Beware.

In the end, this is small compensation for the injustice leveled upon you. Bring them down, Bay. Bring down those who pretend to this day to be your greatest supporters.

And forgive me for the wasted years and the doubt. H.K.

Bay's hands shook as she set aside the letter and began paging through the computer printouts. She lost count of the dollar value after the third page, but it was nothing compared to names on the final series of documents.

She clapped her hands to her mouth. There they were...Basque, Tarpley and Martel. Bought and paid for by Madeleine and company.

Bay almost crumbled under the knowledge that she hadn't been released under ethical means. The only thing that kept her going was more names...Lyle Gessler...Elvin Capps...Lieutenant Ed Gage...she noted several politicians, the chief of police and a district judge. Yes, the very judge who had presided over her case and eventually reversed the verdict.

"Swine," she seethed. "The lot of you feeding on anything and everyone for—"

The buzzing of her phone startled her. She snatched it up off the table.

"Yes?"

"Where are you?" Jack demanded.

"At your house."

"I'll be there in ten minutes."

He made it in seven. Bay opened the garage door and signaled Simon. When they saw Jack pulling in, Simon simply said to her, "Tell him he can come tell me about it when he's rested," and left them to their privacy.

Bud hung around for a minute to soak up some attention. Ever eager for a run and some adventure, though, he soon went bounding off after Simon.

Bay hit the garage door button. Before it was half-way down, Jack grabbed her.

''Don't you ever scare me like that again,'' he muttered near her ear.

''When did I do that?''

''Coming between me and Ridgeway.''

''If I hadn't, he would have had assault charges filed before Stevens finished interrogating you downtown. What happened there?''

''More fishing. He knew he didn't have anything. Unfortunately, Gage heard about it and gave me another royal ass chewing. If he thought he could get away with it, he'd cut me loose. Instead I'm suspended for the rest of the week.''

Bay was grateful to be able to give him some encouragement. ''He won't be doing that much longer.'' Her arm around his waist, she coaxed him into the house.

''Why, is he moving up north to hang with Martel?''

''That's not the wildest scenario. He's on the same payroll.''

Jack stopped. ''What have you found out?''

''The reason Holly needed my help on Sunday. It wasn't just to cover her as she took some last pages of evidence. She needed the time to hide the whole package in my truck.''

His expression went from euphoric to murderous. ''It damn well better be incriminating.''

''Come and see.'' She led him to the table where she had everything organized. Before long, he had to sit down.

"This is why she had to go, too. They knew she had something on them. Reckless kid. If only she would have trusted you sooner."

"She was afraid I was duped by Madeleine. I can't blame her. In the beginning I was."

"Who wouldn't be with that kind of display of power and cash?" Jack shook his head at the lists. "So Martel and Tarpley were paid to lie. Damn… Tarpley's still being paid."

Bay read what he'd just seen. "What do you think that's about, hush money or a retainer for more dirty work?"

"Either way he's dirty. He's also a liability for them. I wonder if they realize that his kind is a no-win investment? Hold it…Gage?" Jack laughed without humor. "Now I realize what you meant. I should have known…and the chief and your judge…there's your release."

"Do you think they know I'm really innocent?"

"They're scum. They don't get a vote."

"I want their admission. When this goes public, people will wonder. The media will stir up the whole mess anew pointing fingers at the threat on the streets. One of those fingers will be directed at me."

"Not more than once."

As sweet as it was that he would defend her with brains or brawn, Bay wasn't amused. "This has to end, Jack. After the last several years, people's trust and faith have been through enough of an ordeal."

He drew her onto his lap and rocked her, but she knew he was trying to soothe himself at the same time.

"You're right. Striking back is a lousy habit to get into. We'll focus on getting this into the proper hands the way Holly said."

"Any ideas?"

"The FBI sounds like a good start."

35

Thursday, June 20, 2001

"Ashes to ashes...dust to dust. We will miss our sister, but we will see her again and embrace in joy."

Bay sat near the rear of the church as Martin Davis concluded his sermon. Although asked to sit up front with the Ridgeways and Holly's parents, she knew she couldn't.

On the altar table was a brass urn and a single color portrait of Holly framed by matching sprays of vibrant red gladiolas. In front of the urn her parents had laid two white Tyler roses grown only a half-dozen miles from where she and they had lived. Bay had heard from Duncan that his mother hadn't been happy with the simplicity of the setting. Sounding unusually bitter, he'd said he was relieved that at least she hadn't brought in camera crews to turn this into a docudrama.

A single violinist began playing and Holly's parents rose and exited through the side door, followed by Madeleine, Duncan and the Davises. Then everyone else started out through the rear exits. Bay kept her seat to wait out the crowd, in no hurry for what she suspected would be the most embarrassing part of this ordeal. She might as well have gone though, because some of the dialogue she overhead was equally embarrassing.

"Hey, I haven't seen you in ages. You look great."

"Lost seventeen pounds. I'll loan you the book."

"Can't we leave now, Mom? I'm starving."

"Daddy needs us to do this for him. We'll go to Chili's right after."

"Bless her heart, it was a terrible way to go, but this is no surprise. I can think of three or four people myself who could have done it. But you watch, they're going to announce a new building and name it after her."

It turned out to be not a building but a garden-park area at the northeast part of the property. At the patio where the KWRD staff ate lunch and took breaks, Madeleine had a display complete with an artist's ink-and-watercolor rendition on an easel, more flowers and huge baskets of teddy bears to give to the children attending. The plans showed a gated area monitored by security so parents could be assured of the safety of their children, an environmentally friendly play-ground, picnic area and jogging track all arranged around a duck pond.

"It will be called Holly's Haven," Madeleine announced to polite applause.

Two mothers up front pushed their children forward to accept bears from Holly's mother. While Martin stepped forward to thank Madeleine, Odessa took charge of Holly's relations, escorting them to

Madeleine's car now parked yards beyond the patio. Bay would have left herself, but Duncan stopped her.

Grasping her hands, he kissed her on both cheeks. "You've been such a stranger, I've missed you."

"It's a difficult time. What with the investigation and this, I didn't think you needed any more company."

The official word had come on Tuesday that Holly had been forcibly drowned. Ever since the case was given news priority, there were reporters posted regularly outside the church property and at the Kirkland house. Once again Madeleine had somehow managed to keep reporters from becoming a nuisance at the estate, but how long she would succeed was questionable. For the first time that Bay could remember the pressure seemed to be wearing on her and Duncan. Despite their groomed appearance, impeccable manners and gracious smiles, they both looked as though neither had slept all week. Then again, she and Jack weren't faring much better.

As word leaked out that an official investigation would be underway, Jack reluctantly banished Bay from the ranch. They were keeping in touch by phone, but Jack even built restrictions around that. He wouldn't say anything relevant to the case if either of them were using the wireless phones due to their unreliable privacy. That meant the only time they really got to speak was late at night, and then she had to take the call in the shop break room.

"You're not company, Bay." Duncan gave her hands a reassuring squeeze. "Come over to the house now. We're having a little buffet for the Kirklands before they leave for the airport."

"How can they leave?" Concerned that she'd exposed too much dismay and not just through her voice, she gently extricated her hands and sought to refine the slip. "I mean, surely the police need them for background data and such, and then there's the house to deal with." Personally, Bay hoped they would be here to see Holly's brave work cited by the authorities.

"Well, they would have, but they don't have a lot of choices. We've been keeping this quiet, honey—Mrs. Kirkland has to undergo cancer surgery next Monday."

"How awful." Bay clasped her throat, aching for the family. "What they've endured. No, Duncan, I couldn't possibly come over, not knowing that. They don't need the added stress. Why, I don't know if they've accepted my being released."

"Don't worry, Mother explained it to them."

It was all Bay could do not to groan. "Doesn't she realize all she did was make Glenn, the man who would have been their future brother-in-law, look unworthy of their daughter?"

"He blundered and paid for it with his life. They're Christians, Bay, they can forgive that."

Bay didn't know if she could listen to this. "I wish she would have spared them at least that." She wondered if Madeleine didn't see this as getting another subtle lash at Holly. The more she was learning about the woman, the greater seemed Madeleine's capacity for treachery under the guise of benevolence.

"Well, it's too late to debate that now. Listen, if you're not coming, I'd better ask you something Mother would have addressed if she'd managed a moment alone with you. One of the brass wires on the gate has been tampered with. We think it was done back on Tuesday by some tabloid freelancer who got into an altercation with Elvin. The obnoxious wretch was annoyed that we wouldn't give him an interview. Imagine. Anyway, you know Mother and her eagle eye. Could you come by as soon as possible and repair it?"

"I'll do it tomorrow morning. I have some extra wire exactly for that reason."

"Thank you. It'll be one less thing to keep Ms. Perfectionist from pacing in her office night after night."

"I noticed she looks less resilient than usual. Detective Stevens isn't giving you and Elvin too much trouble, is he?"

"He hasn't helped her nerves any. He's been to the house twice. Good Lord, Elvin even has a witness, that same nosy woman who fingered Jack Burke. She confirmed she saw and heard Elvin Monday morning trying to get Holly's attention, ringing the doorbell, pounding on the windows. And by the time I arrived there was already one patrol car on the scene."

Bay wondered if he was missing the point or being disingenuous. "I suppose Stevens is more interested in alibis specifically around the time of her death. On the news, I heard the medical examiner says it happened between nine and ten o'clock Sunday night."

"I heard Mother going over her week's itinerary

with Elvin in her office as I went up to my room. Lulu was coming downstairs after having turned down Mother's bed and switched on some lights because Mother hates walking into a dark room.'' A rare spasm of anger darkened Duncan's handsome features. ''Damn it, I happen to know Jack Burke doesn't have any alibi. He claims he was in bed asleep.''

Duncan was right, that wasn't the truth, although Jack insisted to Bay it was the story he would be sticking to. He hadn't been asleep, he'd been making love to her. It had been their first night together in some days and the combination of abstinence, euphoria over the new evidence they had and his agitation at Holly for endangering her had triggered a deeper, untiring passion in him.

''I have to admit, Bay, I worry for you, too, with that man running the streets free. Are you sure you're all right over there at Martel's?''

This time Bay was grateful to have her thoughts pulled back to the present. It wasn't merely the blazing sun that was threatening to make her hyperventilate. ''Of course. I'm fine, Duncan.''

''Has Stevens been to see you?''

''He stopped by yesterday basically asking the same things he did on Monday.'' What she wouldn't share was that he talked to Mike about Nick and then to her again about the assault.

''And Burke? I appreciate you've found it in your heart not to hate him, but I hope you're being prudent and telling him to keep his distance?''

''I haven't seen Jack,'' she said truthfully. ''It appears he's being the prudent one.'' Summoning a small smile, Bay touched the sleeve of Duncan's black suit. The tailoring was so exquisite he looked like a prince...what a tragedy that he was a dark prince. "I really have to go. Mike lent me his car so I wouldn't be humiliated by driving the truck. In return I have to finish a project for him this afternoon. See you."

"Tomorrow. I should be around most of the morning."

Bay hurried off—or as fast as her black, strappy high heels allowed—before he could suggest lunch or something else. Many of the memorial attendees had already left, which was a relief. Unfortunately, the media continued to hang around. The police had run them off church property, but she knew their long-distance lenses could count her eyelashes. Belatedly she worried that they would be checking out the license plates on the black SUV and start bothering Mike. If that happened, she would quit and leave rather than subject him and his family to any of this ordeal.

The vehicle's windows were slightly tinted, but Bay slipped on sunglasses as she nodded her thanks to the uniformed officer and sped by the media. She then took a convoluted route to the shop to be sure she didn't make it too easy for any of them.

Good-natured whistles welcomed her as she entered the noisy shop. She waved at the older guys and rolled her eyes at the youngest. They were a decent group who, after she'd proved herself, accepted her as one of them.

Intent on changing before she returned Mike's key, she was stopped by his baritone, "Butler!"

Backtracking, Bay entered his office and was struck by the rush of hot air coming from the pedestal fan behind his desk. He was on the phone, but he leaned forward to push a small brown envelope at her.

Covering the mouthpiece with his hand he said, "Mailman just brought that for you. Sending yourself Valentines?"

Even as she reached for it, Bay felt her heart in her throat. She recognized that red pen and enviable handwriting. It didn't matter that both the send to and return addresses had her name on them care of Martel's, the envelope was from Holly.

But how? This was Thursday and—with less than steady hands she picked up the envelope and checked the cancellation stamp—it had been run through the system on Monday. How could a first-class envelope take four days to go a maximum of eight miles across the same town? Then she saw it. The zip code was off by one digit. That would have been enough to throw it into the wrong bin and direct it to the incorrect delivery station, causing another day or two delay.

Mike hung up. "Hey, I was kidding. Bad timing, though, huh?"

"Uh…no, that's fine. I'd just forgotten this, that's all."

"Was it rough? The service, I mean?"

"Awkward. I don't think a lot of those people are into cremation."

"Works okay for me." Mike pointed to the envelope with his pencil. ''You know most of us with drafting class backgrounds print pretty good, but our script sucks. I'm impressed.'' Before she could reply he continued, ''That was the bakery on the phone just now. Hint-hint?''

''Uh-huh...oh!'' Bay backed out of the door. ''I'll only be a minute. I'll tell Mackie to load up in the meantime.''

''He's loaded, he's loaded. The flatbed's ready at the side dock.''

What timing, Bay thought hurrying through the shop to the RV. She couldn't possibly take the time to inspect the contents of the envelope right now, but how she wanted to.

The next several hours would have driven her crazy if the job hadn't demanded her complete focus. Fortunately, Mackie was as intuitive as he was talented and he helped things go fairly smoothly by anticipating what tools she would need and when. Nevertheless, it was past seven that evening when they returned to the shop. It was locked up tight and the only vehicles out front were the blue wreck and Mackie's restored Ford pickup.

''You go on and take off,'' Bay told him as he parked the flatbed truck back at the side of the building, next to the big used truck Mike had purchased at an auction. ''You got that tank and everything loaded, the least I can do is unload our tools.''

''Sure you don't mind?'' The young newlywed looked hopeful. ''I'd stay, but if I hurry, I'll just have time to shower and get Rhnea to our second childbirth class.''

''Shoot, why didn't you say so? Git, boyo.'' As he tossed her the keys and bolted out of the truck, Bay called after him, ''You remember to breathe, too!''

There wasn't much to unload, even though the main item was one of those full-size gang boxes that would crush a person if it ever toppled over. But once she got the overhead doors opened, Bay used the electric hoist to lift the heavy thing onto the dock, then rolled it to its workstation.

Within ten minutes she had the place locked down and the alarms set. Buying herself a pair of sodas from the machine in the break room, she ran to the RV. She did take the time to swallow half of one drink to offset her thirst and weakness. It had been 120 degrees up near the ceiling of the bakery, the humidity almost creating rain, and even though she'd ingested plenty of water during the day, she remained dehydrated and dangerously depleted of nutrients.

But she didn't take time to get out of her sweat-soaked clothes. Yanking open the refrigerator, she tugged open the vegetable bin and exhaled in relief at finding the aluminum-foil-wrapped package tucked behind a head of lettuce and a bag of carrots. Ripping off the double wrapping of foil, she dropped down onto the camel-brown leather bench at the dinette table and tore at the envelope. This one had been securely fastened, tape added to keep anyone from toying with the opening. She shook the envelope and out fell a small leather-bound book, and another yellow sheet of lined paper. The book looked like a diary, but she unfolded the note first.

> Bay, it's over an hour since Jack paid me a visit and I've been thinking ever since. He's made me realize a few words of apology aren't enough for my part in making your life hell. Under different circumstances, we should have been friends...if Glenn had lived, if I hadn't been so jealous of you and his awe for your talent. Maybe the enclosed will make up in part for that. I realize now that if I'm putting it all behind me, I don't need this any longer, while it could assist you and the authorities in building your case. At the least, it'll clear up a few mysteries for you regarding the hang-up calls you've received, and my malicious attempt to gaslight you. My only excuse is that I thought you had struck a deal with the Ridgeways over Glenn's grave.

Bay slumped back against the seat. Not Elvin, but Holly had been the one trying to spook her. No wonder things had quieted so quickly once Holly started to have doubts about any collusion. If she hadn't been preoccupied with so many other things, she could have figured that out.

> I'd better change out of my bathing suit and get this to the box outside the post office. If I wait until morning, I may chicken out and burn it instead. Know that I'm ashamed of many en-

tries, but hopefully the added data will offset that. Goodbye—H.K.

The shrill buzzing of her cellular phone in the deathly silence won a brief, "Jeez," from her as a cold hand locked around her heart. Then she added injury to insult and overreached, sending the phone skittering off the table. Grappling under the seats in a unit that was lit by a mere forty-watt bulb by the fixture beside the table, she had to listen to four more rings before she managed to find and answer the thing.

"Yes?"

"Why are you breathless?"

Bay shifted from her knees to her butt and let her head drop back against the refrigerator. "My phone was making like a mouse under the table. What are you doing on this line? You're supposed to call me on the shop phone."

"I have been for the last ten minutes," Jack replied.

"Sorry, sorry." She sighed willing her whole being to downshift two gears. "I honestly didn't hear it. Let me get over to the other phone and I'll call you back."

"No, tell me what's wrong?"

"Not much aside from attending Holly's service this morning and trying to do the psychological gymnastics of accepting that a stunning woman could be turned into ash and a few bone fragments. Then spending the rest of the day in a survivable version of an oven, only to come back here to a visit from a ghost."

After a slight pause, Jack said, "Baby, I know it's been hard, but you can't go emotional now."

"Who's emotional? She sent me her diary."

"You have thirty seconds to get to the other phone."

36

Moments ago in the isolation of his bedroom, Jack had been willing to make a deal with the God that, up until a month ago, he'd about lost faith in. He'd been calling Bay since minutes after five and had a new appreciation for how many seconds were in a minute, how many minutes in an hour. He remembered that she had that project at the bakery, that she'd warned him things could get hairy, that a six-hour job could easily become sixteen or twenty. "Think of all the stories production crews tell about movie making," she'd joked, "and how you wait nine hours to shoot ninety seconds."

None of that computed. Jack had gotten to the point where all he wanted was to hear Bay's voice and know she was all right...and now he had. But no sooner did he hang up than he picked up the phone and redialed.

"You can't count."

He loved that voice that was at once soft and deceptive. He loved that she could find the wit to take the edge off her sharper or worn emotions. He wished for their lives to be so tranquil that right now they could be having phone sex as foreplay to the real thing. But he had sent her a verbal hug and she'd blinded him with a right hook.

"You aren't easy on a guy's heart. You have Holly's diary?"

"I'll save the wrapping, although it's suffering from my less than patient handling once I recognized her handwriting. Jack, she put my address in the return box, too. It's eerie. I know she was thinking she'd hand the house over to a Realtor and zip off to start sipping champagne or boilermakers someplace more exotic, but it gives me chills."

He needed to get her away from that mind-set fast. "What's inside?"

"Hey, I was serious. I just got here and finished her note when you called." She gave him a recap of what it contained.

Jack's insides did an amusement park tour thinking of the field day the Ridgeways' defense attorney—more likely attorneys—would have profiling the kind of unbalanced person who would stalk a dead lover's former friend and partner. Thank goodness they had the documents off Madeleine's computer. They better damned well get the computer itself, though.

To her he said, "Another mystery resolved."

"Don't tiptoe around my feelings. Say what you think."

"I can't. You'd never let me within a hemisphere of you again. That diary better have something useful to us or I'm going to tell you to come out here and accidentally trip and drop it in the burning barrel."

"Are you wanting some bedtime reading?"

"Hell, yes, but not that kind. I miss you, Bay."

"Jack. Did—are you holding back new bad news?"

He rubbed at his face hard enough to scrub off two layers of skin. That admission had been her cue to tell him she'd missed him, too. No, goddamn it, he wanted *the* words, the ones he'd said to her, the ones he didn't deserve hearing back, but continued hoping against hope that someday he might—even if out of gratitude.

"Same old, same old here. I keep getting a recording at the FBI office on Golden, and until they do a litmus test on everyone here, I'm not handing over anything to anyone. Screw Gage's threats, too. Tomorrow I'm driving to the Bureau's Dallas office and asking for help there. Ignore my mutterings. Read."

"You sound tired and you'll need rest for tomorrow. I'll browse starting from the back...her last entry is last Saturday—'Everything is set to pass on. If she isn't there tomorrow, I've decided to mail it to her. A gamble but I have to leave. I feel them gauging and weighing. Eventually, they'll decide there's less risk in silencing me permanently. I don't know if Bay is the right one to take this the next step.'

"Well, that makes two of us," Bay muttered.

"You're doing fine."

"She didn't make an entry every day. Why, that SOB...Jack, the choir director copped a feel at the copier machine. He can't be my age and has six kids."

"There you go. His wife probably beats him off with wet diapers."

"Behave. This is too painful. Her mother doesn't

understand why she's not married yet, while it's left to her father to tell her about her mother's cancer. He's worried they'll run out of money.''

''Like she didn't have enough pressure.''

''Yeah.'' Bay sighed and seconds later sucked in a sharp breath. ''Why this is terrific, she's collected addresses.''

''Whose?''

''Give me a second,'' she replied slowly, as though trying to decipher something. ''There aren't any names. Wait...jeez, I am beat, I thought the initials at the bottom were states, but listen. '33 Mamou Lane, Effie, Louisiana.' And there's a G.T. at the end. That has to be Catfish. Where's Effie?''

''Forget it. Somewhere they don't pave roads, I'm sure. So rural the mail carrier needs a machete to cut the Spanish moss on his monthly trip to deliver the government checks.''

''It can't be too far...or bad. Remember how often she listed outlays of cash in those documents she gave us? He must come to pick them up.''

''More likely Elvin drops a shopping sack over at State Park. Take it from me, he and the crawfish probably cohabit. Why do you think Madeleine needed Martel to pull off your release? Who else does she have listed there?''

''There's a few Houston addresses...some dude who can only be contacted at the front desk at a Corpus Christi hotel....''

''Okay, that's it. Close the book.''

''What did I say?''

"Tomorrow, I want you to meet me out front and hand that thing over."

"You're going to Dallas."

"Well, I don't want you knowing more than you need to about something that's a no-win situation. Listen to me—burn that envelope with your address on it, and the letter. I'll destroy Holly's letter to you that I have."

"Don't you dare. We need that to show her clear thinking and conscience."

"It identifies you as the person she'd entrusted all of her information to."

"So what else is new?"

"Understanding the people Madeleine and Davis have hooked up with. You're thinking this is simple, white-collar money laundering where silencing someone is an occasional necessity, but frowned upon because it attracts attention. Wrong. These fools have themselves neck-deep with a drug cartel."

37

Friday, June 21, 2001
10:12 a.m.

The damage done to the Ridgeway gate was going to take Bay the rest of the morning and into the afternoon to repair. She wasn't thrilled about being out in this grilling sun, but was glad she'd warned Mike of the possible length of the job. Actually, the solitude would do her good; the fewer people she had to deal with today, the better.

Her heart was aching and her head throbbed. It was Jack who got credit for this, though. He'd become like a plastic bag over the head with his orders and refusal to listen, treating her as though she were behaving more erratically than Holly. She wouldn't blame him if he never forgave her for hanging up on him. It had been the hardest thing to listen to the phone ringing, and this time returning to the RV hadn't allowed her to block out the sound.

Elvin shuffled up the driveway mopping at his brow. "Mrs. R. says it's too hot for you to work. She thinks you should come back this evening when it's cooler.''

On another day maybe Bay might have been able to shrug this off, pack up and haul ass. The customer paid, was a good motto for situations like this when a client didn't know what they wanted. Besides, Bay no longer thought anything that Madeleine suggested was for her welfare alone. Today, however, she felt a resolve settle in her.

''Well, you tell Madeleine that I'm here now. I may not be available later, and I respect her *eye for perfection* above any concern for a little sweat.'' Then she drawled, ''Shoot, Elvin, chill out. If she was all that worried, she would have you out here holding an umbrella over me.''

She couldn't be positive, but she thought she heard him say, ''Bitch,'' as he shuffled back to the house.

Of Duncan she saw nothing. That was better yet. Reading Holly's diary until her eyes burned had allowed her to see that at one time Duncan had given her hope of a new love. It was Madeleine who hadn't approved, Madeleine who kept sending him off on new missions, and it wasn't necessarily true that distance made the heart grow fonder. Holly lost respect for her and Duncan, but Bay couldn't see he had experienced any great emotion one way or another.

Removing the defaced brass went quickly. It helped that it was at a level where she didn't need a ladder. However, as she drank from a bottle of cool water, she knew the new wrapping would be hell in this heat, especially since she couldn't wear gloves. Common sense told her to accept when she was wrong and come back this evening the way Madeleine wanted. Elvin wasn't going to get the pleasure out of knowing that, though.

Starting down the driveway to tell him a necessary tool had broken, she had to jump out of the way as a white BMW with a black convertible roof swept by her. Rubbing her twisted knee, she was slow to look up again, and yet when she did, her gaze locked directly on the license plates.

Louisiana.

"Merry Christmas," she murmured.

Instead of going to talk to Elvin, she hobbled to the truck to use one of the water bottles and hold it against her knee. She didn't really need it, except that it allowed her to sit on the edge of the passenger door floorboard and watch what was going on from under her eyelashes.

The man who emerged from the coupe was no sleaze. A tall, slim black dressed with casual elegance in a white linen jacket over pleated, silvery-gray slacks and a whiter silk shirt, he strolled over to Elvin as though he had all the time in the world. The two exchanged a few words Bay couldn't hear and Elvin led him inside.

Catfish? Somehow she doubted it.

Bay packed and thought about hobbling down to the house herself when the bald-headed young man with the diamond studs in both ears reemerged. This time he was carrying an attaché case.

An icy chill ran down her back, and a different kind of déjà vu feeling brought a metallic taste to her mouth. She knew with a certainty above everything else that this had been Glenn's sin. He had seen something all right.

It came back to her with an overpowering rush, his increasing irritability about the Ridgeway account, his talk of getting Holly into a different job once they were married. My God, she thought, he was trying to figure out a way to tell me without getting all three of us in trouble.

Sensing that neither man was paying much attention to her, Bay climbed into her truck. Her mind was racing as though driven by some other force as she eased around and out the service entrance, then down the street to Broadway. There she hesitated.

Which way will he go?

Her gut said I-20 and she turned right up Broadway. When she got near the intersection of the Loop, she pulled into the same parking lot she'd used the other day and circled around to prepare to exit again. The noon rush was in full swing and keeping tabs of any vehicle was iffy. Fully expecting to lose him, she scribbled down his license number. At least she would have something to add to Holly's notes. Maybe the guy was already in there, but now she was a witness to his activity, too. No one could claim now that Holly was an embittered, hallucinating drunk.

About to cut her losses, she saw the BMW glide by. Those gold, spoked hubcaps were a real ego trip, she thought…and would make following him so easy.

She sent up a silent *thank you* for the impulse that made her fill up the gas tank this morning rather than to wait until later. Her challenge for the moment would be to keep up with Mr. Slick. The truck had over a hundred thousand miles on her and that BMW looked fresh off the showroom floor. No contest. If Slick was in a hurry, she would be wasting her time. Her gut said she had to try.

Staying a good three cars back as she'd watched Jack do, Bay didn't try to do any phone calling until she was outside of town and had I-20 in sight. First she rang Mike.

"Don't ask me to explain, but I'm not at the Ridgeways and I may not be back until late tonight. If anyone from there calls for me, tell them I'm lying down with an ice pack on my knee."

"You're hurt?" Mike asked.

"No, but they need to think that."

"Should I be worrying about you, kiddo?"

"Maybe just wish me luck. You've been terrific, Mike. Later."

She disconnected even as he tried to interject another question and quickly triggered her memory dial for the estate. "Madeleine...Bay."

"Darling, Elvin said you left without a word."

"I should have taken his advice early on and quit while I was ahead. Your guest in the pretty car sent me stumbling and I've sprained my knee."

"That's terrible. Are you going to a doctor? Is there something I can do? You must send me the bill, of course."

"That's sweet, but I think it's more uncomfortable than serious. Be patient with me? I have the damaged brass off of the affected lances, the problem is I won't be able to replace them today. Will it be all right if I give it a shot tomorrow?"

"You don't even need to ask. Wait—tomorrow is Saturday. I can't, in good conscience, ask you to give up your weekend."

"Why not? It's not as though I'm going dancing, is it?"

Madeleine chuckled. "I wish others had your sense of humor, and your work ethic. I do so miss our chats. If you're feeling better why don't you come to lunch Sunday? Duncan will pout, but I'll sit you beside me. We do need to talk about your part in the Haven's design."

She couldn't fathom how the woman could refer to Holly without stumbling over her words. "You mean you've changed your mind about the front entrance piece?"

"Not at all. I have great plans for you. Here's my massage therapist, I'd better not keep him. Call me tomorrow, darling."

"Great plans," Bay muttered as she disconnected. "I believe it."

She took a minute to complete her drive up the entrance ramp to the interstate and to regain ground on the BMW. Now she had to deal with eighteen-wheelers and she couldn't afford to let too many of them between her and the car. Once comfortable with her position, she made her most difficult call. Instead of signaling his pager, she dialed the house.

At the end of the message and the sound of the tone, she began, "Jack, it's me. Look, I don't want you to get upset, I'm on my way to Louisiana. I know it's nuts, but there was a guy at the estate a while ago with Louisiana plates. It's a BMW, white with those gold-spoked wheels.'' She recited the plate number and described the guy. ''I don't think this is Tarpley, but listen to this. He went in empty-handed and came out with an attaché case. I think it's important to see where this leads.'' Static began to compromise her signal. ''I'm about to lose my connection. I'll try to check in later.''

The display showed she no longer had a connection and she didn't know how much of what she'd said made it through. Coming upon an eighteen-wheeler, she signaled another pass. Seconds later she spotted the BMW being stopped by a state trooper.

38

I-20 Eastbound
2:33 p.m.

Seven more miles and he would be at the Tyler, Highway 69 exit. Jack rolled his shoulders feeling the stress-of-the-day knot there. He wanted a hot shower and a Scotch, but not as much as he wanted to hear Bay's voice. He'd had no luck in getting through to her phone. It didn't make sense; he should have a clear signal at this point.

He hated the way things had ended between them last night, though he'd be damned before denying he wanted her out of this, and out of Tyler. His so-so reception in Dallas made him resolute. Until they got some commitment from the Bureau, some decisive and positive news, he had to work this as though they were on their own and that meant Bay was going to be moved out of the line of fire.

It struck him that she might be having the same problem with her phone and he called the house to retrieve any messages on his machine. After two marketing calls, and one terse, but unsurprising check-in from Stevens, he heard her voice.

"Jack, it's me..."

The smile that began to spread over his face quickly died as he listened in disbelief and abject horror. She was going where after whom? How could she do something so reckless? The guy she'd described probably had a small arsenal in that vehicle, while she didn't have so much as a water pistol.

"Christ." He slammed the steering wheel with his palm.

His machine reported her call came in about ninety minutes ago. Things were going from bad to worse. Ninety minutes on a highway where people could drive seventy and odds were Mr. Diamond Studs was forcing her to do closer to eighty. She wasn't racing into a spider's web, she was missile launching herself through it and straight toward catastrophe.

Jack struck the wheel again. Then he began praying.

39

South of Alexandria, Louisiana
4:37 p.m.

''Behave, damn it.''

Bay found herself holding her breath until the guy in the BMW cleared the intersection without attracting the attention of a parish police car. They were no longer on I-20, having turned south at Shreveport onto I-49. Now just beyond Alexandria, Slick didn't show the slightest interest in slowing down.

''You drive like a timber hauler getting paid by the load,'' she grumbled. ''Haven't learned one thing from that ticket, have you?''

Talking to herself was becoming her way of dealing with her growing hunger, as well as the stress. She'd really thought the game was over back in Texas, convinced that trooper would take one look at the car, run a license check and start calling for backup to peel that BMW like a banana. The cops on this road were tough and even Mike said he never failed to see a car or truck being checked. When she'd exited outside Longview, she'd been sure she'd seen the last of him and could use the overpass there to head back to Tyler. To her amazement, not a minute later the dude was zipping under the overpass, on his way again. She figured it was her luck that both Slick and the cop had been LSU or UT grads lettering in basketball. The trooper had probably high-fived the guy and sent him on his way with just a caution.

Bay massaged the kinks in her neck. Between Slick's NASCAR driving technique and not hearing from Jack, her spine was turning into a chiropractor's dream. Just to give herself something to do besides worry, she tried her phone again, but couldn't get so much as a single blip on the display panel. Of course, she hadn't seen any microwave towers lately, either.

"And if we don't come to Effie or wherever soon, I'm going to be forced to give up on this joyride out of necessity."

The red indicator bar sliding toward E on her fuel tank gauge made that the likely outcome. Naturally, gas stations would be few and far between on this side of the city.

"What do you have in that white leopard you're driving?" she asked the man ahead of her. "An extra fuel tank in the trunk?"

Tossing the phone on the seat beside her, she almost missed seeing the sign.

"Ha! Effie, two miles."

Now all she needed was for Effie to be situated on the highway and not located some sixteen miles back in the woods. Something else had her insides writhing: either Slick *was* Catfish after all, or he knew him.

She soon discovered that Effie wasn't directly on

the highway as she'd hoped, but the tiny, two-traffic-light community wasn't far off the main road. And when Slick pulled up to the side of a ramshackle general store at the second light, Bay almost clipped a teetering senior citizen as she ducked into a gas station/convenience store at the first intersection.

The pumps were slightly receded from the other buildings in town and that proved as much a liability as an asset. Bay had to peer around an abandoned building to see what Slick was up to. That's when she noticed the worn but still readable address painted on the decomposing side wall of the store—33 Mamou Lane.

This was Catfish Tarpley's residence? Hoping she had a minute or two to figure it out, she dashed into the store and handed over a twenty to the gum-chewing teenager behind the counter.

''Go ahead,'' the girl said, more interested in watching Britney Spears on the tiny TV on the other side of the cash register.

As soon as Bay had the pump locked on automatic, she checked down the street again. Slick was coming out of the building and two men were with him. They looked as backwoods as Slick did a *GQ* ad, but the three seemed to know each other well enough. At least the good old boys in the matching torn T-shirts were laughing.

Slick used his remote to pop open the trunk on the BMW and tilted his head in invitation. The two men looked inside and Bay didn't figure they were admiring the roominess. Sure enough, each reached in, simultaneously taking off their hats and tucking something behind them. Bay just knew they were guns, but the trio created their own protection, not that there was anyone else on the streets to pay attention. So far not three vehicles had driven past them.

What happened next had Bay's mouth going dry.

From an inside pocket Slick withdrew a bundle of cash, which he handed over to one of the men. The guy then climbed into the passenger side of the truck parked next to the BMW, while his partner headed for the driver's side. Bay wished she could make out the license plate, but Slick was moving again.

Certain that he would be pulling up to the pumps to fill up himself, Bay rushed back to the truck and shut off the unit. She didn't even take the time to replace the fuel tank cap; tossing it into the bed of the truck. She hopped into the cab and backed up into the side street. The truck's gears protested as she shifted into drive and gunned the engine, making the first left around the block.

At the next intersection she made another left and in the distance she saw the red-and-white pickup driving down the dusty road. The BMW was gone. When she eased up to the blinking traffic light she saw it pulling into the gas station.

Pursing her lips she blew rather than whistled.

Now what? Slick's job was apparently done. What were the other two up to in these backwoods? Was one of them Catfish? She hated to admit it, but that transaction she witnessed appeared to be a payoff for a hit.

Wetting her dry lips, she rushed through the light after the pickup. She didn't have to worry too much about keeping her distance on this unpaved road. There was enough dust being kicked up by the truck ahead of her to make them invisible.

They were soon in woods again and still the dust churned. About a mile farther down the relatively straight road, the dust started building to the right. Bay braked and saw the truck had turned into a narrow driveway. Easing up to it, she saw the mailbox and barely made out the name *Tarpley.*

The Tarpley mailbox was the only one she'd noticed thus far and from what she could see ahead, there wasn't another close by. The only place to turn around was either this driveway or what appeared to be a garbage dump in the woods across the street. Glad it wasn't raining, Bay pulled in there. She shut off the air conditioner and rolled down the windows to check the ground in front of her to make sure she wasn't about to drive over something that would lacerate her tires or gouge a hole in her oil pan. It was slow going and then just as she almost completed a turn around a pile of old rusting appliances, she heard it.

Popping sounds…and screams…and more gunfire.

Bay braked hard. She hadn't imagined it, but she didn't want to believe what she'd heard. As she sat there debating what to do, she vaguely saw through the vegetation the pickup coming back out of the Tarpley driveway. Would they spot her? Hoping they wouldn't, she scooted down in the seat and held her breath.

The red-and-white pickup sped back up the street kicking up a new dust storm.

Shaken, Bay sat up and wiped at the cold sweat beading on her forehead and upper lip. Her hands were shaking like someone with palsy. They'd killed him, she thought. First Glenn, then Holly and now Tarpley...who else needed to be silenced in order to keep their secret?

No way was she going back up that road yet. The sun was sinking fast and in another hour or two it would be dark. She would be harder to recognize in the dark if Slick was still around. However, the idea of sitting across the street from a dead body was too much a reminder of those terrible minutes with Glenn while waiting for the police to arrive.

Bay slumped over on the seat and picked up her phone. "Work," she ordered it. "Work!"

The greenish-gold display merely replied No Signal—Low Battery.

"Jack. Oh, Jack..."

She closed her eyes against her rising panic. Rest. She would have to be alert on the drive back home; she needed to conserve her energy and stay calm.

Sitting up, she adjusted the windows. She didn't want to asphyxiate herself, but she didn't want to share the cab with any snakes or rodents, either. Then shifting the seat back as far as it would go, she closed her eyes so she wouldn't have to see the driveway across the street.

The moon was up. Bay immediately raised her hand to protect her eyes. Then she realized it wasn't a moon, it was the beam from a flashlight.

Opening her mouth to scream, she heard, "Bay!"

Jack? "Jack!"

Frantically, she rolled down the window. Had she imagined him? How had he found her? He in turn was moving the beam over her.

"Are you hurt?"

"No, but I think Tarpley is—"

"Dead. We have to get the hell out of here. How much gas do you have?"

"About two-thirds of a tank."

"That'll do. Stay right behind me. I'm going to stop in Alexandria and use a pay phone to call the sheriff's office. You stay in your truck. Then we're going to drive at least until we get to Shreveport where our license plates won't stick out so much."

He was talking to her as though she were a stranger, a stranger he didn't like very much. She agreed that she deserved a good tongue-lashing, but couldn't he do it after he hugged her for a minute?

Instead he returned to his truck and backed into the street. Bay had a million-and-one questions racing through her fuzzy mind. She dreaded passing the store at the corner until she saw that it was dark, locked up for the night with no one around. The entire town was empty save the cars at the convenience store. It was apparently the teen hangout and music and laughter drifted on the evening as she and Jack drove by.

They passed few vehicles before Alexandria. Once there, she waited as Jack made the call and while she stayed in the truck as ordered, she didn't miss that he was careful to discreetly wipe down the phone afterward. Bay watched him with hungry eyes. However, an ache built in her chest and rose in her throat as she noted his stony countenance in the harsh floodlights.

The next part of their trip took longer, and it was almost two in the morning when Jack led her off the interstate and pulled into a small hotel on the west side of Shreveport. It crossed her mind to keep going; she didn't want a confrontation with him and she wanted the familiarity of her own bed, borrowed though it was, but she stayed right behind him.

"I'll get a room," he said, reaching for his billfold as she circled around his truck. He nodded to the all-night restaurant that shared the same parking lot. "You go get us something to drink and eat. I haven't had anything since yesterday, and I'm guessing you could use something too."

Bay backed away from the money he tried to give her. "I have some."

"Take the goddamn cash."

It was bad enough that he was seething, to see he couldn't bring himself to look at her hurt unbearably. Her own vision blurred by tears, Bay snatched the money and stalked off.

He'd said room. Singular. How was she going to get through the rest of the night with his resentment pounding at her like waves on a seawall? She would check the bathroom while she waited for their order. Along with freshening up, she might be able to find enough aspirin to drug herself to sleep.

Uncertain what to get for him, she stuck with the staples: cheeseburgers and fries with two large unsweetened teas. Business was bustling, understandable considering their location by the highway and all of the clubs and casinos. Bay ignored everyone and everything and retreated to the rest room to kill time.

When she exited the restaurant, Jack was standing outside the farthest room on the ground floor. Without a word, he pushed the door open for her and equally mute, Bay entered. As soon as she was inside, he locked and bolted the door.

She could feel the explosion coming and hoped the walls were thick enough to contain it. She vowed not to be the one to start, though. The least she could do to repay him for coming after her was to take it without rebuke.

"Would you just tell me why?" he ground out at last. "Was it a way to make me pay one last time?"

Confused, she turned around to see him leaning with his palms flat against the desk next to the TV. His back to her, his head bowed, he was the picture of defeat.

"I guess I can't make you care enough about anything, about me, to want to live, but do you think I could go on if something happened to you? So help me God, if I had to see them putting you in the ground, I'd be going there the next day."

"No." Bay crossed the room and wrapped her arms around his waist. "You're wrong. I do want to live. Jack, I love you. I know I didn't want to, and that I fought it with everything in me, but I do."

He pulled free of her grasp, but only to enable himself to wheel around. Then he framed her face in his hands. "Again. Say it again."

"I love you."

In the next instant he was smothering her with

kisses. From her scar to her chin, each eyebrow and eyelid and both corners of her mouth, he blessed every feature with his lips, sometimes whispering her name, sometimes the affirmation of his own love. It was sweet and dizzying, but nothing compared to when he slanted his mouth over hers and let her see the full depth of his desire and need.

Bay leaned into it, reached for more of him and was almost lifted off her feet as he tried to get her closer yet. The next thing she knew she could feel the bed at the backs of her legs. Immediately, she pulled at the buttons of his shirt, he tugged her T-shirt from her jeans. Sometimes their hands bumped in their eagerness to touch, moments later one would guide the other where their needs burned the greatest.

They parted only briefly, for Jack to yank the bedspread and blanket off the bed and onto the floor and to shove back the sheet. Bay toed off her sneakers and reached for the snap on her jeans, but that's as far as she got. Taking control again, he slipped his hands into the waistband of her jeans and panties. Shoving them down, he followed with openmouthed kisses to her breasts, her waist and thighs, until he could help her step out of the tangle. Then he swept her up, urged her legs around him, and lowered her to the bed.

As he caressed and teased her breasts, he shoved his own slacks and briefs down. Gazing deeply into her eyes, he whispered, "I need you so damned much."

She took him into her, a delicious shiver racing

through her body that won a groan from him and had him burying his face against the curve of her shoulder.

"I still can't believe it—your responsiveness to me."

"Just love me, Jack."

"Forever."

Words were unnecessary after that. Driven by their lonely souls and their hopeful hearts, their bodies merged again and again in a sweet, intense dance of their own creation. It defied their exhaustion, building on itself to culminate in joint cries of pleasure. And in the peaceful aftermath they held each other with the purest joy.

40

"I know this is a cliché, but I never expected this for myself, Jack."

The admission brought a smile to his lips, which was nothing compared to the lift under his ribs. Shifting to brace his back against the pillows, Jack eased Bay over him. "You think you're going to get any complaints from me? I want to hear it all, the confessions, the bewilderment, and I accept all IOUs of gratitude. I'm not proud where you're concerned."

But rather than laughing, Bay's look was serious. "You found me. You didn't just come after me, you did something no one else could have done. How?"

Jack didn't want to go back to those dark moments, and yet if it locked her more firmly to him, he would force himself. "The damn cellular didn't work."

"Mine, either."

"Hoping you'd somehow managed to contact me at the house, I checked my machine there. You don't want to know about those few minutes."

Bay pressed a kiss to his chest. "I'm truly sorry. In hindsight I don't know how I dared risk it."

"I do. You're too damned brave for your own good."

"No. It was when I accepted how deep my feelings went for you. I've seen you growing more and more frustrated and desperate to get the right proof to the right people. I thought if I could track down that proof we could say, *There. Now, once and for all, do something.* I never meant to get trapped by my own fear in those woods."

"You did the smartest thing under the circumstances. You laid low. When you said Tarpley, it took me some time, but I finally remembered enough of the address to ask directions to Effie at the visitors' center at the state line. Once I got there, seeing the Mamou address was a cinch. Thing is, it was locked up tight and there was no sign of any BMW, let alone you. I needed gas and stopped at the convenience store. The kid clerking there was bragging about the ten-buck tip she'd made when some crazy woman ran off without getting her change. I described you and your truck and when she could confirm it, I asked which way you went. The only reason she could tell me was because she did try to run outside and give you your change."

"My God, Slick was there by then. She could have inadvertently put him onto me." Bay explained how she avoided him by detouring around the back block, ultimately following the two killers.

Jack's arms tightened around her. "When I found Tarpley, I almost lost it. I just knew they had you, too. It was only as I was getting out of there that my headlights picked up a little of your pickup. A part of me dismissed it. Trucks in that shape aren't unusual especially in rural areas like that. I made myself go check it out and then wished I hadn't. The way you were lying there—'' He closed his eyes, but knew it would be a long time before he forgot the fear.

Bay stretched to kiss him. ''I went to sleep saying your name.''

His managed a smile. ''So maybe I heard you.''

She brushed his whiskered jaw with the backs of her fingers. ''Tell me about Dallas. Did you have any luck?''

''Oh, they're interested. They're just cautious as hell and not thrilled that I'm a rogue cop, which muddies the lines of communications.''

''You're a rogue because of inside corruption.''

And that corruption was his greatest worry next to wondering about Madeleine's next move. ''You know we can't wait for the Bureau to get up to speed, don't you? I have a hunch Stevens is getting strong pressure from Gage and elsewhere to get a warrant for me and I'm sure he's figuring out how to plant supporting evidence if he hasn't already. From there to arranging for a humiliated and despondent cop to commit suicide in his cell is easy.''

''No!'' Bay sat up, her striking blue eyes huge in her small face.

''My little warrior.'' He wanted to stop this discussion and coax her into straddling him. Her nipples puckered from his gaze alone. ''You need to know what's waiting for us back in Tyler, baby,'' he said sadly.

''Then we have to take the initiative based on what we know. You aren't saying it, but I know if they're willing to kill you, it won't be long before they recognize I have to go, too.''

''Not if you let Duncan seduce you.''

''I can't believe you're still on that chorus. No, Jack. Never. There has to be another way.'' Bay leaned forward, all of her passion directed to justice now. ''I kept reading Holly's diary last night. She wrote that Lyle Gessler has had more than one heated argument with Madeleine. She quotes words like *excessive wealth* and *unsubstantiated revenue.* He once yelled that she could flush herself into federal prison if she liked, but that he wouldn't be joining her. Supposedly, Madeleine took great pleasure in reminding him of the illegitimate baby and underage mother he was supporting outside of town.''

Social dirt, Jack knew from his own years in investigation, was abundant. But he was forever fascinated at how it rose like stirred silt with the slightest shift in political agendas. ''Then he's our man. In the morning we'll head back to town and convince him to meet with us. Once he sees his culpability in this mess, we're going to shuttle him to Dallas as fast as we get his agreement to cooperate.''

''Jack. Tomorrow is Saturday. He's not going to be in his office.''

''I don't know. I have a hunch that when you work for Madeleine Ridgeway you're on call 24/7. At any rate, a call to his home that there's smoke coming out of his office building is bound to do the trick.''

Bay eyed him with new respect. ''You've been hiding this devious side of yourself from me. What else don't I know?''

Drawing her back over himself, Jack arched into her moistness. ‘‘That when I’m in love, I don’t need all that much sleep.’’

Bay rubbed her breasts into his chest hair until their nipples caressed. ‘‘Exactly how many times have you been in love?’’

‘‘This is the first time...and the last time.’’

41

Saturday, June 22, 2001
Tyler, Texas
9:11 a.m.

''Ready or not, here we go....''

At Jack's warning, Bay glanced over her shoulder to see Lyle Gessler's Mercedes turn into the parking lot of the three-storied office building off of Old Bullard Road. When he saw that not only weren't there any smoke or flames pouring out of the building, there also weren't any fire trucks, he ripped off his sunglasses and squealed to a halt before the front door.

''What the hell?'' he demanded, bursting from the steel-gray car.

The moment he spotted Jack coming out of the office breezeway flashing his ID, he went slack-jawed and began to retreat to the Mercedes.

''Wouldn't do that if I was you,'' Jack said.

''What is this? Extortion? Blackmail?''

''An early Christmas present. Hands up where I can see them, please.'' Jack eased to the side of Gessler and cautiously checked him for a hidden weapon.

"This is the deal. You cooperate and as a reward, you don't get buried as deeply into the federal penal system as Mrs. R., Junior, and the rest of your playmates do."

"Get lost," Gessler replied. But his Adam's apple rose and fell several times.

"Don't believe me, huh? What would you say if I told you that last night Catfish was murdered by order of your boss?"

Lyle remained silent. Only his pasty coloring exposed any loss of bravado.

"Not moved to tears? We weren't either...except that it suggests that some corporate housecleaning is under way. Think about what that means. Oh, you're apt to shrug off troublemakers like Ms. Kirkland and dredges on the bank account like Catfish...and you won't miss Ms. Butler, who spotted you for the worm you are from the beginning. But Catfish was a useful soldier, and so would Ms. Butler be if she could be groomed into the proper cheerleader. The fact that Mrs. R. is willing to change her mind and sacrifice people she's invested a considerable amount of money in tells me you're on the short list to go. Need proof? Bay, love, come down here and show Mr. Gessler what else we have."

Bay stepped out of the shadows and carried the red leather diary down to the car. "Hi, Lyle. Slumming this morning?" she asked, taking in his starched tennis clothes. "Here's some summer reading you might be interested in. It's kind of a diary and something of an exposé about a holier-than-thou attorney who has a sweet tooth for underage girls."

Gessler bowed his head, his hands falling limp over the edge of the car door. ‘‘What do you want?’’

‘‘Take a trip with us to Dallas.’’

‘‘Why Dallas?’’

‘‘Because that’s where the main FBI offices are.’’

‘‘Why can’t we go downtown to the police station? I’ll turn myself in.’’

‘‘So Ed Gage and a few others can come to your aid? Sorry, pal. It really is over. Now what we’re going to do is give you some incentive to behave,’’ Jack added bringing out his handcuffs.

He got no farther. A silver sedan swerved into the parking lot.

‘‘Bay,’’ Jack yelled. ‘‘Down behind the car.’’ At the same time he shoved Gessler to the ground and drew aim.

As the Town Car braked and the tinted windows lowered, Bay saw Elvin pointing an equally impressive automatic back at Jack.

‘‘Thought as much. Gessler, you’re such a sap. Mrs. R. had her suspicions right off and called a friend at the fire department. You could have thought of that, too.’’ He motioned to the two men. ‘‘Inside the car. Bonnie Bay! C’mon, honey. Come to the big house and tell Mrs. R. why you’d want to treat her so bad after all she’s done for you.’’

‘‘Stay put, Bay,’’ Jack ordered.

But she wasn’t going to take that kind of risk again. Bay came around the Mercedes.

‘‘Good girl,’’ Elvin drawled. ‘‘Now take those handcuffs and put them on your boyfriend.’’

Bay knew Jack wasn’t about to let that happen and

sure enough he tossed them over the Town Car and into the empty field across the road. Elvin wasn't pleased.

"Gessler, do you think you could pick up that gun and hand it over, then get behind this wheel while I make sure these two don't try any more funny stuff?"

On any other day, this street would be teeming with people. Even in another hour Old Bullard would be an expressway full of shoppers and weekend revellers. But for right now the street was back in its lazy Southern morning mode. Bay and Jack exchanged glances knowing they had to hope for an opportunity to change their luck somewhere else.

Lyle locked up his car and slid behind the wheel. As he wove his way back onto Bullard and then zigzagged onto Broadway, Elvin made a phone call.

"You're right, it was a hoax. I'm bringing in Burke and Butler."

42

Bay didn't care about Madeleine's cold glance as they were brought into her office. All that mattered was that Elvin's automatic was pointed in Jack's back.

"Bay, dear, I'm seriously disappointed."

"So am I. It's over Madeleine. The FBI are onto you, Catfish isn't going to rot and be eaten by varmints in his woods."

Wearing her own tennis outfit and looking bronzed and fit, the older woman circled her desk and studied the group before her. "The Tarpleys of the world don't interest me. Do you realize what we're doing here, Bay? Detective Burke? We have become a successful recycling center. No, don't smirk, give it some thought. As the Bible says, 'The poor will always be with you.' Well, so, too, the weak, the lazy, the predators of those poor souls. Do you think I like the idea of drugs? Bay, you know except for my wine, I don't even allow aspirin into my system."

"You killed Glenn. Why?" Bay demanded.

"Holly told him lies about us and he attempted blackmail."

"Try again."

''Do not speak to me in that tone of voice. You don't understand the big picture.''

''People are not chess pieces, Madeleine,'' Bay intoned. ''They're not commodities on the stock exchange of life. They dream, they hurt, they bleed. What right do you have to micromanage that?''

Madeleine placed her hands together as though to start some chant. ''Last year, we saved dozens of children from starvation in South America and a pair of twins from being sold to a child pornography ring in the Far East. In Mexico all of our schools teach viable trade skills. In Nicaragua, a little girl who was severely injured in a farming accident has teeth for the first time. What do I care if the scum of the earth want to burn their brain cells with narcotics? They are the percentage lost anyway.''

''One could make the same argument for your little girl on the farm or your children in such a unloving home that their parents are willing to sell them. Where are those children today, Madeleine?'' Bay demanded. ''What if their parents ran out of money again? What about the addicts and junkies who prey on the innocent to support their habit? You have entrepreneurs in your congregation. What if one of them was shot because of some expendable junkie needing a fix?''

'''Many are called but few will answer,''' she replied.

The office door opened again and Duncan stood frozen in the doorway. He stared at Elvin with his gun and then at Bay. Swallowing, he shook his head at his mother.

''You promised me.''

''Darling,'' Madeleine replied with a maternal smile. ''Please, let me handle this. Everything will be all right. Why don't you take Bay into the garden and I'll join you as soon as Detective Burke and I come to some amicable agreement?''

''The only resolution to this situation is that you're being shut down,'' Jack replied. ''You think getting rid of me and trying to brainwash Bay is going to work? Holly got into your computer, Madeleine. It's all been shared with the FBI. Your payoffs to the police, the judge in your pocket, the money laundering...they have it.''

''He's bluffing,'' Elvin said, raising his gun.

Bay sensed Jack about to launch himself at him, but she was closer. And yet even as she moved, she was yanked backward. Duncan had gone into motion before any of them.

''No more!'' he shouted at Elvin and reached for the gun.

In the next instant the room exploded. There were screams and scrambling...Jack grabbed the nearest object, a crystal ashtray and flung it at Elvin, who was already off balance due to Duncan slumping against him. It struck him in the temple giving Bay an opportunity to keep the gun pointed toward the ceiling until Jack could punch Elvin again and gain full control of it.

As quickly as the eruption began the room grew eerily quiet. Elvin crawled into a corner. Lyle Gessler lowered himself into one of the armchairs, crossed his legs and rested his forehead against his hand. As for

Madeleine, she stood frozen in her place. It was Bay who dropped to Duncan's side to see if she could help.

"Oh, Jack," she whispered.

"Get on the phone," he said gently. "Call 911."

Epilogue

Wednesday, July 4, 2001
Jack Burke's Ranch

While they'd expected it, the arrival of the unmarked police car dampened everyone's spirits. Simon immediately excused himself and said he had to give the calves their supplements. Even Bud, who'd been trying to impress Bay and Jack with his ability to bury and rebury a favorite bone a record number of times, turned shy and hunkered between Bay and Jack's deck chairs.

Lyon Stevens emerged from the black sedan without his suit jacket and with his tie tugged low enough to release his collar button.

Bay glanced at Jack and murmured, ''That's a good sign, isn't it?''

''Better yet will be the sight of his taillights when he leaves,'' Jack drawled. But he was smiling as he began to rise.

Stevens motioned for him to stay put. ''I won't intrude but a minute.'' His wheat-white mane looked wind-whipped and his broad forehead glistened. ''I hope to salvage what's left of my Fourth, too. Just wanted you to know I've come from the hospital. The doctors don't expect Odessa to come out of her coma and we've put out an APB on Davis, but he does have a significant amount of cash on him. He could be out of the country by now.''

''He'll surface again,'' Jack replied with confidence. ''Probably suffering from a new case of amnesia and with a new wife at his side.''

To Bay it was one more tragedy. Only days after Duncan's funeral, Odessa suffered a terrible fall on the stairs in their home. Or so Martin explained to the police and those in the Mission of Mercy congregation who remained steadfast—a dwindling number. But as soon as the authorities announced they intended to prosecute, Davis obviously decided this was one challenge too many, even for a miracle worker like himself, and he ran.

That left Madeleine who had been arraigned and denied bail along with Elvin and Lyle Gessler. They were all in jail. Madeleine was awaiting news on a venue change. Through her attorney, she had asked to see Bay, but Bay had refused. She couldn't forget the image of Madeleine standing over her son's body. The woman appeared to have emotionally severed herself from the loss.

''He didn't have enough of my blood in him,'' she'd said with the dispassion of someone discussing a poorly performing stock. ''Too sweet, like his father.'' Then she'd looked at Bay and her smile had warmed. ''You and I could have been something special. I wanted a daughter, you know. Females understand survival better, and daughters are such a comfort in one's old age.''

Bay knew she would have to testify at her trial, as well as Elvin's and Gessler's, but listening to that insanity brought a relief that it wouldn't be this month.

''What's the news on the stateside members of the cartel?'' Jack asked Stevens.

Bay knew that was his chief concern. Upon learning the courier she'd called Slick had vanished and that none of the international officials at the schools were being helpful—what with the financial assistance they were getting drying up—he'd taken a leave of absence to stick close to the ranch, and her.

Stevens shrugged. ''The Bureau's being close-mouthed as usual. They're promising an update soon. I can tell you that what we're hearing in town via the grapevine is that the power players south are pulling back and waiting for a new market to open.''

''Maybe since we didn't get any of their people, they could care less about us and Tyler.''

''Wouldn't be surprised.''

It was a waste, though, Bay thought, and the impact of all of this would be deep felt and prolonged. Locally, the police department was undergoing a shake-up and several elected officials were squirming under media scrutiny.

Stevens cleared his throat. ''I wanted you to hear it from me first. I've been offered Gage's position.''

That brought Jack to his feet. He'd told Bay that while Stevens had been tough on him, he'd been fair.

As she watched the men shake hands, she thought she saw a new friendship in the making.

"I need a second in command I can trust. Interested in the position? Horne wants an answer ASAP."

Lieutenant Alan Horne was being moved up to the chief of police position. It would be a different department, Jack had said when he'd discussed his future.

"I'll discuss it with Bay and let you know tomorrow," Jack replied.

"Fair enough." Stevens checked his watch. "I'd better get moving before my wife starts the barbecue without me. You don't ever want to let her near lighter fluid and matches."

Once he was gone, Bud sprang up and went back to playing as though he'd been locked in a kennel for a week. Bay was fast concluding it might be a good idea to get him a playmate to help him burn up some of that energy.

"Did I assume too much?"

She turned to Jack and smiled seeing no reason to start being coy at this late date. "Hardly. Thank you for saying what you did, but the answer would be the same regardless. I want you to do what makes you happy."

He drew her onto his lap. "Being with *you* does that. Why don't I retire and you can support both of us?"

"You'd be bored within weeks." Nevertheless, at his prompting, she was taking her time making decisions about her professional future, too. Mike was offering her a partnership, but Jack wanted her to know he would love having her open a small shop here and be more selective and artistic in choosing her clients. Bay was leaning toward staying with Mike for a while, as much to pay him back for his help during this ordeal as to give her and Jack more time to get used to being an official ''couple.'' And who knew? She might take him up on that partnership in time. He was proving to be a good friend as well as an honorable man. As saddened as he'd been to learn of Nick's involvement with Madeleine Ridgeway, he'd been more embarrassed and angry that a relation might be going to jail and tainting the family name.

''Come back to me, Bay,'' Jack said softly.

She laid her head against his shoulder. ''I'm here. I'm just sad that it couldn't have been different for Glenn and for Holly.''

Elvin had confessed that Razor Basque hadn't killed Glenn, he did. Razor backed out of the deal upon learning Elvin wanted Bay killed, too, without Madeleine's knowledge. Elvin explained he'd recognized what his boss couldn't admit—that Bay was strong and faithful and would never accept Glenn's death without digging up all their secrets. Despite her earlier, eerie feelings about the man, Bay had been devastated by the revelation. Poor Duncan had never stood a chance trapped between his Black Widow mother and her equally ruthless henchman. Maybe he'd been guilty of too much denial or protection, but she would never forget him for finding the courage at the end that saved her life, and Jack's.

''All we can do is go on,'' Jack continued, lifting

her hand to his lips. ''And you know I can't do that without you. I need your love as much as I needed your forgiveness.''

Following her impulses as well as her heart, Bay took his hand in both of hers. ''You have it all.''

Helen R. Myers

Helen R. Myers is the bestselling and award-winning author of over thirty-four novels. She lives deep in the Piney Woods of East Texas—a place still known to some natives as "renegade country" in the house she and her husband built together.

MHRMBIO